EVERY SHADE OF BLACK

Love Luigi

EVERY SHADE OF BLACK

LINZI DREW-HONEY

Matador
9 Priory Business Park,
Wistow Road, Kibworth Beauchamp,
Leicestershire. LE8 0RX
Tel: 0116 279 2299
Email: books@troubador.co.uk
Web: www.troubador.co.uk/matador
Twitter: @matadorbooks

ISBN 978 1789013 863

British Library Cataloguing in Publication Data.
A catalogue record for this book is available from the British Library.

Printed and bound in the UK by TJ International, Padstow, Cornwall
Typeset in 11pt Aldine by Troubador Publishing Ltd, Leicester, UK

Matador is an imprint of Troubador Publishing Ltd

'We can't always choose the music life plays for us, but we can choose how we dance to it.'

Unknown

PROLOGUE

TATIANA

Tatiana Berisha retouched her lipstick a perfect sticky scarlet. Admiring herself in a black polished Chanel compact she puckered up and swished her fine blue-black hair. It tumbled down her back like an exquisite crushed velvet drape. As she slipped the mirror back into her handbag, she surveyed the sumptuous luxury of the first-class cabin of the Arab Emirates flight. Destination London. Under her breath Tatiana purred. It felt like she was coming home.

It had been three long months since she'd left in a hurry. She was looking forward to going back. It wasn't that she didn't enjoy Dubai. She loved the constant sunshine and the constant sex. But no matter how hard she fought against it, it annoyed her that she was whoring again. She'd presumed that that life was in her past, that she'd left that world behind when she met Edward Jackson. But no. Once again, when she had sex, she had sex because she was told to. It was her job, not her choice. When she lived in comfort and opulence in Surrey with Eddie, she had the lavish lifestyle she craved and she could play around with whoever she wanted, whenever she wanted. That was until Suzanne Perry-Jackson, the yellow-haired bitch, ruined everything. A cruel smile parted lips as shiny red as nail polish. Revenge would be sweet.

She rolled her eyes. Eddie, the silly man, was besotted. It was as simple as that. It had been so easy to win him round again. He'd promised to pick her up from Heathrow. He'd be waiting for her at the airport like a foolish little lap dog. She giggled as she thought of him. Once she'd drawn Eddie back in, she'd had to work on Angelo. He'd cashed in on her beauty and insatiable appetite for sex. She'd made him big money, so it was in his best interests to keep her sweet. The premier gentleman's club with the richest clientele in Dubai needed her outstanding talents. So, after much discussion, Tatiana was rewarded for her first-class efforts with a fortnight's leave and a first-class return ticket to London. If all went to plan, she wouldn't be returning. Dubai would be in her past.

Tatiana had caught Eddie just right, had been working on him for several weeks, on the phone and on Skype. When he was down and desperate for some company, he had talked. Like an erupting volcano, he had talked and talked. She liked that he was now living in a penthouse in Chelsea Harbour. She fancied a bit of that. She'd made all the right noises as he sounded off, angry and bitter as he told her the St George's Hill mansion was now sold. She fancied a bit of that as well. Stupid, smitten Eddie would have so much more spare cash to spoil her with now.

Tatiana's ears had pricked up when, sounding irritated, Eddie had told her that his soon-to-be ex-wife had a new man in her life. She'd clucked sympathetically before casually asking the new lover's name. As soon as she'd hung up, she googled Sebastian Black and got lucky. She liked what she saw; a handsome as you like, blue-eyed doctor. Remembering those online images of him, she smiled. *Fuck; he was something very special!* Surely, he had to be Suzanne's 'Knight in Shining Armour', the one who'd gallantly rescued her when Angelo pulled his amusing little stunt! She grinned wickedly, and an orange-tinged warmth spread through her and settled hot and pulsing in her groin. She'd managed to steal one man from right under the bitch's stuck-up nose, and she intended to do it again. This time, with a great deal more satisfaction. Let's see if this one can resist the sweet scent of Albanian pussy.

Just contemplating doing the very gorgeous doctor was making Tatiana horny. She needed to be fucked. She'd join the 'Mile High Club', she decided, her pussy dampening at the mere thought of some pure animal gratification. Licking her glossy lips with the tip of her tongue, she glanced across the cabin and spotted the perfect candidate sitting across the aisle: a businessman travelling alone. She studied him for a moment. She guessed him to be European and pretty old, perhaps thirty years older than her twenty-one years, but Tatiana thought him suave and sophisticated in his sharp expensive suit and shiny shoes. He had a full head of pale grey hair which was long and floppy. His angular face was clean-shaven with a strong jaw. She knew he'd be appreciative. The old ones always were.

Tatiana concentrated her gaze on his mouth. She hoped he liked oral sex as much as she did. Picturing him on his knees in the confined space, his tongue busy inside her, she unbuckled her seat belt and stood up showily. The stranger's hazel eyes were all over her now. It made her heartbeat quicken. After he'd licked her to orgasm, she'd make sure he'd fuck her hard and fast. Tatiana's heart was thumping as she moved toward her prey. Making a conscious effort to slow down her breathing, she smoothed her figure-hugging, vermillion red dress around her curvy hips as she struck a pose beside him. Her waist was tiny, her ass was wide. Tatiana knew only too well that men found it an irresistible combination.

Moving in incredibly close, invading the stranger's space with her presence, Tatiana leaned into him. Her heady Valentino Intense perfume saturating his senses, her Balkan accent exaggerated for added effect, she whispered huskily in his ear: "I've always had this fantasy about joining the 'Mile High Club'."

The man looked up at her and gulped, blind confusion registering in his heavy-lidded eyes. He swallowed hard for the second time and then opened his mouth slightly, responding with nothing more than an embarrassed cough.

Tatiana's lips a big red pout, she murmured: "Follow me to the washroom and I'll be waiting for you." She winked and then turned away. Panther-like, Tatiana slinked off down the aisle, her green eyes feral and gleaming with triumph as she heard the stranger hurriedly rise from his seat.

ONE

SUZANNE

Suzanne's office in Covent Garden was situated on the third floor above a young and trendy women's fashion store. Through sash windows, the shadows lengthened as afternoon segued into early evening and darkness descended, even though it was barely 4.30. An anglepoise lamp on her desk surrounded her with a halo of golden light and made her section feel snug and cosy in the diminishing natural light. Up in the eaves, the workspace could be described as *bijou* or, being somewhat less complimentary, as downright poky, but Suzanne loved it. It felt fantastic being back at work; back in the driving seat once more.

This was to be a new year with a new start. Suzanne was determined to lay the ghosts of her past behind her and celebrate the present. The last six months had been a crazy rollercoaster of a ride. Dumped after almost two decades of marriage and, while still reeling from the shock, abducted by a sadomasochistic one-night stand. Suzanne's sybaritic world had been shattered, and yet, she'd managed to come through it and rise from the phoenix. Her divorce was proceeding according to plan, and she'd set up a new home for her and her boys. Back from boarding school, they'd shared Christmas with Suzanne and her wonderful new partner, Sebastian. The two of them had fallen so easily into coupledom. And yet, even after being together for almost four months, his name on her lips made her tummy turn somersaults. Of course, she'd had some wobbly moments, but now she considered her life was back on track and she felt happier than she could ever remember. Kind of born again.

Although bustling, below on the square, there was an almost cheerless air. All the vibrant colours, the reds and the golds and the emerald greens of Christmas, had vanished over the weekend, leaving the cobbled streets, all of a sudden, a little spartan and sad. It had been a glorious crisp winter's day, the first working day for many after the extended festive break. Keen to get to grips with working again, Suzanne had already spent several days the previous week getting things just so in the tiny office she would be sharing with her Uncle Jack; her late mother's only sibling. Since Suzanne's parents' death, he'd always been there for her. This time, coming to her rescue with a job offer. Uncle Jack was a travel writer. Over the years, he'd handed over plenty of assignments to Suzanne, whose skilfulness with the written word impressed him greatly, as did her English language first which she managed to achieve while pregnant with the twins. Now Jack was hitting retirement age, he seemed only too pleased to be able to lighten his load and offer some work to his favourite niece.

In a slate grey tailored pencil skirt teamed with a cashmere sweater and sporting her mother's pearl necklace, Suzanne looked chic and businesslike. She peered at her PC, her green eyes, dusted in smoky shadow, sparkling vibrantly. Her mass of flaxen hair caught up in a comb, she fiddled lazily with the feathery wisps that tumbled free as a wide grin tugged at her mouth. *Perfect!* They'd emailed through the confirmation. She knew she'd just talked her way into an amazing deal, knew Sebastian would love what she was planning for his birthday.

"You're looking very pleased with yourself," Uncle Jack observed after hanging up the phone.

A heavy smoker, his gravelly voice a dead giveaway, Uncle Jack was a big handsome man with twinkly eyes framed with horn-rimmed spectacles and deep laughter lines. He had an abundance of silvery hair which was overly long and flicked up untidily over the button-down collar of his maroon corduroy shirt. There was an aristocratic air about him, and the way he tilted his head to the side when he looked at her, reminded Suzanne of her mum.

"I've got a fantastic deal on an upgrade for me and a club world seat for Sebastian."

"Well done, you." Uncle Jack leaned back into his seat. "You're going to love the Fairmont."

Suzanne smiled at her uncle. "And I'm guessing we'll get treated pretty well there, so they get the review they want." She gnawed her bottom lip in concentration as she checked the data on her screen. Satisfied it was all correct, she sat back, beaming.

"Done," she announced and set the wheels in motion for the document to print.

"Does Sebastian ski?"

"Of course! He plays it down, but I bet he's brilliant at it like he is at most things. He's never skied in North America though, so I'm hoping that will give him a buzz."

"What time are you off?" Uncle Jack asked, pushing up out of his chair and heading towards the small kitchen area tucked in a corner under a low sloping ceiling. Before she had time to answer, he added: "Coffee?"

"Yes, please. Just a small one." Suzanne's face creased into a warm smile. "We fly out early Friday afternoon and we're back on the overnight Tuesday. Should give us plenty of time to hit the slopes and get the feel of Whistler. I'm so looking forward to a bit of five-star luxury."

"You'll certainly get that at the Fairmont."

Looking at his niece fondly, Uncle Jack filled the dinky cup and handed it to Suzanne.

"Thanks," she said, taking it from him, before adding earnestly: "Don't go worrying, Uncle Jack. It won't all be about celebrating Sebastian's birthday. I'll do a good job, I promise." Suzanne experienced a wonderful physical ache saying her lover's name out loud.

"I don't doubt it for a minute, love. I just hope he appreciates you."

Suzanne's smile was enormous. "No worries there. Sebastian treats me like his princess." She grinned, and, cradling the cup between threaded fingers, she sipped at her coffee, before fixing her gaze on her uncle. "D'you mind if I finish up here now? I'm dying to get home and surprise him."

"Of course, love. Have the boys gone back to college?"

4

"Yes. Last night. Did I mention that Rayan made head of house and Christian is captain of rugby?"

"No, but that's marvellous news, Suzanne. Good for them! You must be very proud."

"Yes, I am. It's been a tough few months for them too. But they both seem fine. They're great kids."

"Great men more like. They're bloody huge! I don't know who they get it from. Yes, love. You get off and enjoy your surprise."

"Thanks, Uncle Jack," Suzanne mouthed as she leaned over and began gathering up the recently spilled-out paperwork. Speedily, she stapled the sheets together at one corner, and then folding them in half, slipped them into her handbag.

Standing, she shrugged on her boxy Karen Millen suit jacket and buttoned it from the bottom to the top. "See you tomorrow," she said excitedly as she knotted a black silk scarf around her throat.

Keen to get home and set up her surprise, Suzanne downed the rest of her coffee in one thirsty glug and then kissed Uncle Jack's soft veiny cheek before bustling out of the door, still jostling her arms into her winter coat.

TWO

SEBASTIAN

Sebastian had finished for the day, but remained at his desk as if glued to his seat, unable to haul his weight up and out of it. The room was stark white and brightly lit. The slatted blinds were angled open, and outside the full-length windows fell the murky darkness of night, illuminated only by the headlights of the many passing cars. It was rush hour in Wimbledon, south west London. His legs crossed beneath his desk, he jiggled one leg nervously on top of the other and stared at the official-looking letter in his hand. His fingers were long and sensuous, and his nails neatly trimmed and scrubbed immaculately clean. He had the kind of hands any woman would welcome on her body, and the kind of intensely colourful eyes that dazzled those he met. He was an exceptionally attractive man. Startlingly so.

Sebastian exhaled abruptly and air rushed out of his lungs audibly. The General Medical Council had finally set a date for his preliminary interview. Exactly one month away. Sylvia Hamilton was going ahead with her ridiculous allegation that he touched her inappropriately during an examination. The lying bitch.

Sebastian threw the letter down in disgust. The paper fluttered onto the surface of his workstation. After a few seconds filled with nothing but silence, he raised his large frame up and out of his chair. He was tall and muscular with broad shoulders and not an inch of spare fat on his waist. Arresting blue eyes surrounded with luxuriant ebony lashes lit up a truly beautiful chiselled face. His cheekbones were high, his mouth sensual and interesting, due in the main to a set of pointy, elongated incisors. He wore his jet black hair long and deliciously messy. He looked more like a movie star in his prime rather than a well-respected orthopaedic surgeon.

Sebastian's shirt was pristine white, the collar heavily starched and knotted with a slender tie in a peacocky purple that seemed to turn his magical blue eyes an eclectic shade of violet. From the back of his office chair, he collected his jacket; grey and single-breasted, it was a perfect fit. Once he was wearing it, he retrieved the letter from his desk, folded it methodically, and sighing, he slipped it inside his breast pocket. Grabbing his mobile from his desk, he hurriedly typed a text to Suzanne.

Just leaving, baby. See you very soon. Love you X

A hint of a smile lifting the corners of his lips, Sebastian opened the door of his consulting suite and walked into the reception area.

"I'm off now, Pauline," he said. His voice was deep and plummy.

Pauline looked up from her computer cheerfully. Her hair was the colour of burnt toffee. She was mumsyish, carrying a few extra pounds, and was in her mid-forties.

"Okay. I'm almost finished up here. Have a good evening."

Sebastian smiled back at his secretary. "You too," he said warmly.

Sebastian walked past her desk and out of the door. Long-limbed, he descended the stairs, taking them two at a time towards the ground floor exit.

He flicked the remote and from some distance unlocked his sleek white Porsche. The black roof glistened. He shivered. It was a chilly night with a definite bite of frost in the air. Sebastian hadn't bothered with an overcoat. He'd be at Suzanne's and warm soon. He grinned to himself as he thought of his sexy partner. As he hurried to his car, he noticed a pearlescent white Range Rover Evoque that he didn't recognise, parked at an unusual angle across a couple of the empty bays. The car was shiny and new, high spec with tinted privacy glass and flashy twenty-two inch alloys. The driver's window was halfway down, and an extremely beautiful young woman was just sitting. Long red fingernails on display, she was smoking a cigarette, very theatrically. Shimmering rings of smoke exuded from her blood red lips. The circles of smoke rose dramatically and floated skywards, lingering in the cold night air. As their eyes met, she rewarded him with a seductive grin. She looked foreign, Sebastian thought as he chucked her a courteous smile in return.

"Excuse me." The words seemed to glide from her lustrous mouth.

"Yes?" Sebastian answered, a little surprised that she'd addressed him.

"Sebastian Black, I presume?"

Her accent was hard-edged, and each word was emphatically pronounced. Sebastian felt like he'd suddenly stumbled into the opening act of a play. The encounter seemed staged. The woman was Eastern European for sure, and a real *femme fatale*.

Even more intrigued, Sebastian answered cautiously: "Yes, that's me."

"Ah, that is good I have found you." The young woman giggled, throwing her head back melodramatically before taking another long draw on her cigarette.

Sebastian transferred his weight from one leg to the other, trying to retain some heat. His toes were cold in his thin silk socks and Prada loafers. He watched her, waiting for her to continue, waiting for the scene to play out.

"I was hoping to make an appointment with you, but I see you are finished for the day. That is a shame." Her gooey red lips formed a gentle pout.

"Yes, I am," Sebastian confirmed, wondering who the hell she was and why she was just sitting in her car in the near-deserted car park, smoking in the darkness.

The whole encounter seemed staged. Sebastian eyed her suspiciously. He couldn't help but notice that she was a striking young woman. She was young, very young indeed. Possibly, just barely out of her teens, and yet, he detected an aura of knowingness about her that somehow belied her tender years. She was dressed in black, her neckline was low, and her cleavage boldly displayed, rounded by a push-up bra.

His fingers stinging with the cold, Sebastian fumbled for a business card. Moving in and offering it to her through the open gap in the car window, his hot breath rising like steam into the frigid night air, he said: "My contact details. Call my secretary, Pauline, tomorrow. She'll be able to help you."

The mystery woman took the card, her fingers making a split second contact with his. Sebastian felt a rush of electricity zip up his arm. He could smell her then; a pungent, female scent, vaginal and strangely lewd. Like she'd recently had sex and hadn't showered.

Swishing long, fluid coal-black hair, she smiled demurely and ducked her head like a fine pedigree cat waiting to be petted. "Thank you, Sebastian." Her words were drawn out and breathy. Vivid green eyes flecked with a glint of silver latched onto his, unblinking. She took another deep drag on her cigarette. The orange light from the lit end blazed in the gloom of her car.

For Fuck's sake! Not another one! Sebastian swallowed hard. There was no doubt about it; this one was truly gorgeous and definitely coming onto him, but he didn't need this. With a brisk nod of his head signifying their conversation was concluded, he slid into his Porsche and powered it up. He loved that throaty growl of the powerful engine. The woman made no move to drive off. She stayed put. Sebastian had the distinct impression that her heavy eyes were following him as he put his foot down and eased out of the car park to join the ribbon of slow-moving traffic.

Suzanne's house was only a five-minute drive from Sebastian's surgery. He was heading over to hers straight from work, as he did most evenings. An incoming text tinkled in his ears. Stationary at a red light, a handful of streets from her home, Sebastian opened the text.

Love you too, baby. Hurry up. I've got a surprise for you! X

The lights changed so Sebastian didn't have chance to reply. Grinning, he threw his phone on the passenger seat. One of Suzanne's dynamic blowjobs would definitely ease the pain. Sebastian chuckled to himself as he put his foot down and pulled away. Catching the tail end of the seven o'clock news on LBC, Sebastian tried to pay attention, but somehow the newsreader's onslaught of information just wouldn't go in. The scheduled grilling with the GMC played on his mind even though it was weeks away. Every time he thought about it, he was filled with a gut-wrenching fear. It twisted his stomach in knots. He hadn't so much as touched the stupid woman, so surely the truth would out. But he knew that it would always be hanging over him unless she could be persuaded to retract her allegations. Perhaps he could appeal to her husband and make him see sense? He must be aware his wife was some kind of nymphomaniac, surely?

Determined to store his problems away, Sebastian indicated and steered the Porsche onto the side road, taking the corner hard and sharp, the low profile tyres smooth on the turn. He spotted an empty parking space less than thirty metres from Suzanne's townhouse and reversed into the gap with ease. He cut the engine and exhaled noisily. He rubbed his eyes with his fingertips before combing them through his hair. Shaking off his black mood, Sebastian clambered out of the car and hurried the short distance to her door. He opened it with his own front door key.

"Hey, baby," he called out as he stepped inside.

Before him, Suzanne was a sight to behold. She was waiting for him in the low-lit hallway. Amber light danced on her golden hair which was ironed straight and cascaded around her bare shoulders. Naked, aside from white gold jewellery and classic patent Louboutin

11

stilettos with their deep red trademark soles and matching heels, she was standing at the bottom of the staircase, one hand on her hip. Her legs were spread wide in a delicious triangle, her shaved sex bared brazenly for his pleasure. *Now that's what you call a welcome!* Sebastian grinned. He wanted her at once. Every other thought was swiftly despatched from his brain. He kicked the door shut behind him, leaned on it and groaned. Hurriedly, he shrugged off his jacket and loosened his tie. Suzanne parked her bare bottom on the stairs and arched backwards, thrusting her pubis out for him; a total tease. He moved in on her, dropping to his knees, breathing hard.

"Aw, baby," he mouthed.

With tentative fingers, he opened her sex and stared longingly. He loved to look at her. She was wet and ready for him. He gave her one long, slow lick from her anus to the uppermost seal of her sex. Suzanne shivered visibly at his first touch. She tasted of heat and passion.

Kneeling between her splayed legs, Sebastian inserted a forefinger into her mouth. Suzanne sucked on it voraciously, washing her tongue around his knuckles, slurping noisily, saliva escaping from her lips. Gripping Sebastian's hair, she pulled him in. They were so close his hot breath fell into her open mouth. He trailed saliva-drenched fingers down through the valley of her waist and across her soft, flat belly, caressing and nipping small handfuls of flesh on his travels. He moved away from her, his eyes locked on her pussy as if transfixed with sheer lust. Sebastian thought Suzanne had the sweetest, most beautiful pussy he'd ever seen.

"Baby, baby, baby…" he mumbled, his cock bulging and cramped in his snug-fitting boxers. Sebastian breathed in deeply and savoured the incredible visual spectacle and the wonderful aroma of his lover. His sensuous mouth quirked at the corners.

Biting her lip and whimpering softly, Suzanne brushed his hands away. "Not yet." The words spilled out in a contented cat voice, a sleepy purr. "Take a look at your birthday present first." Her waterfall of hair rippled around her as she handed him several sheets of paper.

Running lazy fingertips over Suzanne's hard, tight nipples, Sebastian stared at the paperwork for a few seconds: two business class flights to Vancouver and a four-night stay at the Fairmont Chateau, Whistler, with ski passes included. He took it all in with a slow, unravelling smile.

"Sweetheart, that's incredible. I'm the luckiest guy in the world!"

Still clutching the booking confirmation, Sebastian rubbed his mouth gently over Suzanne's. His lips tingled as they made contact. Discarding the papers on the stairs beside her, Sebastian kissed Suzanne on the mouth, harder now, his lips forceful and urgent, his ruffled inky black hair entwining with her sleek, golden locks as they exchanged feverish kisses.

Sebastian gingerly inserted a long, slim finger into Suzanne. She was so wet for him. It was a hell of a turn on. He shivered. Pulling back, his eyes held hers tantalisingly as he deliberately eased his digit in and out. Suzanne moaned softly and grabbed his tie, dragging him back in. Ensnarling her fingers in a wild tangle of his hair, she hauled him in close until their lips were just a few centimetres apart. The two lovers panted frantically in time, their eyes locked together. Sebastian slotted his middle finger in alongside the forefinger and Suzanne's sex swallowed it up hungrily. Her wetness and the smell of her excitement were making him dizzy.

His eyes still fixed on hers, Sebastian gasped for air, his mouth hanging open. He leaned in and kissed her again, sealing her lips with his and chewing on her bottom lip. He got a blast of Listerine as their tongues entwined. He widened Suzanne's legs and then concentrated on her clit, pleasuring her with the flat head of his thumb, smothering her in suffocatingly deep kisses as he toyed with her. His chest heaved and his heart pounded out of control. His cock as hard as granite, it throbbed and twitched, growing with every erotic second. Suzanne teased trembling fingertips up and down his shaft, the shape and size of his desire clearly evident through his suit pants, as his whole body shuddered at her touch. At that moment in time, Sebastian wanted nothing more than to be embedded deep inside his her.

His grip firm, Sebastian crushed Suzanne's nipples together in one hand. He knew just how to drive her crazy. Suzanne squirmed and moaned beneath him, her voice no more than a hesitant whisper. Her golden hair fanned out exotically, dancing like flames around her. Sebastian gazed down her naked body, his eyes caressing her as they flowed over her tummy to her open thighs. Her breath caught as she watched him strum her like a flamenco guitarist, his wickedly-gifted fingers making her writhe, making her lose all control.

"You love watching me do that, don't you?" Sebastian murmured, his voice a deep growl.

14

"Yeah, I love watching you finger me," Suzanne breathed, her body already starting to shake. Collapsing back onto the stairs, she encircled him with her red stiletto heels. She tugged at his hair. "Oh fuck! You're going to make me cum," she snarled, biting down hard, battling to control the imploding orgasm that was roaring within. Her voice softening, she begged: "Do me with your tongue, baby. Please!"

Sebastian raised Suzanne's legs up onto his shoulders and groaning throatily, he sank his mouth onto her weeping sex. As endorphins exploded in his head, a flood of remembrance flashed in his brain: Vancouver. That was where his estranged father lived. The distraction only remained with him for a split second before the exquisite taste of his lover banished it and Sebastian surrendered to a feast of pure gluttony and sex. As his tongue worked Suzanne to climax, his only conscious thought was to make her cum and then flip her over and bury his cock inside her.

THREE

SUZANNE

Tonight's dinner was a Chinese takeaway. Half a crispy duck plus a selection of side dishes had been picked at on their laps in front of the dancing tawny flames emanating from a mound of smooth white pebbles. The setting was warm and relaxed. The drapes were drawn. They were the colour of a deep rich Merlot. Suzanne's lounge was brightened only by the flicker of the contemporary gas fire and several red table lamps in a variety of tones and sizes that were positioned around the comfortable room. The ultra-slim flat screen TV that hung above the cream, marble hearth was on but was barely audible, the screen filled with a generic cookery show, the kind that never fails to give you 'the munchies'.

Sprawled on the sofa, Sebastian and Suzanne cuddled up on a harem of multi-coloured cushions. On the modern coffee table in front of them, stacked dirty plates and cutlery sat alongside several half-empty silver foil containers. The glass top was smeared with tiny remains of their meal. Minute flakes of fluffy rice and dribbles of sticky sauce pooled on the surface, but they were in no rush to clean up. In His 'n' Hers white fluffy robes, they sipped ice cold Chablis and relaxed in each other's arms.

Suzanne adored this man, adored absolutely everything about him. She truly loved the way he made her feel. He made her feel desired. He made her feel alive. Sometimes she just couldn't believe her good fortune after all the shit that had happened. Sebastian had, in a matter of months, transformed her into a confident, sassy woman, who felt good about herself and knew exactly what she wanted from life. With him, she was tactile and sensual. Their lovemaking was so intense, it almost felt spiritual. Suzanne shivered dreamily, still basking in the aftermath of their session on the stairs, her pussy still hot and tender and deliciously raw. She could barely believe it, but already she wanted more.

Suzanne rewarded her man with a sleepy smile as he affectionately stroked her feet. Before the break-up with Edward, sex rarely crossed her mind, but since the split, Suzanne couldn't go a few moments without thinking about the next time she'd have her lover. She wanted to experience everything with Sebastian. She wanted to push the boundaries with this beautiful, erotic man.

Deep, dark memories of the dangerous stranger who introduced her to the delights of sadomasochistic sex bounced around her head. They sent tingles dashing through her body. Despite the ordeal she had suffered at Angelo Azzurro's hands, Suzanne still hungered for that all-consuming intensity of uncontrollable lust she had shared with him. She had to admit that for a short moment of madness she was totally intoxicated by the man's charisma and presence. The sex they'd shared was truly off the scale. Suzanne still craved those unbelievable highs but certainly didn't want them with Angelo. Unsurprisingly, she never, ever wanted to lay eyes on the psychotic asshole again. But the very idea of Sebastian blindfolding her and rendering her helpless and totally at his mercy while he used her body for his pleasure, was becoming her ultimate fantasy.

The dominance and the decadence of her first sexual encounter outside her broken marriage evoked within her a need that she was now determined to explore with the man she had fallen in love with. Suzanne hadn't yet suggested it to Sebastian. She was biding her time. The fact that he was the one who tracked her down and rescued her, had witnessed her imprisoned and shackled to a bed, had stopped her from going there, somehow. Awful memories for them both, but she had put it all behind her, had erased the terrifying moments of craziness from her mind. Suzanne was ready to play those wild sex games with a man she trusted totally. Until now, she hadn't wanted to seem blasé about what had happened and didn't want to push it. But tonight, was the night. The mood was right. The time was right. She hesitated for just a moment and chewed her bottom lip nervously.

"Sebastian?" The inflexion at the end of her word spelled out that she was after something.

"Not again. You're insatiable, woman," Sebastian laughed. A determined hand slipped beneath her robe and moved steadily up her thigh.

"You know I trust you," she paused, "implicitly."

"Yes?" Sebastian stretched out the single word as he answered. He grabbed a handful of her smooth bare flesh.

Suzanne let out a fleeting moan before picking up her thread again. "And you know I want to experience everything with you. Since we met, I've just felt so… " Suzanne faltered.

"Horny?" Sebastian interjected and grinned broadly. He leaned in and tilted her lips to his. Their mouths came together in a hungry kiss.

Suzanne was floating all of a sudden. The softness of his mouth. The heavenliness of his breath. The taste of his tongue. She closed her eyes and disappeared into the kiss. She fingered his hair upwards from the soft nape of his neck, twisting strands in her fingers, tugging at it. Sebastian held onto the kiss. Nimble fingers circled her inner thigh. Goosebumps glided up her spine.

Sebastian's breathing picked up as he found her and cupped her throbbing mound. He held her pussy in his grasp like he owned it. His thumb more pressing now, he probed inside, locating Suzanne's swollen clitoris that bulged between puffy pink sex lips. He stroked her unhurriedly and then curved a finger inside. His brilliant blue eyes fixed on hers, Sebastian pleasured her. Suzanne felt as if she might melt under his delicious and intense scrutiny.

As her robe fell open, instinctively Suzanne eased her crotch upwards and her upper half sank further back into the comfort of the sofa. Her breathing was ragged, and her voice had a tremor of excitement laced through it. She looked up at him with half-lidded eyes and took a deep breath. "Okay. I'm just going to come out and say it."

Groaning softly, eyes heavy with longing, Sebastian stared back at her as he continued to finger her.

She gripped his moving wrist. Her voice was soft. "I want you to tie me up. Blindfold me. Take charge of me, baby." Suzanne stared at him with a lopsided smile.

Sebastian's hand froze. Only for a heartbeat.

"Do whatever you want to me. Please, baby?" Suzanne gasped, her words just a breathy whisper.

Sebastian stared at her hard. "Okay," he said quietly as he slid his finger from her sex.

Suzanne took his hand in hers. "Come on. I've got everything we need." The words fluttered out of her mouth, sugar sweet like candy.

With her heart pounding in her chest, Suzanne giggled nervously and dragged Sebastian up off the sofa. Breathing hard, she led him to her bedroom.

FOUR

SUZANNE

Suzanne's bedroom suite took up almost half of the middle floor of her stylish rented townhouse. The door was shut. The curtains were drawn. Fashionably long aubergine brocade drapes spilled in a fold over the cream deep pile carpet. The walls were painted a soothing soft matt ivory. The room was a fairly compact double but had an air of sumptuous comfort about it, with lots of little touches of luxury. A huge silver floor mirror leant against one wall, while framed family photos completely covered another. Edward didn't feature in any of the shots. A tall cut glass vase of highly perfumed lilies graced a whitewashed, shabby chic side table that was a favoured piece of Suzanne's from her old life. When she'd split with Edward, she wanted only a few possessions from her marriage.

Centre stage in her bedroom was Suzanne's new bed. Grand and opulent, it was hand painted silver with flashes of gold leaf. Italian and extravagant, it had cost her a small fortune. Although it was probably a little too large for the room, she'd selected king sized and dressed it with crisp Egyptian cotton bedding with a barely

21

discernible white stripe. Suzanne was an accomplished housekeeper, so normally the bed looked like it had been made-up by a professional and belonged in a show home. Tonight, however, it looked very different. Wearing nothing at all, Suzanne lay spreadeagled on it. PVC cuffs wrapped around her wrists and ankles, she was chained to her bed with her arms and legs spread wide, her hands clenched in small, nervy fists. Suzanne had bought everything she'd needed online. She had Angelo to thank for introducing her to bondage paraphernalia.

Illuminated only by a dozen flickering candles, the bedroom lighting was dramatic and shadowy, and the sweet giddy smell of vanilla infused the still air. Blindfolded, Suzanne couldn't see a thing. In her sightless world she found it difficult to stay still as her other senses came alive. She breathed deeply and inhaled the wonderful fragrance of the flowers combined with the musky aroma of the perfumed candles, distributed all around her. The scent floated into her nostrils. It filled her head, her lungs and her blood as she lay on her back tethered and tied, barely able to move more than a few inches in either direction.

Wrapped around her soft honeyed hair, two silky black stockings covered Suzanne's pretty eyes. Her lover had used two for extra thickness. Her eyes squeezed tightly shut, Suzanne had no vision whatsoever. The sheer nylon tickled her feathery long lashes. A cold inky blackness surrounded her, and an all-consuming sense of vulnerability made her naked body bristle. Already her toes felt numb. Sebastian hadn't bound her quite as tightly as she might have liked, but Suzanne was so turned on and tuned in, she was trembling. Every nerve within her was taut with expectation.

Sebastian hadn't said a word since he'd fed the fine denier stockings around her head, widened them and secured them in position. He'd fumbled with the procedure before smoothing down her hair tenderly, taking his time. Suzanne wondered if he felt completely at ease with this, wondered if he was just going along with it because she had arranged everything, had wanted it so much. Suzanne dispelled her doubts swiftly. She could sense arousal in his silence. She could feel the tremor in his body as a delicious quietness hung between them. Suzanne was too deeply immersed to give in to halting reservations. All she could hear was the sound of her own expelled breath and the heavy thunder rising in her chest as she waited.

The weight of Sebastian's body dipped the mattress, causing ripples beneath her. Dreamily, Suzanne rolled her head from side to side, whinnying softly as she slid off the pillows. Sebastian gripped her hair, wrapping golden strands around his fingers, tugging her up forcefully, as he threw the pillows to the ground and then lowered her down into a central position. The pillows discarded, she was now spreadeagled before him, totally flat. In her dark world, his roughness made her scalp smart, but his strength and brutishness excited her, made her wet. Suzanne wondered what he was planning. The anticipation of what was to come made her pant. Her twisting body rallied against her chains and she shivered visibly. A giant shot of adrenaline coursed through her veins. White lights seared in her brain as she sensed his big masculine body closing in on her smaller naked form. Suzanne felt helpless and yet bizarrely empowered.

Her heart pounding wildly, Suzanne ached to reach out and touch her man, to feel his biceps and the blistering warmth of him on her and in her. Skin on skin. She needed to caress his chest, rake her long fingernails over the knots in his shoulders and tease the familiar velvety smoothness of his skin at the top of his spine. She longed to fist his cock in her hand and play with the sensitive tip until it began to dribble at her touch. Suzanne wanted to touch him there. She just needed to feel his raw passion for her. She fought against her shackles, each hand balled into a tight fist as she thrust her hips upwards and a low guttural roar broke free from her parted lips. Sebastian responded. Suzanne felt his lips surround a nipple and draw it forcefully into his mouth. His firm hands trailed slowly down her wanting body, tracing every contour of her naked curves.

As his fingertips stopped on her sex, Suzanne moaned softly. Sebastian's perfect white teeth clamped together on her swelling bud, nipping and biting, working in unison with his tongue. As he gorged on her nipple, his hand stayed stock still, and Suzanne's pussy thudded with the blinding pressure of his touch. He was driving her totally crazy. She yearned to feel his fingers inside her. She wanted to grab his hand and make him finger her to orgasm. She wanted a finger in her ass. He'd barely touched her, but she was already skating on the edge.

"Sebastian. Touch me, baby. Please." It was the first words spoken between them in several minutes.

Sebastian said nothing. Aside from his harsh breathing, he remained silent. Suzanne's nipple puffed up in his mouth as his teeth tightened around it. Suzanne groaned, her mouth open and wide like a giant letter O. The pain was exquisite, ebbing and flowing like frothy turquoise waves rolling to the shore. Sebastian grabbed both of her upturned breasts, and then like a man with a purpose, shifted around until he was knelt either side of her body, his knees tucked close beneath her armpits.

The blackout of her world was comprehensive, and the agonising sweetness of her smarting nipples swelled through her very being. Suzanne knew what was coming once the smell of Sebastian's cock seeped into her nostrils. She breathed deeply and lapped up his manly odour as she sensed him closing in on her open mouth. She adored sucking Sebastian's cock, loved playing with his tight, heavy balls as she worked him with her hands and her lips and tiny nibbles of teeth.

Sebastian fed his cock into Suzanne's mouth. She knew it was about to happen, but somehow, it still shocked her. His silky, smooth cock felt bigger than ever and tasted incredible. She savoured the sharp citrus note of his shower gel combined with her lover's own special taste and smell. As he plunged into her, Suzanne started to gag. With both hands, he squeezed her aching nipples. They felt tender and inflamed and wonderful, all rolled into one. Suzanne imagined how beautiful and powerful he must look straddling her face with his wide shoulders thrust back and muscled arms busy as he pulled at her nipples, rolling them between his thumbs and index fingers. Erotic images vibrated in her head. Scorching shivers of pain forced an animal growl from her lips. Suzanne gagged and smothered Sebastian's cock in a shower of saliva.

The intoxicating aroma of sex rushed at Suzanne as Sebastian pounded her mouth. She welcomed every inch of his cock even though it seemed like she would choke on the sheer length of it. Her head thrust back at an angle, her chin high, she felt him all the way down her throat. Her mouth was overflowing. Breathy mewls resounded in her ears as she struggled to catch each breath. Every fibre in her body was tight. Suzanne welcomed the saltiness of the first dribble of his cum. The magic moment overpowered her, as her lover, with total dominance moved in her mouth, fucking it with a wild abandonment, fucking it hard like a pussy, as he ascended to his peak.

Suzanne was spellbound by the steady rhythm. Her hands fisted, she squirmed on the cool cotton bedding as Sebastian, tearing at her hair, grabbing at her breasts, was falling headfirst into his climax. She could feel her excitement literally trickling down her legs. She hadn't yet cum and wondered how she could be so astonishingly wet. Realising she was close, she tightened all the muscles in her abdomen and thighs and pulled strongly against all four restraints. Her muscles felt deliciously fatigued, and excitement pulsed in her groin with a hypnotic steady beat. Suzanne was sailing on the brink of heaven.

All of a sudden, Sebastian withdrew, leaving Suzanne's mouth wide open and empty. She was bereft momentarily, but a split second later his slickness moved down her. His body against hers was searingly hot and slippery with perspiration. He caressed her cheeks, his touch as gentle as a whisper. He cupped her face and covered her mouth with his, swallowing up the sound of her joyful exclamations as his hard cock slid easily inside her. His chest was on her and his cock was in her. She was full to the brim with heat and sex and happiness.

Gripping her manacled hands powerfully at the wrists, Sebastian started his slide to sweet oblivion. As he pumped his cock in Suzanne's pussy, he laced his fingers through hers, clutching both her small hands in his larger ones. He smothered her with his frenzied mouth and tongue, biting and sucking the perfect bow of her lips.

"Oh my God! Oh my God!" were the only words spoken. Suzanne spat them out between a shower of stiflingly hot kisses, as her orgasm began to engulf her.

Sebastian only managed half a dozen more vehement thrusts before he let out an almighty roar and erupted, his hot seed rushing into her, filling her up. Suzanne was with him all the way. It was as if an electric storm that had been gathering between them had finally combusted. The force of finally having Sebastian's cock inside her in a world of absolute blackness just rocketed her over the edge. The wait had been the sweetest surrender; an unbelievable agony. Suzanne's heart thudded out of control and her tightening pussy began to explode. As she started to cum with him, her exhausted muscles contracted rapidly, intensifying the highly emotional orgasm that literally took her breath away. When Suzanne started cumming, she thought she would never stop.

FIVE

SEBASTIAN

The heavy curtains were drawn, the candles extinguished and the handcuffs and restraints tucked neatly away beneath the mattress. The lights were turned off. It was dark and quiet and warm. Suzanne was breathing deeply in slumber. Sebastian snuggled in behind her, spooning his nude body tight up against her smooth nakedness, his arms wrapped around her. Suzanne was snuffling softly, tousled and smelling of fruity shampoo, her golden locks sprawled out like a mass of wild yellow flowers on the white pillow beneath her sleeping head. She was dead to the world. But Sebastian couldn't sleep. His mind was running on overdrive.

What the hell had just happened there? He'd never been rough with a woman before. Not that Suzanne was just any woman. She was the love of his life. His soulmate. He was sure of that. He absolutely adored her. And that deep bond of love made their brutal lovemaking session seem even more alien to him. He'd fucked her mouth like he was angry with her, like he was totally out of control. There was very little preamble, no steady build up. He was like a wild animal taking what he wanted.

And it was shockingly pleasurable. The truth was, he'd loved it. Loved Suzanne's submissiveness. Loved her being his very own personal plaything. His orgasm was absolutely mindblowing, so intense, and yet, when he'd been hammering away in her mouth while she was gagging, lying there blind and in chains, well, it just struck him as wrong on so many levels. It seemed so misogynistic, without warmth and love. Just an animal coupling. Amazing for sure, but, just not right that the utter ruthlessness of it all had excited him so much. Especially considering what had gone before.

It had only been a few months since Suzanne had been grabbed by the sleazeball who took his revenge for her running out on him by kidnapping and imprisoning her. Suzanne had certainly picked the wrong kind of creep to get mixed up with, however briefly. But understandable, of course. When her husband had walked out on her, Suzanne had been fragile and lost; the perfect prey for this controlling asshole. The memory of his beautiful Suzanne locked up and in chains in that basement apartment, her eyes red raw from crying, her body marked by the Albanian's vicious hand, still freaked him out. Even though saving her had undoubtedly moved their relationship onto another level.

Sebastian sighed softly. *Maybe it was just too soon for him.* Her ordeal had terrified them both at the time. But somehow the dominance had awakened something in Suzanne. So much so that she now lusted after more of the same, but controlled and with him, the man she trusted and loved. She'd moved on. *Suzanne had managed it, so why couldn't he? Why couldn't he just enjoy it for what it was? Amazing consensual sex with his lover.*

He consoled himself with the fact that he did what he did and behaved as he had because Suzanne wanted it. She'd planned the whole thing. She'd even bought the handcuffs. *How on earth did she manage to get the under-the-bed restraints beneath the heavy mattress?* Sebastian wondered. Probably got Ayman to help her, he decided, and then worried what the hell their good friend and neighbour would think if he actually had.

Sebastian repositioned his forearm slightly and slid it upwards to Suzanne's right breast. Lovingly, he held onto her sleepy nipple. He was glad he hadn't bruised her at least. He couldn't bear to think of his healing hands disfiguring her glorious body. Suddenly, a thought hit him. With bondage play, weren't they supposed to have a safe word to share? In case it all got out of hand. He thought he should mention it to Suzanne if they were going to go down this road again. And he had the distinct feeling that they would. And soon. His fingers cupped Suzanne's breast as he pushed air out of his lungs emphatically in another breathy sigh. Surely, he was supposed to be the one in control, but somehow it didn't feel like that at all.

Determined to get some sleep, he nuzzled in closer, Suzanne's fragrant hair tickling his nostrils as he drank in her calming smell. He hooked a leg around her and clung on. He shut his eyes tightly, but still sleep wouldn't come. There was just too much churning around in his head. As usual, he just couldn't switch off.

Being careful not to move too much and wake Suzanne, Sebastian glanced at his blue dial Breitling timepiece. A yellow wedge of light from the streetlamps in the quiet suburban road peeped though a gap in the curtains, affording him just enough light to learn that it was almost two. The realisation that it was so late made him even more anxious. He had a busy clinic in the morning and needed to pop home first. He knew he must stop overanalysing and get some sleep. Easier said than done, though, of course.

His mind coasted and he thought of their trip to Whistler. What a fantastic birthday present. Suzanne was incredible. He'd never met anyone like her. No one had ever given him such a generous and thoughtful gift before. He'd been so busy with work that he hadn't skied last season, so the opportunity of hitting the slopes again was very welcome. And he'd never visited Vancouver before. Never been to the marvellous city that his father emigrated to twenty years ago. Sebastian hadn't had any contact with his father since then. Since that summer when he was sixteen years old and at Eton and had smashed his GCSEs. Eleven A stars in total. Even his father couldn't complain at that. Though Sebastian couldn't remember if he saw him once he'd got his results. He was pretty sure he hadn't. He didn't miss his father at all. But the reality of heading to Vancouver in a few days brought his absent father to the forefront of his thoughts.

He presumed he was still alive, as surely, he'd have been notified if he'd passed. He'd be his next of kin, of course. Unless he'd started again with a brand new family in Canada. It was certainly possible. Donald Black was a big, handsome man; a charming exterior disguising the brooding darkness within. Sebastian pitied the new family if he had started afresh. He wondered if his father had mellowed with age or was still that angry tyrant who drank too much and talked with his fists. He'd made Sebastian's mother's life a misery and his childhood a nightmare. He'd feared his father for most of his growing years. Being sent away to boarding school at the age of eight had got him out of harm's way. And he was grateful for that. Donald Black was a drunk and a bully and clearly not the least bit interested in his only child. Sebastian suppressed a sigh. Thinking about his father hurt.

Completely out of nowhere, like a hard slap around the face, Sebastian came to a decision. It was time to see his father again. He wouldn't tell his mother and he wouldn't mention it to Suzanne, but he'd seek him out on this trip. Perhaps confronting him now he was a grown man would give him peace, would give him closure. His mind made up, Sebastian closed his eyes and waited for sleep to come.

SIX

TATIANA

Perched on a stool at the breakfast bar in the stylish open-plan kitchen, Tatiana gazed out over the River Thames through impressive windows that overlooked the sludgy, grey, undulating waters. It was a dull day, and the early morning winter sky was sooty black with heavy rain clouds. The threat of a wet and miserable day ahead did little to dampen Tatiana's bright mood. Breakfast today in the airy silver and maroon kitchen that wrapped around the vast white living space was, as always, a freshly squeezed orange juice and several Camel Blues.

Tatiana sucked on the last couple of inches, drawing her cheeks in severely, before stubbing a fair length of her cigarette out alongside many other dog-ends in an overflowing jumbo ashtray that sat before her on the gleaming granite worktop. Their cleaner had been in yesterday, so the kitchen was looking much neater than usual. With quivering circular smoke rings leaking from her flawlessly made-up ruby red lips, Tatiana smiled contentedly. Her smile was so wide it almost reached her ears. She was feeling very pleased with herself. Since arriving back in London, everything had gone to plan.

33

She loved being back in the UK, adored living in the swanky riverside apartment in fashionable Chelsea.

Of course, Eddie had welcomed her with open arms as Tatiana had known that he would. He was truly under her spell. He had, in a matter of days, spent a fortune on his 'baby girl'. He'd wined and dined her in London's most expensive and exclusive restaurants and bought her her dream car. He'd financed an entire new winter wardrobe too. *Well, what was a girl to do when she only had bikinis and sandals and flimsy see-through summer dresses?* And of course, there was the Cartier love bangle and that wonderful sapphire pendant she'd set her heart on. She fingered the dazzling blue jewel as it sat neatly in the crook of her delicate throat.

Tatiana swished her luxuriant hair and grinned as she stood. She hugged Eddie's shirt around her nakedness, covering the bubble gum pink hummingbird tattoo that decorated her smooth young skin above her left breast. Her bare bottom flashed between fluttering white shirt-tails as she padded into the bedroom. It was spacious with high ceilings and a blingy, bejewelled chandelier that glittered spectacularly as light bounced off a cluster of jewels. The room Tatiana now shared with Eddie wasn't showy enough for her liking. The black leather bed with its pop-up TV was perfect, of course, but the bedding was something Eddie had bought from a chain store; cream and bland. Maybe she'd buy something more exotic for their bed and get a fancy designer in to fix the place up to her taste. Brighten it up with a fresh lick of paint and throw in some animal print. Replace the boring beige carpet with something snowy white, deep and sumptuous. Something comfortable to fuck on doggy style. Doggy style was Tatiana's favourite sexual position.

Tatiana peeled Eddie's crumpled dress shirt from her to reveal her stunning young body, her skin darker now since her time in Dubai. She loved having a winter tan and thought her white bits, where her minuscule thong had covered her up, looked extra sexy and emphasised the curve of her sex. Caressing herself languidly, she admired her upturned breasts in the bedroom's full-length mirror. Silicon, of course, but Tatiana knew they looked so much better than the real thing, and they'd lost none of their sensitivity.

As Tatiana's fingertips connected with her nipples, her pink buds tightened and grew at her touch. She rolled her tongue around her lips, coating them with saliva and mewing softly. She was still feeling horny even though Eddie had fucked her twice before he left for his job in the city in the gloom of dawn. He'd fucked her in bed on waking, on all fours like a randy little dog. She loved the deep penetration, Eddie's fingers working her clit in time with every thrust of his cock. She loved it when he grabbed her bouncing ass cheeks and slapped them hard as he sensed she was about to cum. Eddie couldn't fail to notice. Tatiana was a very vocal lover, after all. As the thought struck her, she pursed her lips in a narcissistic pout, and her thumb and forefinger squeezed tightly together on her throbbing nipple.

The first fuck of the day was always her favourite. It made waking up early worthwhile. Today when she was on her knees with Eddie's thick cock filling her, she came three times in quick succession. Wonderful blow-your-head-off climaxes that morphed from one into another, until she could take no more; and her knees gave out and she collapsed gasping for air.

When Tatiana had got her breath back, her pussy still burning up and sticky and dribbling with cum, she wanted more. So, just as Eddie was going out the door, all suited and booted and ready for work, Tatiana grabbed hold of his tie and stopped him dead in his tracks. On her knees, she unzipped him, reached in and took his flaccid cock out of his suit pants. She fed his fat dick into her mouth and it grew hard instantaneously. Her full lips and bold twirling tongue had magic powers; she knew only too well. Tatiana snickered. Eddie had an important breakfast meeting today. But he'd just have to make up some excuse for being twenty minutes late. Her smile grew wider. Eddie would never say no to her. He simply couldn't resist her when she wanted him. Not a chance. One minute he was all business, about to walk out the door; the next, he had her backed up against the wall, fucking her hard and fast and deep, the clock ticking. It was so good. She giggled when she thought of Eddie turning up for his important business meeting dishevelled and reeking of sex.

Time for her to take a shower and wash away all that wonderful cum. Tatiana hated condoms. Hated the loss of sensation and the absence of semen, hot and steamy inside her. As a professional, she missed out on all that, but being back with Eddie, she wouldn't be bothering with rubbers now. When she was dressed with her full face on, Tatiana planned to ring Sebastian Black's office and set up an appointment. Meet him face-to-face again. His card was carefully tucked away in her bedside drawer. She didn't want Eddie discovering her little plan. She intended to nail that good-looking son of a bitch just as soon as possible. Payback time, Suzanne. *You tried to fuck it up for me and now, you loser, I'm going to fuck it up for you.* Tatiana's smile was expansive and cruel, her lips set in a mocking twist of triumph.

Images of Sebastian, cold and breathy in the frosty early evening air, hovered in her head. Without question, he looked even better in the flesh, testosterone oozing from his every pore as they talked, his startlingly blue eyes all over her like a rash in the darkness of the car park. Of course, he wanted her. Men always did. Self-assured and confident, Tatiana knew she could have him. She pictured herself riding him, her breasts jutting, her thighs parted. Tatiana fingered her breasts idly as she daydreamed about impaling herself on Sebastian Black's cock, sucking him dry with her tight young pussy as she gazed into his magnetic midnight blue stare. *Oh yes! Revenge would be sweet.*

Tatiana welcomed the burn between her legs; a smouldering, delicious ache. She pulled at her engorged nipples, lengthening them till they were rigid and tight and almost an inch long. Soft growls bubbled from her lips as she twisted them. Releasing an animal moan, she shrugged the shirt from her shoulders. Dropping it where she stood, she headed to the shower, one hand already playing between her legs.

★

With Sebastian's business card in her grasp, sitting propped up on the bed, Tatiana keyed in the number. The room was messy, the bed unmade. Piles of discarded clothes littered the bedroom floor. The air smelled of perfume fused with cigarettes and the unmistakable sweet smell of sex. Seductive and flawlessly made-up, her sultry lips a slash of her trademark crimson, Tatiana was dressed all in black. Smug and contented like a pampered moggy, she stretched out long and lean against the padded headboard in simple skin-tight leggings and a silk shirt, tucked out. The shirt was tapered at the waist and unbuttoned to show off her prominent cleavage. Her latest trinket, the sparkling blue jewel, was decoratively exposed, glinting at her throat. Her feet were bare; pedicured and pretty.

Tatiana wriggled her perfectly painted toes impatiently as she waited for the phone to be answered. As expected, a woman picked up. Pauline, the secretary, of course.

"Good morning. Mr Black's office," the female voice said brightly.

"Good morning to you. My name is Tatiana Berisha and I wish to make an appointment with Dr Black. For today," she tacked on almost like an afterthought.

Pauline was all business as she replied: "Hello, Ms Berisha. This is Pauline, Mr Black's secretary. Today's not possible, I'm afraid. One moment please. I'll consult Mr Black's calendar for the first available appointment."

There was a short pause on the line.

"I'm afraid the first appointment I can offer you is Thursday the 17th. At say, 2 pm? Would that be suitable?"

Tatiana realised at once that that was the day after she was due to fly back to Dubai, but of course, that wasn't going to happen now she was back with Eddie. She noted the secretary kept referring to Sebastian as Mr, not Doctor. She decided to do the same. Tatiana sighed irritably and said: "So there are no appointments with Mr Black for more than a week?"

"Yes, I'm sorry. He's away for a few days, so there's nothing I can change, I'm afraid. Do you happen to be free at short notice, should a patient cancel?"

"Yes, I am," Tatiana replied, sounding slightly less sulky.

Pauline continued: "Okay, well, I'll make a note of that then. But if you are in need of an urgent consultation, perhaps I can recommend one of Mr Black's colleagues?"

"No, that is not an option. I need to see Mr Black," Tatiana cut in swiftly.

"Okay," Pauline responded calmly. "Would two o'clock on the 17th be suitable then?"

"No. Not really," Tatiana said churlishly. "Later in the day would work better for me," she added, her voice softer again.

"Well, his last appointment is also free that day. At six o'clock. How about that?"

"Yes, that would be perfect," Tatiana rasped, rolling the 'R' on her tongue, making her accent even more brittle and Slavic and sexy. Her sex goddess tone was totally wasted on Pauline.

"There's no late clinic on a Thursday, so will a half-hour appointment suit you?"

"A half-hour will give us plenty of time," Tatiana replied, moistening her lips and smiling knowingly.

As Pauline began to take down some details, Tatiana had already switched off. She was miles away, contemplating a shopping trip maxing out another of Eddie's credit cards.

SEVEN

TUESDAY 8 JANUARY

SUZANNE

Suzanne was grateful to be back in the comforting warmth of her office. She had the place all to herself as Uncle Jack was out for the day. She closed and locked the door behind her, and dropping the stiff brown bag containing her lunch onto her desk, she flicked on the lights. Even though it was the middle of the day, the small room needed additional illumination. Outside, it was bitterly cold and miserable; the sky the colour of brushed steel, the dense clouds dashing across the sky propelled by a wind that was both icy and brisk. Popping to the corner of the square to the sandwich bar had chilled her to the bone. She was pissed off at herself for forgetting her gloves.

Suzanne rubbed her hands together to try and get some movement back in her smarting fingers, and then unwrapping her scarf, she wondered if snow was forecast. It certainly felt cold enough. She smiled. Either way, she'd be surrounded by the beauty and serenity of snow in just a few days. The thought warmed her from the inside out. Slipping off her black pure wool Chanel coat and draping it neatly over the back of her uncle's

40

battered swivel chair, she hummed cheerily to herself. At the coffee machine under the eaves, she pressed buttons and waited for it to spring into action; blue lights flashing as it spewed out hot black liquid.

Heading back to her desk with a cup of steaming coffee, Suzanne checked the time. One fifteen. Perfect timing to call Sebastian. She'd text first to check he was free. Suzanne couldn't wait to speak to him. They'd barely had time for a proper cuddle that morning. Though they had managed a delicious little quickie on waking, Sebastian spooning her from behind, his hands firm on her waist and her breasts as they made love in the warmth and the darkness, before they'd exchanged a single word. *So fucking horny!* The very thought of their swift early morning lovemaking made Suzanne shiver. Now she would be working in central London most days, she hated getting up in the darkness and heading out into the chill of winter. She consoled herself that at least she woke most mornings with Sebastian holding her or inside her. And, it was only a matter of hours before she'd see him again. A half-smile escaped from her lips. She wanted him again already.

Relaxing into the springy chair and leaning back into the headrest, Suzanne pushed away from the desk with both feet and scooted a few inches across the shiny wooden floor. She was wearing medium heeled, black leather ankle boots with soft fake fur cuffs teamed with a sophisticated Elisabetta Franchi dress. It was tailored, with a neat polo neck and sleeves that finished half way across her biceps. As she glided, the hemline of the black knitted dress hitched up to reveal the darker band of her stocking tops.

Suzanne giggled. She was in the mood for nylons today; sheer and black and sexy. The very same stockings that had doubled as her blindfold. She dipped her head and inhaled deeply. She was certain she could still detect the aroma of last night's lust, the sweet scent of their shared passion unlocking the exquisite memory box in her head. Last night had been something else. Something magical. Something she wanted to experience again, and soon.

Suzanne fished in her food bag and came up with one half of a chicken Caesar wrap. She took a large mouthful and started to text.

Hey, baby! X

While she waited for Sebastian to reply, she texted her girlfriend, Abi.

Hi Abi, thanks for the dinner invite. We'd love to come. 8pm? Looking forward to meeting your new man. Finally! Lol! X

Her text to Abi had just sent when a reply pinged in from Sebastian.

Hey, sweetheart. Just having lunch at my desk. Too cold to go out. You okay? X

Suzanne texted back straight away.

I'm doing the same. Been thinking about last night! X

She took another bite of her wrap and washed it down with a ladylike sip of hot coffee.

And? X, Sebastian answered immediately.

And it's distracting me. Making me horny!

Suzanne added several emoji smiley faces with winking eyes and lolling tongues to her text before sending it.

Squirming in her seat, Suzanne leaned back and

parted her thighs. All of a sudden, outside, the day had brightened considerably. Watery sunlight hit her face and warmed her. The shaft of winter sun that peeped through the skinny gap in the blinds collided with the smattering of freckles over her nose and made them glisten like tiny grains of demerara sugar. Suzanne squinted as she combed long fingernails through her hair which she wore loose around her neck. Twiddling golden wisps, she waited for a reply.

Now you're getting me excited and I've got a patient at two. X

That's ages away, baby. You know the stockings you blindfolded me with? X

Indeed, I do. X

Suzanne bit her bottom lip as she texted.

Well, I'm wearing them today and I can still smell you on them. I swear I can smell you right here, right now. X

She typed quickly on the tiny keyboard and then checked her message, a naughty smile tugging at her lips. She hit send and crossed her legs. Her fingers fidgety, she squeezed a hand between her thighs.

SUZANNE! X

What are you doing to me? X

I'm getting hard now! X

Sebastian's short texts were arriving thick and fast, one after the other.

I'm getting wet. Call me! X

Suzanne trailed a languid hand over the lace front of her black thong and then placed her phone on the desk. She snaked her fingers beneath the triangle of fabric. It was damp and sticking to her pussy. Suzanne's probing digits gravitated to that special place on her clitoris and she stroked it dreamily, her legs spread, her head flung back, her eyes closed. As her fingers accelerated, Suzanne's phone rang. Sebastian's own personal ringtone; the soothing sound of a harp. She blinked her eyes open and snatched up the phone with her free hand.

"Hey, baby."

"I want you!" Sebastian breathed into the phone.

Hearing her man say those words did it for her every time. Suzanne felt her pelvis clench. Sebastian's need for her reached deep into her core. She shuddered. "I want you too, baby," she gasped as she slid two fingers inside her.

Down the wire, she heard his sharp intake of breath.

"My fingers are inside me, and I'm daydreaming that it's your beautiful cock, Sebastian." Suzanne's voice was as soft and smooth as cashmere. She was enjoying herself, and then, for a single moment, a flashback of Angelo Azzurro trying to dominate and control her over the phone months before, flickered at the back of her brain. Her eyes darkened as she swiped the negative imagery away.

"I can smell you, Suzanne. I can taste you too. I've got a beautiful chemical memory of how you taste and smell," Sebastian growled down the phone. "I want you, baby. Take off your clothes and bend over the desk for me." His voice was low and his words smoky with desire.

Suzanne placed her iPhone on the desk in front of her and switched it to loudspeaker. Her lover's sensual voice filling her office made her feel weak and feverish, like she was drugged. She was breathing heavily as she shrugged her dress above her head, her hair falling back over her shoulders like a shawl of fine golden silk. She eased her thong down her legs and kicked it off. She thrust her bare bottom out expectantly and waited for further instructions.

"Is your bra off?"

Suzanne felt as if Sebastian was watching her. She unclipped her bra, her pendulous breasts tumbling free as she arched over the desk.

"It is now," she purred. They were both speaking in whispers.

"Now widen your legs. I want you to imagine I'm touching you and then sliding inside your beautiful wet pussy."

"Oh God, Sebastian!" Suzanne's breathing was heavy as she slithered a hand between her legs.

"Stick a finger in your ass, Suzanne," Sebastian ordered. "You love my finger in your ass, don't you?"

"Oh yeah. I love it," Suzanne whimpered, her voice sugar-coated with passion.

Suzanne was finding it difficult to breathe. It felt as if she had to unlock every single breath. Her chest was tight and constricted. She couldn't believe that Sebastian was becoming so masterful. Last night had been an astonishing catalyst, it seemed. Their sadomasochistic lovemaking had really cranked up the eroticism to a new level. Suzanne adored the change in her man. Loved the dominant streak she had unearthed.

Her legs like jelly, and unable to stand any longer, she sat. Pushing her crotch towards the edge of her chair, Suzanne propped one leg up on her desk. She slid a finger back into her sex. The intensity of her wetness shocked her. Her lust was leaking onto her office chair. Biting her bottom lip, she did exactly as she was told.

She sucked on a forefinger to lubricate it, and then elevating herself slightly, she cautiously inserted it into her bottom. Moaning softly, she rhythmically worked her fingers in her ass and pussy simultaneously. The skin between her two openings felt as sheer as gossamer. She savoured the exquisite friction as her busy fingers rubbed alongside each other. It felt so good. Better than good. It felt out of this world.

As she played, Suzanne fantasised how it would feel to be doubly penetrated by two cocks. Maybe Sebastian could stick a dildo up her ass while he fucked her. At that decadent thought, her nipples seared, white hot. She was losing it already. She sensed an orgasm escalating within. It was whooshing up from the tip of her toes and ascending her legs at breakneck speed. As it hit her groin, Suzanne cried out, her entire body convulsing as she squirted in a tumultuous gush and her orgasm overwhelmed her.

On the line there were no more instructions. All Suzanne could hear was the steady drumbeat pulsating in her head and her chest, and the hard rush of Sebastian's jerky breathing.

EIGHT

SEBASTIAN

"So, how've you been, Sebastian?"

The woman posing the question had a soothing voice, laced with a disingenuous edge. She was in her late thirties, with rich mahogany hair cut into a fashionable layered bob that tapered into the small of her neck. Her unblemished creamy white skin was framed by a choppy fringe. Sitting in a wingback chair face on to Sebastian across a small coffee table, she wore a baggy black pantsuit and a tight smile. Her teeth were exceedingly white, and her eyes were widely spaced and the colour of blended army fatigues. She was very attractive in a quirky kind of way.

Sebastian exhaled, puffing up his lips as he did so. "Yes, I've been fine, thanks, Sara," he answered with a false brightness.

He fiddled with his hair nervously, his long, tapered fingers teasing black unruly strands out of the starched collar of his baby blue shirt. His legs were crossed and he bounced one leg on top of the other. He was clearly uncomfortable; his body language screamed 'tense'.

"Actually, it's good timing that we have this

appointment today", he said, hesitating slightly before continuing. "I'm planning to look up my father."

Sara's eyebrows arched in concern. "D'you think that's a good idea?"

Sebastian said nothing.

"Things have been settling down for you lately. Maybe meeting your father will unsettle you?" Her words came out flat and with very little intonation.

Sebastian planted both feet on the floor and thrust his head in his hands. He stayed in that position, head down, for a few seconds before straightening up again and delving into olive green eyes, which stared right back into the penetrating blueness of his own.

He'd been coming to see Sara weekly for a few months now. She was detached and businesslike, and Sebastian wasn't at all sure he warmed to her. She wasn't his first shrink, and she probably wouldn't be his last. Since finding Suzanne chained up in that basement, he'd been suffering from severe bouts of insomnia and having nightmares again; the night terrors depriving him of sleep as they intertwined Suzanne's ordeal with deeply suppressed childhood memories of his violent father. The timing was ironic. At almost thirty-seven years of age, just as he'd found love for the first time, instead of being deliriously happy, he still sometimes felt like he was falling apart. He knew he needed to talk to someone discreet and professional who would listen. He wasn't sure if the sessions were helping. But still here he was, spending yet another secret hour with Sara and her incredibly frustrating manner.

Sebastian tilted his body back into his chair and glanced around him. The room was cold and uninviting. Lined with shelves stacked with alternative medical books, the walls were painted an uninspiring wishy-washy grey. There were a couple of half-decent oil paintings on the wall and a vase of yellow-tipped red tulips that flopped and hung their heads. The flowers and art did little to improve the ambience of the treatment room. Sebastian wondered why he'd come. For a moment, anger pulsed a featherlike beat in his temple.

When he spoke, his voice was hushed and measured. "I'm going skiing in Whistler with Suzanne at the weekend. We're flying into Vancouver. That's where he still lives, I think." He paused, searching for the words. "I don't know. I just think it's time. It's been more than twenty years."

"How does Suzanne feel about this?"

"She has no idea. I haven't really told her that much about my father."

Sara chucked him a toothy smile. "So, how are you two getting along?"

"Fantastic. She's perfect. I can't imagine anyone being more perfect."

"But?"

Sebastian stared at Sara, his eyes hard. *How the hell did she recognise there was a 'but'?* He answered her falteringly. "Well, it's worrying me, I suppose, because even though those awful things happened to Suzanne, she seems absolutely fine, whereas I'm…" Sebastian's words dried up. He seemed incapable of finishing his sentence.

"Go on," Sara pushed.

Sebastian sighed heavily. He screwed up his handsome face. He was embarrassed. He didn't want to be discussing his intimate moments with Suzanne with this woman, and yet, he considered he must, if he was ever going to get anything out of their meetings. There was a long silence before he answered.

"Suzanne wants me to be rough with her sexually. I go along with it, but it just kind of freaks me out."

"It really bothers you?"

"Yes. Yes, it does," he said, leaning forward and lowering his head again. Sebastian stared down at a section of the cold tiled floor in his line of vision. He didn't look up at Sara as he continued: "It's only really happened the once. Last night, in fact."

"And?"

"Well, it felt great at the time, but then I felt as guilty as hell afterwards. Couldn't sleep at all. It's like I didn't want to do it but couldn't stop myself." His words trailed off. "Like being in control makes me feel totally out of control."

"We're talking consensual sex and role play here, I'm presuming."

"Of course." Sebastian looked up and shook his head exasperatedly. He sighed and then his words spilled out haltingly. Quietly. "Today I went into sort of control mode on the phone with her. I instigated it. In my lunch hour. In my bloody consulting room!" he added, each short sentence, clipped and late, as if he really couldn't believe what he was saying.

Sebastian was sure he detected a stifle of a grin on Sara's face as she spoke to him soothingly. "If you're troubled by your feelings, perhaps you should tell Suzanne exactly how you feel."

"Yeah, I know; of course I should!" Sebastian retorted

crossly, meeting her gaze firmly. His striking blue eyes full of barely suppressed impatience, he spoke evenly: "Picking the moment isn't easy. I just don't want to mess things up when everything seems so perfect. The problem's me. Not Suzanne." He exhaled heavily again.

"I think perhaps you should choose your moment and discuss it with Suzanne as soon as possible. Anyway, we can talk more about the feelings of guilt you seem to be carrying about this at our next session, but for a moment let's get back to tracking down your father. Will you tell your mother what you're planning to do?"

"No. No, I won't," he said, shaking his head vehemently, his tousled hair flicking around his cheekbones. "If I do manage to meet up with him, then I'll talk with her about it afterwards, I guess."

"Okay," Sara said smoothly. "Have you got any idea what you'll say if you do track him down?"

Sebastian finally managed to muster up a weak smile. "Nope, none whatsoever, but I don't think I'll be lost for words somehow," he stated determinedly.

NINE

SUZANNE

Just before five there was a firm rap on the office door. Suzanne looked mildly alarmed. She wasn't expecting anyone. Outside, darkness had fallen, and it was almost time for her to head home. *Who the hell is that?* she asked silently as she sprang up from her desk.

Hurrying towards the locked door, she called out warily: "Hello?"

"Hey, sweetheart, it's me." Sebastian's rich cultured voice floated into the room and into Suzanne's head. Her mouth widened into an enormous smile, and her heart clattered in her chest. *Oh my, have I got it bad!* she giggled.

There was no time to check on her appearance. She'd had a wash and tidied up her hair and make-up in the office's tiny cloakroom after her brazen behaviour in her lunch hour. As she'd carefully reapplied her bronze lipstick, a 'Little Miss Sensible' voice in her head firmly rebuked her for acting so shamelessly. But now Sebastian was there in person, knocking on her door, there was no such inner voice ticking her off. All Suzanne cared about was that she looked good. For him. She wanted

52

him to make love to her, and she'd put money on it that he wanted that too. Why else would he come to her unexpectedly. The very idea that he couldn't wait a couple more hours and had trekked all the way to central London for her made her heart sing with happiness.

Suzanne unlocked and opened the door. Sebastian stood a little over six feet tall, and with her heels on, Suzanne almost matched him for height. Barely pausing for a single breath, she literally fell into his arms. His cheeks were icy cold, and he smelt of spearmint and musky cologne. His glorious scent wafted in her nostrils as their lips came together and she tasted his tongue. She kissed him passionately, their mouths forceful and hungry. Suzanne shrugged Sebastian's overcoat and jacket off, peeling them down as one along his arms, her lips hardly drifting from his for a moment. Still devouring her man's mouth, she stroked his face, warming his cheeks with her hands before taking hold of him by his shoulders and kneading the knots of fused bone atop his torso. Eye to eye, she dragged fingers through his windswept hair as they continued to feast off each other. The intensity of Sebastian's kisses made Suzanne feel like she was tumbling from a clifftop.

"Baby, that is some welcome," Sebastian murmured, drawing away.

"What are you doing here?" Suzanne asked, encircling his waist, her hands dropping to the cheeks of his bottom as she drew him into her. Sebastian had the most marvellous ass, round and tight and wonderful. She could feel a hint of his hard-on pressing against her, the shape of his shaft resting on the mound of her sex. She let out a groan and pushed back against him.

"Missed you so much," he whispered, his voice loving and warm. Sebastian nibbled Suzanne's ear. "I had to see you. Just couldn't wait," Sebastian disclosed and then continued to shower her mouth with a swarm of tiny kisses.

"Have you come to christen my desk?" Suzanne teased, cupping his face again and breathing hard as she gazed into his magnificent, densely lashed eyes. The nearness of him was making her pussy throb. He was making her feel lightheaded.

Sebastian kissed her once more. A firm kiss planted on her needy mouth, a 'let's-calm-down' kind of kiss. He withdrew and gazed at her, desire flickering in his eyes.

"Actually, I came to invite you for an early dinner. Somewhere nice in Covent Garden maybe?" He paused for effect and dazzled her with that disarming smile. "But, now you mention it…"

Suzanne grinned back. Her heart was thumping. And fuck, yes, she was getting wet. She just couldn't resist this man. Her man. And he simply couldn't keep his hands off her either. That was such an incredible turn on for Suzanne. Sebastian wanted her at every opportunity, and it was abundantly clear he wanted her right that minute. The sexual tension in the compact office was palpable.

"But, now I mention it," Suzanne repeated and chuckled softly before moistening her bottom lip with her tongue.

"Yes, I do want you, baby, very, very much," Sebastian groaned, and then he kissed her mouth lightly.

He stepped back and stared at her for a moment, his chest rising and falling as his breathing accelerated. He looked almost like he was battling to resist her allure. Suzanne giggled and continued licking her lips, and then it was all over. He took hold of her dress and yanked it up and over her head. Her honey blonde hair tumbled to her shoulders and she shook her head lazily. She knew it made an impact, knew Sebastian loved her gilded hair. He stroked it gently and then moved a little further away while his eyes journeyed downwards across her womanly body.

"You look so beautiful, Suzanne. Sometimes I can't believe you're mine."

"Believe me, I am all yours," Suzanne replied softly, under her breath.

Suzanne felt herself evaporating under Sebastian's worshipping gaze. His eyes could melt her soul. He stamped a forceful kiss on her mouth and then massaged her shoulders rhythmically. His hands moving steadily down her body, he stroked the arc of her back, his fingers soft and delicate as he explored her, his hands rubbing her lower back, his thumbs splayed wide on her hip bones. Further south, his hands settled on Suzanne's bottom. He kissed her neck, his sharp white teeth nibbling at her throat as he gave her bare buttocks a hint of a squeeze. Suzanne threw her head back and whimpered as her lover spread her pussy from the rear. Goosebumps sprang up all over her trembling body as he unclasped her bra. Purposefully, he let it drop to the floor. He stared deep into her eyes as he rolled her nipples around with the flat palms of his hands. Tight pulses travelled from her swollen nipples to her groin. Suzanne felt like her knees might give out at any second.

As if reading her mind, Sebastian grabbed Suzanne

and lifted her easily onto the desk. She scrabbled to the edge as he tucked in between her parted legs. He touched her face, his fingers as gentle as a summer breeze. He kissed her again, slowly and reverentially, his hands raking upwards through her mane of shiny hair, fanning it out and then twisting golden strands around his fingers. Suzanne could smell the scent of soap on his skin and the spicy aroma of his Tom Ford aftershave. She breathed him in and closed her eyes. She was lost in the moment, cocooned in a bubble of sheer bliss. Cupping his cheeks, she took in huge gulps of him.

Suzanne raked long fingernails over Sebastian's chest. She pulled off his tie and then gripped the fabric of his shirt. She'd never seen it before and thought it might be new as the buttonholes were stiff. Her fingers fumbled on each button. She wanted it off and fast. She wanted to be skin on skin with her amazing lover. Sebastian assisted, shrugging it off from his shoulders once unbuttoned and then hastily unfastening the shiny silver cufflinks at his wrists. Suzanne licked the centre of his broad chest, stopping momentarily to bite and suck his nipples. With the taste of his bare flesh sweet on her tongue, she tugged at his belt. As she did, Sebastian caught her with a look; his eyes flaring like bright sunlight on an ocean. Suzanne was so aroused she was finding it difficult to breathe. She unbuckled his belt and then seized the zipper on his midnight blue suit pants and lowered it. A gasp of relief erupted from Sebastian's sensuous mouth. Their eyes locked as she released his hard cock and right away took him in hand.

With Sebastian's cock in her grasp, together, they fell back onto the desk. Sebastian lowered his forehead to

Suzanne's. His face hovered above hers, his black hair falling onto her face, tickling her cheeks and her chin. His hand roamed beneath her garter belt, stroking her warm flat belly as she tightened her hand around his shaft and started to work it gradually from the base to the engorged head. Sebastian growled and moved in for another kiss, bearing down on her, dipping his tongue in and skimming it around the inside of her teeth. As he feasted on her mouth, he fingered the lace tops of her stockings and the tempting slash of uncovered flesh between stocking top and underwear.

Gliding a hand smoothly up and down Sebastian's cock, rolling her fingertips over the purply head, Suzanne delighted in the knowledge that he was now fully erect. He felt huge in her hand. The fine skin of his cock was fiery hot, and the more she wanked him, the more breathless he became, air rushing from his mouth between gritted teeth. Half sitting and half lying now, Suzanne whimpered softly as she instinctively spread her legs wide for him. She wanted to be full of him. And she didn't want to wait. The suspense was driving her crazy. She pecked his lips eagerly as his fingertips moved tantalisingly slowly towards her sex. The pressure of his touch on her skin was so intense, it felt as if his fingertips might sear her and leave a telltale scar. She cried out softly and gripped his chin, her fingernails fanning out across his face. She licked him, biting and slavering at his mouth as his fingers finally homed in on her pussy. With a firm hand, he brushed the tiny scrap of fabric away and ran an index finger from the tip of her opening to her bottom, and then slowly back again. Sucking the finger into his mouth greedily, he stared at her, all eyes and teeth.

"I love the way you taste." The words oozed from his drenched mouth, his incisors sharp and sexy and noticeable as he spoke. "And you're so fucking wet!" he added as his index finger delved back within the folds of Suzanne's pussy.

Suzanne groaned. Eyes closed, she writhed. Rolling her head from side to side, her hair was a swatch of golden sunshine. The delicateness of Sebastian's finger fluttering over her clitoris was a sweet torture. The scent of him and the way he touched her so dexterously drove her insane. Suzanne squeezed her eyes tight. Flashes of bright colour sizzled in her brain. Powerful pheromones took her and elevated her to another dimension. She was desperate to be fucked. Wasting little time, she guided Sebastian's cock to her, teasing the head up and down to lubricate the tip with her wetness. He emitted a soft roar, and, barely pausing for a second, he took charge and penetrated her fully, in one easy manoeuvre. Their fit, as always, was perfect.

Hoisting Suzanne's long legs up on his shoulders, Sebastian dragged her to the very edge of the desk so that the lower section of her ass hung in mid-air. Like a rag doll, she complied. A willing victim to her lover's pleasure. He took a moment to kiss each stocking-clad calf adoringly before concentrating solely on making love to her. He laced his fingers through hers and held on tight, his arms locked and strong, his biceps taut and bulging as he moved inside her. He gazed down at Suzanne, his eyes brimming with a lethal combination of love and lust. Concentrating hard, she contracted her muscles, so her pussy rippled around his driving cock. Sebastian's captivating eyes held hers as she squeezed him.

Panting softly, Suzanne elevated her bottom so Sebastian could thrust even deeper inside her. His cock felt enormous, and she loved every single inch he gave her. They mirrored each other's movement as he fucked her, Sebastian dragging himself almost all the way out, tormenting her with every new insertion, his blue stare fixed on her as she ascended to climax.

"I'm very close, baby," Sebastian spat out as he continued to move steadily within her, the symbiosis of their bodies perfectly in tune.

"Do it, Sebastian. Cum inside me," Suzanne hummed, her words low and soft and warm, pushed from pouty lips in sync with each spirited shove of his cock.

Sebastian squeezed Suzanne's hands tightly in his. "I love you, sweetheart," he cried out as he thrust into her one final time and the lovers came together; noisily, joyously, their body's slick from their exertions, their lips meeting in a cornucopia of feverish kisses.

"I love you too, Sebastian," Suzanne breathed, as a tumultuous orgasm flooded her tremulous body and her spasming pussy filled full of her lover's seed.

She started to shake, her knees turned to jelly and every single one of her ten toes felt numb. Suzanne kept her eyes firmly closed as the sound of her thunderous heartbeat slowed in her chest and her head, and she relaxed and wallowed in a moment of pure euphoria.

TEN

SUZANNE

Dressed again, and with her flaxen hair brushed and sleek, Suzanne emerged from the shower room. She glowed. Her green eyes gleaming as dark as mint sauce, she shot Sebastian a dazzling 'cameras-are-on' smile. He was sitting, balanced on the front edge of her desk, his long legs stretched out in front, propping him up. He was busy on his phone. He rewarded her entrance with an easy grin and immediately tucked his mobile into the inside breast pocket of his suit jacket. The move was swift and measured, but, captivated by his engaging smile, Suzanne hardly registered her lover's mildly furtive actions. He adjusted and tightened his smoky blue tie, and then, combing fingers through his tangle of hair, Sebastian stood and offered her his hand.

"You looked beautiful," he said softly and planted a peck on her sticky bronze painted lips.

"Thank you," Suzanne replied almost formally, ducking her head a little after the kiss. She looked up at him coyly, all big-eyed, lashes fluttering. She still couldn't get used to being showered with compliments day after day. Taking his hand in hers and squeezing it fondly, she kissed him again, her lips curving into a contented smile when she was done. She dotted the wave of his knuckles with a smattering of baby kisses and then grinned at him girlishly: "I'm starving, baby. Shall we go and eat?"

"Yes, of course," Sebastian said smiling. "I came here to take you out to dinner, not to do you across your desk. Honestly!" Sebastian chuckled and shot her a wry smile. "Where do you fancy?" he asked, sneaking another kiss before grabbing his overcoat.

Together they bundled themselves into their winter coats. As Suzanne switched off the lights and locked the office door behind her, the pair were discussing their dining options.

★

To make their return train journey home as swift and as simple as possible once they had eaten, Suzanne and Sebastian chose to head for a favourite haunt of theirs in Waterloo. Sebastian hailed them a black cab. They didn't have to wait too long before he secured one, which was a blessed relief on such a bitterly cold evening. Since the sun had dropped, the temperature had plummeted. After just a few moments of standing around with the raw wind whipping fine strands of hair around her face, Suzanne was freezing. In her fashion boots, her feet were so cold her toes felt like icicles.

Once they were settled in the taxi and on the move, Suzanne switched the heater on full and snuggled up to Sebastian. As hot air blasted the small compartment, she closed her eyes and savoured the moment. She felt so relaxed, so happy, like she was the luckiest girl in the world. She adored Sebastian, loved every damn thing about him. He was the love of her life.

Even though rush hour was at its peak, their journey through the London traffic to the H10 hotel took little more than fifteen minutes. The hotel with its asymmetric architecture and funky design sat proudly on Waterloo Road, a little south of the busy railway station. It was just after six thirty when they pulled up outside. Sebastian helped Suzanne out of the cab, handed the driver a ten pound note and a couple of coins, and then arm in arm the couple hurried through the automatic glass doors into the warmth of the elegantly designed lobby.

Newly built and part of a Spanish chain, the hotel's reception area was fashionable and bright. Trendy artwork filled entire walls. White canvases sketched in black with splashes of garish yellow looked like they'd been daubed in English mustard. Sofas and chairs were plentiful in shades of taupe and pale orange. There were lifts cut into the wall formulated from brushed steel. A bank of laptops set up for complimentary use faced the front window of the hotel, and there was a compact bar tucked away in the far corner; modern and light, it featured shiny black décor illuminated with fuchsia pink neon. The whole place had a truly European feel.

What Suzanne and Sebastian loved best about the H10 was the Waterloo Sky Bar; a chic cocktail bar situated on the eighth floor. Heading straight there for an aperitif, they made their way across the lobby. Their hands laced together, they summoned the ultra-modern lift. It arrived soon after, spilling out a bunch of young tourists all muffled up sensibly, ready to do battle with the frigid weather.

The only occupants of the ascending lift, Sebastian waited for the doors to close and then moved in and stroked Suzanne's face. Her cheeks were still icy cold. He framed her face with his warm hands and then tucked blonde threads behind her ears, his touch tender and loving. He kissed her softly on the mouth just as the elevator doors glided silently open. Sebastian stood back gentlemanly and they filed out. Together they followed the winding corridor, removing their outside coats as they did so. Splitting up, Suzanne headed for the powder room, while Sebastian made his way to the bar.

★

Returning from the ladies, Suzanne glanced across the bar at Sebastian. He was seated on a stretched sofa with their drinks and a small bowl of nibbles on the table in front of him. The stunning vista of the brightly lit London night sky was his backdrop. Vibrant and classy, the sky bar had extensive, far-reaching views. A riot of vivacious colour in various shades of electric turquoise, the bar was designed specifically to make the most of the night panorama. London landmarks such as the London Eye, the Gherkin and the Shard commanded centre stage in the impressive skyline and appeared almost godly amongst thousands of lesser illuminated structures that crammed the vast expanse of horizon. The vast floor-to-ceiling windows that framed the amazing outlook were dressed eclectically in shimmering, diaphanous silver chiffon.

The place could easily accommodate a couple of dozen guests on bar stools, easy chairs and massive window seats, though tonight, early on a weekday evening there were less than a dozen patrons. Beyond the expanse of glass, a stylish roof terrace could seat another twenty or so and was kitted out with patio heaters. Complimentary knitted blankets for the daring were piled high in wicker baskets just inside the door. The outside space was largely uninhabited aside from a couple of smokers braving the elements for a quick fag and a closer unobstructed view of the smorgasbord of twinkling luminosities, lighting up the London square mile.

Sipping from a glass of red wine, Sebastian seemed totally engrossed with his phone screen. Deep in thought, he didn't glance her way as Suzanne arrived at their table. She noticed he was frowning.

"Everything okay?" Suzanne enquired as she plopped down beside him, crossed her legs gracefully and took hold of the large glass of Spanish rosé that awaited her. She sipped it. It was perfectly chilled, fruity and delicious; just what the doctor ordered. She stared at Sebastian and waited for his reply.

"Yes, all good." He blew her an air kiss and smiled with his eyes. "Just checking my emails. I've had a cancellation tomorrow, but Pauline's filled it with a new patient. So, all's fine, but it's first thing and I'll need to get in early to make sure I'm up to speed." He conjured up a faux sad face. Dropping his phone into his pocket, he added: "I'll need to go back to mine tonight."

"Okay, no problem," Suzanne said, replicating the same sad face, before smiling widely to conceal her disappointment. These days, she hated sleeping alone.

Sebastian took a large glug of Rioja. Grinning at Suzanne, he said: "I asked the barman to ring through and book us a table for seven. Seeing as my girl is so hungry."

"Thanks, baby." Suzanne squeezed Sebastian's hand and then took her phone from her handbag. "I need to text the boys. See how things are now they're back at college."

"I bet it's a shock to their system being back after having all that time off," Sebastian commented.

"Yes, I'm sure, but they'll have to stop their partying and get themselves sorted as their exams are coming up fast."

"And then they'll be off to uni before you know it. That's if they don't decide to take a gap year."

"We'll see. But if they do, I'm sure Edward will be happy to finance it as he's desperate to get back in their good books." Suzanne rolled her eyes. "Did you take a gap year before Cambridge?"

"No," Sebastian answered. His reply seemed tinged with regret as if he felt he'd totally missed out. "My father was long gone by the time I got into uni, so there wasn't much chance of a gap year. My mother's parents were always very generous and helped me out financially, but I still had to cram in several jobs while I was studying."

Suzanne sipped her wine again and then dabbed her lips with a paper serviette. "What kind of jobs?"

"Umm, mainly in bars. I was rather good at tending bar, if I say so myself." Sebastian laughed and flashed his sharp, impossibly white teeth at her.

"Ah, so that's where you learned to make such a good mojito?"

"Of course!"

Suzanne smiled sweetly and then asked: "Are your grandparents still around?"

"I barely remember my father's parents to be honest, so I've really no idea, but I'm guessing not. On my mum's side, they both died within a year of each other, only a few years ago, actually. My grandfather and I were very close. I suppose he was the father figure I never had."

"Was he a doctor as well?"

"Yes. He was an orthopaedic surgeon too. From when I was very small, I wanted to follow in his footsteps. I even had one of those children's doctor's kits. You know, all in a little case with a plastic stethoscope," he laughed. "I spent a lot of time with him when I was a child, and he was always talking about his work. He loved it. Of course, he was delighted when I decided to study medicine." Sebastian seemed wistful, momentarily caught up in his past. He took another mouthful of wine and then asked: "Do you have grandparents?"

"No. No grandparents. Aside from the twins, Uncle Jack is my only blood relative now."

"That's tough."

Suzanne glanced down and sighed heavily; tiny gusts of air surged from her quivering nostrils. Her bottom lip trembled. "Not half as tough as it was when I took the call about the pile-up on the M4. It was like my world had suddenly imploded. The boys were very young, but it crushed their world too. They adored their grandparents." Suzanne's voice became very small.

Sebastian leaned in and with gentle thumbs brushed tears from her cheeks that she didn't even realise were there. She felt his warmth embrace her. "Sorry," she sniffed and squeezed his hand.

"It's okay, baby. It's fine." Sebastian fiddled with her hair and then kissed her lips softly. "You've got me now, okay?"

"Okay." Suzanne took a deep breath. Sebastian's tenderness slipped around her like a warm coat. Looking at him earnestly, she said quietly: "I know I've got you, but sometimes I really can't believe my luck." She caressed one side of his cheek with the back of her hand. "I do love you, Sebastian," she breathed gazing into his eyes.

"And I love you too. Very much," he whispered, a mesmerising smile lighting up his face. He stared at her for a moment, his startling blue eyes full of affection. He squeezed her hand gently, and then grabbing his wine balloon, Sebastian drank the last of his wine in one thirsty swallow. Beginning to stand, he said: "You text the boys. Send them my best, eh? I'll just go and pay and then we'll head down for dinner."

ELEVEN

WEDNESDAY 9 JANUARY

SEBASTIAN

Although it was past midnight, Sebastian was still up. Dressed in suit pants and a shirt, his tie loosened, his sleeves rolled up, he sat in his home office huddled over the computer. His legs crossed, he bounced his uppermost leg jumpily and stared at the screen. A heavy sigh broke free from his lips. It hadn't taken him long to find his father. Even though Donald Black was a common name, his father's high-profile profession as a world-renowned research scientist had made his task a fairly simple one. He'd even managed to find several photographs of him online, smiling down the lens, looking professional and relaxed. To Sebastian, his easy grin seemed grotesque and mocking. He'd aged well, Sebastian judged begrudgingly as he gazed at his father's images. He couldn't detect a family resemblance aside from the fact that they were both big men. In a flashback to his childhood, he remembered how his father had always seemed so enormous to him.

The secretive trawling of the net in the early hours made Sebastian feel like shit, made him feel like that abandoned kid all over again. Regrets began to flare, burning and hissing in his head as he stared at the various news clippings. Why had he let this slide for so long? Why had he let it eat him up with heartache for so many years? One report mentioned Donald Black was a resident in an upmarket harbourside area in West Vancouver called Bayridge. In the photo he looked tanned and healthy, seated on an outside deck which overlooked the navy blue water. Wondering if his father still lived there, Sebastian shook his head slowly.

A deep sense of loss enveloped him. How could a man treat a woman the way he had treated his mother? Where did all that unsuppressed rage and anger stem from? And how could anyone bring a child into this world and then just abandon them, walk out of their life like they never existed? If Sebastian ever became a father, he knew damn well he'd always be there for his kids. Even though Sebastian hated his father for what he did to his mother and didn't want anything to do with him, ever, he still felt the need to see him. For closure. He just couldn't understand why any father wouldn't want to keep in touch with his only son; his own flesh and blood. The abandonment hung heavy on his heart. Somehow, it made Sebastian feel less of a man. Like a failure. It hurt like hell.

Sitting staring at the screen, he sighed heavily and attempted to rub away the tension throbbing at the back of his neck. As his fingers massaged the area, Sebastian wondered if his father had made a new start with his life. He stretched and then scrolled down through the article. He soon learned that his father had remarried but, it seemed, had sired no children.

"Well, that's a fucking relief!" Sebastian blurted out loud as he stood up from his desk. In anger, he kicked a wastebin out of the way.

Still leaving his father's smirking image filling his monitor, Sebastian padded barefoot to the kitchen. He flicked on the under cupboard spotlights and a warm amber light washed across the large white expanse of units and granite. He took a small bottle of San Pellegrino from the fridge, uncapped it and took a large swig. Wiping his mouth with the back of his hand, he stood stock still, breathing deeply. There was a kaleidoscope of butterflies swarming around his tummy and a beating edge of a migraine tapping away in his head. He felt drained. He took another long sip of fizzy water. All of a sudden he felt very alone.

Holding the water bottle by the neck, Sebastian headed back to his office. As if in slow motion, he lowered himself into his seat and set the bottle down beside him on the desk. He combed a hand through the crown of his jet black hair. After a few moments of just sitting, Sebastian clicked on the link to the online email address he'd unearthed, and slowly, he started to type.

TWELVE

SEBASTIAN

"Coffee," Pauline announced as she set down a steaming mug on a smiley faced coaster.

It was a bright morning and the glorious, cloudless winter sky streamed sunlight across the consulting room, leaving dazzling pools of light illuminating the tiled floor. Wearing a cashmere Hugo Boss suit in charcoal grey, his unruly hair looking smooth and sleek for a change, Sebastian looked up at his secretary. "Thanks, Pauline. Just what I need this morning."

He rubbed his eyes gently. He felt exhausted. He'd gone to bed late and hadn't slept well, kept awake through the small hours with a pounding headache and a thousand unanswered questions pirouetting in his head. These days, he didn't like sleeping alone either.

"All the information for the new patient is on your system. A Ms Tatiana Berisha. I wonder if she looks as scary as she sounds." Pauline said, sounding amused.

Sebastian stopped mid-slurp, all at once the name setting off alarm bells. Surely, this had to be the woman in the car park? The woman that Edward had set up home with? The money-grabbing hooker. The name

71

was anything but commonplace. He thought she'd disappeared without a trace some months ago, making a complete ass of Suzanne's ex in the process. Quite literally taking off immediately after it all kicked off with her old buddy, Angelo Azzurro.

Pauline was staring at him, waiting for an answer.

Sebastian feigned a smile. "Yes, she is actually. I sort of bumped into her. She was just sitting in her car in the car park when I was leaving a couple of days ago."

"Really? Now that is odd." Pauline hesitated, as though picturing the scene in her mind's eye. "I'll buzz you when she arrives."

Pauline returned to her station in the outer office, and Sebastian checked his emails, for about the tenth time since waking. No reply from his father. He shook his head resignedly and then clicked on the information his secretary had taken from Tatiana Berisha. As he read through her notes, a text pinged in.

Morning, sexy. Thought I'd try and catch you before your first patient. Missed you sooo much last night! My bed's too big without you! X

Preoccupied, Sebastian texted back immediately:

Missed you too, sweetheart. Text later. My first patient is imminent.

At once he felt guilty for being so distracted. He started another text and typed in:

Love you lots.

He added a stream of kisses and then hit send.

He was rewarded with a reply just a few seconds later.

Love you more. X

He grinned. Suzanne did that to him every time. But niggling concerns washed the smile away almost as soon as it appeared. Suzanne didn't know Tatiana was back or she would have mentioned it, he was sure. They'd both presumed she'd disappeared for good with that asshole, Angelo. *If she was back, perhaps he was too? Fuck! That was a worry!*

Sebastian exhaled noisily and stood. Hands on hips, he paced. He had no idea how to play this. Perhaps he should call Suzanne and tell her? Or maybe, he should leave it for a few days so they could enjoy their break without this playing on her mind? He took off his jacket and arranged it over the back of his chair and then wandered into the small washroom off his office. He rolled the sleeves of his stylish floral rose pink shirt up to his elbows and began washing his hands. By the time he'd finished the methodical process, he'd decided to just hold back for the moment. See what news, if any, came out in the consultation. Then he'd make a decision.

After refastening his cuffs, Sebastian headed back to his desk. He sat down and began to skim through Tatiana Berisha's scant notes. As he digested the fact that this self-assured seductress was only twenty-one years old, Pauline's voice drifted through the intercom.

"Your eight o'clock, Ms Berisha, is here, Sebastian."

He hit the reply button. "Thanks, Pauline. Give me a couple of minutes and then send her in, please."

With clicky heels announcing her arrival, Tatiana Berisha strutted into the consulting suite a few moments later. Sebastian stood to greet her. Now she was before him, he took in the whole package and had to acknowledge the young woman was absolutely stunning. She exuded the confidence of extreme beauty coupled with the arrogance of youth. Her raven hair black and shiny, it

73

was rolled and tucked into a neat French pleat pinned up at the back. Her make-up was light aside from highly glossed lips. She wore a tailored black suit teamed with a deep pink silk blouse with too many buttons undone. Her cleavage and hummingbird tattoo were blatantly on display. When Sebastian spotted the distinctive tattoo, he was in no doubt whatsoever who this young woman was. She looked sleek and sexy. She was a head-turner all right, but Sebastian sensed her presence in his office could spell nothing but trouble.

Tatiana smiled graciously at him, the smile never quite extending to the depths of her almond-shaped eyes. Just like their first meeting, she gave him the impression she was playing a part; an actress hamming up her role. She stood before him like a fashion model striking a pose.

Sebastian shook her hand. It was small and fine-boned and adorned with several expensive rings. On her slender wrist, Tatiana wore a gleaming yellow gold Cartier Love Bangle encrusted with masses of tiny diamonds. *More jewels courtesy of Edward, or some other sugar daddy, perhaps?* Her grip was strong and her hands were dry and silky smooth. Tatiana held onto Sebastian's hand and didn't let go. A few brief seconds later he extricated his hand from hers.

Wearing his most businesslike smile, Sebastian invited Tatiana to take a seat. She countered with silence and a sexy lick of her lips which she swiftly converted into a pout. *This girl can get away with a pout, that's for sure*, he thought as he watched her. There wasn't a single line on her lovely face. Flashing green eyes flecked with silver, Tatiana dropped dramatically into the patient's chair. She crossed her legs, the rustle of her stockings clearly audible. Staring at Sebastian earnestly, she flapped long jet black lashes heavily coated in mascara.

"So, we meet again, Ms Berisha," Sebastian stated with a trace of James Bond irony.

"Yes, indeed we do," Tatiana replied. Her voice was breathy and seductive and unmistakably Eastern European. Tatiana's puckered lips transformed easily into a girlish smile. "And it is so much warmer and more comfortable in here." A soft tinkle of laughter escaped from her glossy mouth. She shifted in her seat slightly, uncrossing her legs before sliding her knees together modestly.

Sebastian couldn't help but notice Tatiana's legs. They were encased in fine black nylon. Her ankles were trim and her calves were lithe and shapely with great muscle definition. Her skirt was short and tight. She wore high heels with ankle straps which only served to make her wonderful legs look even longer. He diverted his eyes. He decided to bite the bullet. Confront her.

"I think you know my girlfriend, Suzanne Perry-Jackson?"

Sebastian always thought her double-barrelled name sounded sophisticated and sexy when he voiced it. He wasn't sure if mentioning the connection was a good idea, but he didn't give a fuck. He wanted to know what was going on. Information was King. So, he posed the question anyway.

"Ah yes, the very lovely Suzanne; Eddie's ex." There was an unmistakable slap of spitefulness wrapped up in her reply. "Of course, that is how I know about your expertise," she added flirtatiously. "You looked after my stepson, Rayan." She held his gaze, unblinking, waiting for him to challenge her.

Sebastian digested her reply without comment, thinking that Suzanne would probably have a fit if she heard Tatiana referring to Rayan as her 'stepson'. He considered Rayan wouldn't be too overjoyed either. Convinced he wasn't going to get far with his questioning, he decided to move on. Get this over with. "So, what can I help you with today, Ms Berisha?"

Her response was soft and husky. "It's my crucial ligament. I damaged it in a skiing accident."

"Okay. Well, let's take a look. Please take a seat on the couch."

Tatiana slithered a pink tongue around her mouth. It was a very controlled action. She got up and smoothed her fitted skirt down over her thighs before strolling over to the couch. Heavy-lidded eyes fixed on Sebastian, she elevated her body onto it, bottom first, and then stretched her legs out, making herself comfortable. Sebastian walked to the far end and waited as Tatiana offered up her right leg. He took hold of her right ankle, his hand holding it aloft and just above the ankle straps of her Manolo Blahnik shoe. Her stockings felt as sleek as velvet. The touch of sheer denier triggered a cache of memories spinning in his head. Wonderful recollections of his lover, her pretty eyes covered in stockings like these, her lovely legs wrapped around his neck wearing stockings just like these. The erotic reminiscences exploded in his brain momentarily. Sebastian batted them away and cleared his throat. Tatiana looked up at him, her face expectant, and yet, there was something else. Something Sebastian couldn't quite put his finger on.

"I'm just going to bend this slightly and I'd like you to tell me if there's any pain."

He pushed her leg back towards her body, gently forcing a bend into her knee. Tatiana let out a tiny whimper.

"Does that hurt?"

"A little." The way Tatiana pronounced the word 'little' made it sound as if the letter 'i' was replaced by two 'e's.

"Okay," Sebastian said and lowered her ankle back onto the bed. "When you had the accident, was this operated on?"

"No. It wasn't completely torn, so they said it would probably heal itself."

"And when was the accident?"

"A couple of years ago." Tatiana smiled indulgently. "In Méribel. Have you been?"

Sebastian couldn't help releasing a genuine smile. He was really incredibly excited about going skiing with Suzanne.

"Many times," he answered, his blue eyes twinkling. Taking hold of Tatiana's ankle again, he said: "Okay, Ms Berisha, could you try to push against me as I push against you. I need to test your resistance to see what's going on in there."

Tatiana sat up a bit. "Do call me Tatiana, please." She locked her eyes on his.

Taking a strong stance, Sebastian nodded briefly and averted his eyes. He looked down as he took hold of Tatiana's sexy ankle once more and, with a fluid pushing motion, moved her elevated knee steadily towards her, back and forth. It took him about two gentle shoves and a couple of seconds to realise that Tatiana wasn't wearing any underwear. It was just a quick glimpse of flesh but was enough to learn that Tatiana kept her pussy clean-shaven. Sebastian made no comment whatsoever, but Tatiana was well aware he had seen exactly what she wanted him to see.

"Sorry about that, Sebastian," Tatiana trilled familiarly, choosing her moment to use his Christian name for the first time. She was clearly not sorry at all. "I don't believe in underwear," she laughed and stared into his eyes confrontationally.

Sebastian stared back momentarily and then ignoring her intimate revelation, said curtly: "I think a course of anti-inflammatories might do the trick. If you'd like to wait in reception, Ms Berisha, I'll print you up a prescription."

★

With Tatiana gone, Sebastian hunkered over his computer and made some notes on her file. He had to laugh. *Did that stupid young woman really think coming here with some old skiing injury was a plausible excuse for checking him out? And then flashing at him! For God's sake!* Sebastian hoped it was just curiosity and mischief that brought her here. He hoped that her visit had nothing to do with Angelo Azzurro and that she wouldn't be back. But he had a horrible feeling she just might. What with her and bloody Sylvia Hamilton, it was becoming a nightmare. Sebastian sighed heavily. Fuck it, he refused to worry about it, but he made up his mind to tell Suzanne. She really needed to know that Tatiana was clearly back in

Edward's life. But not by text. He'd tell her tonight face-to-face. As he typed at the computer, a new email sprang up in the corner of the screen. Sebastian caught his breath as he saw it. He clicked it open with unsteady fingers.

Hello, Sebastian, you're right; it's been a very long time. And yes, if you are in Vancouver, please do look me up. Give me a call when you're here and we'll arrange something. Here's my cell phone number...

Sebastian's hands were steady, but his heart was beating wildly as he carefully added Donald Black's phone number into his list of contacts.

THIRTEEN

TATIANA

Tatiana was heading home in a black cab. The London traffic was dense and tiresomely slow, and she was becoming increasingly frustrated as the car inched slowly through the streets of London northwards towards Chelsea. She wasn't particularly happy with the way her consultation with Sebastian Black had panned out. It just didn't go as she'd expected. He'd seemed aloof and reserved. But there would be a secondary opportunity; she would make damn sure of that. She'd call the secretary and rebook the other appointment she'd been offered. As a follow-up. That cow, Suzanne, was going to get a nasty surprise. It was merely a matter of time. Tatiana yawned and settled back in her seat. She gazed out of the window as her cab crawled over Battersea Bridge, the diesel engine idling noisily in stationary traffic.

She had no plans for the rest of the day, but she knew exactly what she'd like to be doing: spending all day getting laid. When she was growing up and had first discovered the joys of sex, she thought that fucking many times, every single day, was the norm but soon discovered that none of her adolescent girlfriends felt quite the same way. Tatiana was still a very young woman when she accepted she had an incredibly high sex drive. Eddie would be out at work all day and she was bored. She needed some excitement. Scanning the exhilarating London vista bathed in the early morning winter sunshine, Tatiana smiled. *How hard can it be to get laid in this big, beautiful city?*

Tatiana's phone vibrated in her bag. She fished around for it and grabbed it. Her screen showed a new text message. From Angelo. She swiped and swiftly typed in her passcode. Concern rippled across her face as she read it.

Hey, Tatiana. Make sure you let me know what time your flight lands on the 16th, so I can collect you from the airport. Need you back. Ciao Bella! X

Tatiana stared at the text for a few moments before replying. She wasn't ready to tell Angelo that she had no plans to return. Not yet. She typed quickly:

Of course, Angel.

She added a couple of kisses and an emoji set of luscious lips and then sent the text. She slid her phone back into the new season Mulberry handbag that Eddie had bought her at the weekend, dropped it beside her feet and flopped back against the seat. Spidery black lashes pulled heavy lids downwards as she closed her eyes in silent contemplation.

★

Tatiana even surprised herself at how little time and effort it actually took to source some action. As she exited the elevator at the Chelsea apartments, she bumped into two burly workmen in matching paint-splattered overalls teamed with white T-shirts with round necks, stretched tight across wide brown necks. They were unloading a trolley parked up outside the adjoining penthouse. When she saw them, she chuckled softly under her breath. The lobby which serviced the two penthouses was roomy and carpeted in lavish black wool carpet, dappled with twinkles of silver. Huge windows allowed the light to flood in and cast shadows on walls of palest grey. The guys seemed in no hurry with their task and slowed to a standstill as Tatiana approached, both sizing her up appreciatively as she sloped towards them like a large exotic cat.

Both men's skin tones were the colour of Galaxy milk chocolate, rich and sexy. African, Tatiana decided. They had a kind of tribal regalness to their demeanour. She guessed they were probably just a few years older than her and looked like they worked out. Tatiana picked up a waft of fresh sweat mixed with an unfamiliar cologne as she neared them. The taller of the two men had closely cropped wiry hair and bore a passing resemblance to Lewis Hamilton, with his boyish good looks and meticulously shaved sideburns that tapered below his chin. He wore a diamond stud in one ear, and both arms were covered in sleeve tattoos. His slightly shorter, stockier mate was blessed with amazing muscular biceps and a shaved head; smooth and round like a brown snooker ball. Her eyes flashing, Tatiana reduced her grin and awarded them a sultry pout as she came alongside them.

"Morning, Miss," 'Brown Ball' said and threw a sly wink her way.

Tatiana felt a satisfying warmth inside. *This was going to be so damn easy!*

"You guys need coffee? I'm just next door. Give me ten minutes and you can come and ring my bell."

Her innuendo hung in the air, hovering like a thousand dust motes in rays of dazzling sunshine. There were a few seconds of silence as Tatiana fiddled in her handbag for her keys. Her eyes darted over the men. She liked black men. Actually, she liked most men. The idea of a wild and dirty threesome danced in her head.

The decorators glanced at each other then back at Tatiana. "Cool. See you in ten," 'Lewis' confirmed, his voice deep and full of south London bluster. His teeth were pearly white and straight and his dark eyes glossy.

Beside him, his friend grinned confidently, his massive arms folded casually over his barrel chest. Tatiana glanced back over her shoulder. She knew exactly what she wanted and knew without question the men were up for it too.

"Look forward to it, guys." Tatiana's softly spoken words floated away behind her as she pushed open the door and then kicked it shut after her. Very dramatically.

Striding down the hallway towards the bedroom to prepare for her visitors, Tatiana laughed out loud at the thought of her neighbours returning home that evening and wondering why their guys had made little progress with the decorating.

★

When the doorbell chimed ten minutes later, Tatiana was ready. She opened the door wearing her sexuality like a beacon. She looked truly irresistible. She had let down

83

her hair and it fell luxuriantly in inky waves around her shoulders. Coated in her favourite perfume, her flawless skin was thick with the floral bouquet of Valentino. With another button popped on her fitted raspberry crush shirt, her breasts looked perky and ready to escape at any moment. Looking very pleased with herself, she stood back to make space for her visitors to enter.

'Brown Ball' stood on the threshold, his beefy arms still crossed in front of him. He sported an amused grin and said nothing. His workmate beside him was silent too, though their hungry eyes said it all.

"Come on in, guys. You want coffee?" Tatiana purred, her green eyes as inviting as a spring meadow.

'Brown Ball' answered this time. "Yeah, that would be nice." Glancing down at his boots caked in ancient grime and splashes of paint, he asked: "You want us to take our boots off?"

"No, no." Tatiana paused and ducked her head. Raising her eyes and turning her gaze from one man to another, she added: "Not yet anyway." She smirked and then licked her perfectly painted lips, drawing the tip of her tongue around the crimson shine of her mouth.

The air crackled with raw sexual tension. All three players were well aware of the game. What was on offer was way more exciting than a cup of instant coffee. Tatiana ushered them in and led them down the short corridor towards the impressive open-plan kitchen that adjoined the large living space. Still wearing their workman boots, the men trudged behind her wordlessly. Once in the kitchen 'Brown Ball' kept on walking all the way to the window and, with his back to them, gazed out at the far-reaching views.

"Okay, coffee!" Tatiana announced brightly, as she leaned over the sink to fill the kettle.

As the water rushed into the spout, Tatiana stuck her bum out and gave it a gentle twerk, which didn't go unnoticed. 'Lewis' took the bait at once, moving in behind her, a hand straying tentatively across her buttocks, his large brown fingers brushing the temping booty. Tatiana giggled naughtily and abandoned the half-filled kettle in the sink. Giving the green light, she pushed back against his wandering hand and exhaled noisily, her breath coming in short gravelly pants. 'Lewis' took her cue and there was no more hesitation. He moved in and snaked both arms around her, trapping her in a bear hug. Nosing her hair out of the way, he began nibbling her neck, his hands cupping her breasts, his cock hard against her trembling ass. 'Brown Ball' stood a few metres from them watching intently, his arms still folded, his nostrils flaring. His overalls were starting to look tight around the crotch.

'Lewis' seized a handful of Tatiana's hair and tugged her round to face him. She offered him her tongue. Latching onto it, he sucked it hard into his mouth, overpowering it with his as he plunged a hand down her blouse. He connected with her nipple in an instant. He met her eyes as he flicked her swelling bud with a rapidly moving forefinger. He was toying with her, daring her to resist. His hot breath surrounded her as she dragged him in for another frantic French kiss.

With both perfect breasts hooked up and over her La Perla push-up bra, Tatiana struggled to catch her breath. Being groped at the kitchen sink by a complete stranger made her wet between the legs. Made her so fucking horny. She could feel her juices moistening her inner thighs. She could smell the musky scent of her passion. It filled her head. She felt intoxicated. One by one, 'Lewis' unfastened the remaining buttons on her shirt to reveal a pretty-as-a-picture brassiere which was fashioned of lace and luxury silk and was the colour of soft summer fruits. It was a perfect colour match for her puffed-up nipples which his large brown fingers gripped firmly and fed into his voracious mouth. He ravaged one and then the other while his free hand snuck up her skirt. Tatiana slammed her eyes shut and threw her head back in ecstasy as he touched her between her legs. She was so sexed-up, she was shaking.

She heard movement, and when she glanced over towards the windows, she saw 'Brown Ball' heading towards them. He carried his swollen ebony cock in his fist, his meaty fingers working their way up and down its thick shaft as he approached, his eyes like two Minstrel chocolates; tight and hard and brimming with arrogance. Tatiana couldn't drag her eyes off his magnificent weapon.

"Ah fuck!" Tatiana let out a raspy groan.

She stared in awe at the monster let loose from his navy overalls. Her heart thumped as he moved towards her. Greedy green eyes roamed his extensive length as his buddy began playing with her. Expert fingers spread her lips and slipped inside with ease. It felt awesome, like an appetiser for greater things to come. *Fuck, that cock is nearly a foot in length,* Tatiana estimated. Shuddering at the mere thought of it, she tightened her pelvic muscles around the fingers squelching inside her. She spat out a soft roar and bit at the delicious full lips that sucked at her mouth. She tasted menthol cigarettes on his darting tongue. The concept of screwing these guys all day was the indulgence she deserved. She'd have her fun and they'd be long gone before Eddie got home, and then she'd play the perfect girlfriend again, ready for Eddie when he wanted her. Tatiana could fuck all day and night, no problem.

"Get on the sofa," 'Brown Ball' barked.

Tatiana was loving being fingered and adored having her tits played with, but the gigantic cock on offer was just too much to resist. She was drawn to it like a magnet. She locked eyes with 'Lewis' who reluctantly withdrew his fingers and slapped her hard on the bare ass. On unsteady legs, her tight skirt bunched up around her waist, Tatiana obediently tottered towards the sizeable seating area.

"Get your clothes off," 'Brown Ball' ordered, still stroking his cock languorously.

Tatiana unzipped her skirt. It puddled at her feet. She stepped out of it and then shrugged off her blouse. She stood before the two strangers in high heels and hold-up stockings with her breasts jutting out of her pretty underwired bra. Her nipples looked enormous.

"And your bra," 'Lewis' snarled from behind, watching her, admiring her ass. His eyes were all over her as he unhitched his overalls, freeing himself ready for the games to begin.

With fumbling hands, Tatiana unfastened her bra. Her wonderful rose-tipped breasts bounced free as firm hands pushed her onto the sofa. Kneeling, facing the back of the couch, her knees widely spaced, she arched her back and leaned forward. She longed to be filled to the brim with a massive black cock. She didn't have long to wait.

Tatiana closed her eyes and wailed as she felt the bulbous head of a thick ebony cock spread her lips wide. Hot flesh sizzled against her bare back. Big, rough hands covered both her breasts. *It's fucking huge!* throbbed in her brain as she sat back onto it, savouring every inch. Once 'Lewis' was all the way in, he rocked her back and forth on it, slamming it into her hard, time after time. Tatiana was lost in the moment of pure animal gratification. She felt a surge of adrenaline ignite her body. She started to let go, started to cry out but was abruptly silenced when an even bigger cock was forced into her open mouth. She felt like she might choke.

Seconds later, Tatiana was cumming. It hit her quickly. A colossal jolt of elation lifting her as she relinquished her mouthful of cock. As her body convulsed on undulating waves of euphoria, she was vaguely aware that she was being moved around. Two pairs of strong hands positioned her so that she was now kneeling over 'Lewis' and parallel with the back of the sofa. Still riding the flood of orgasm, Tatiana sank down hard on him. She gritted her teeth and growled like a wild beast as the blistering heat of his cock filled her again. Her orgasm just kept on going.

Tatiana exhaled hard and slowed the pace. She was huffing and puffing from her exertions, and sweat weaved a lazy trickle between her hanging breasts. As she began to calm down, fingers slipped slickly into her ass. One at first, followed by another alongside it, both working together to stretch her sphincter little by little. It felt so fucking good. The friction of the fingers so close to the cock that she was riding was driving her insane. The fine skin separating her two most intimate openings felt almost invisible, as the cock and fingers worked in harmony. She was loving it, coming down from one climax and already creeping up to the next.

'Brown Ball' removed his fingers and then seemed determined to lose his tongue in her ass. He thrust it deep into her puckered hole, flexing it open. He sucked on her sphincter, his busy mouth sending shivers running all over her. 'Lewis' screwed her steadily. He snatched at her hair and hauled her down towards him. He swept stray strands of flyaway hair aside as he feasted on her open mouth and grazed on her bare shoulders. Tatiana growled like a lioness. She adored being rimmed. The nerve endings around her asshole were so sensitive it sent shockwaves all over her body. Being rimmed and fucked simultaneously was incredible. As she drifted in ecstasy, her whole body tense with excitement, Tatiana got it. The guys were preparing to do her in the ass and pussy at the same time. No sooner had the thought struck her and they were putting their DP plan into action.

'Lewis' fucked Tatiana in an unhurried steady rhythm, while his mate clambered up from his knees and onto the sofa behind her. Clammy breath hit her back, and big hands gripped her waist as he got into position.

"Lean forward, babe," 'Brown Ball' grunted.

Tatiana was incapable of answering now. She was totally losing it. She did as she was told, releasing a collection of soft, indecipherable moans as she leaned forward and crushed her breasts flat against the broad chest of 'Lewis'. He was sweating, and the film of moisture on his coffee-coloured skin mingled with her own. Her bottom thrust in the air, her asshole was in prime position to be filled. Tatiana released an extended wail as big hands held her buttocks apart. She clenched the cock inside her, savouring every spirited jab. Her asshole felt delicious; stretched and open and vulnerable. A sweet stabbing pain moved through her as the head of the gigantic cock entered her sphincter. She felt an intense burning sensation that brought tears to her eyes as he gradually worked the entire length into her ass. When it was all the way in, Tatiana felt like her whole body was aflame.

It wasn't the first time Tatiana had been DP'ed, but it was the first time she'd gone 'dark' for a double penetration session. She wished she could view the spectacle in a mirror. Black on white on black. The imagery would be amazing, she decided as her body trembled with waves of pure pleasure. Never before had she taken such a big cock in her ass. The very idea of being doubly penetrated on her sofa mid-morning, by two complete strangers, was a major head trip, and the reality was even better. She gritted her teeth and squeezed her eyes tightly shut as she let go. As she bounced on the two oversized cocks that rubbed up alongside each other so intimately and feverishly inside her, Tatiana sensed a massive second cumming just moments away.

She let out an almighty shriek as her climax took her. Her howls spurred on the guys, who, working together, increased their tempo as one. A few seconds more and then they were all at it. Tatiana felt like she was cumming for ever, floating on an unbelievable high, as first 'Lewis' exploded into her pussy, followed a split second later when her ass was filled with hot semen. 'Brown Ball' collapsed on top of her, his heavy breathing pounding in her ear. Three bodies perched precariously on the edge of the couch in a tangle of sweaty lust, Tatiana's smaller pale body sandwiched by the two black men that surrounded her.

★

Naked and still breathless, Tatiana lay on her back on the sofa, a beatific smile plastered on her face. Staring up at the ceiling, she caressed her tingling, sticky body languidly with both hands. The guys were washing. She'd catch her breath and then take them into the bedroom. For more. Out of habit, she reached out and grabbed her phone. She swore out loud when she noticed a text displayed on her screen.

"Fuck!"

Not sure if U R around, babe, but just popping home. I forgot some papers. Love you lots and lots! X

Her heart pounding, Tatiana checked the time it was sent and calculated that it had been almost an hour ago. "Fuck! Fuck! Fuck!" she mouthed.

Springing up like a gazelle, Tatiana dashed to the shower room off the hall. Swiftly shutting the door behind her, she screeched to the guys: "My husband will be arriving any minute. Please get dressed and stay in here. When you hear me shut the bedroom door behind us, then just get the fuck out of here." In her panic, Tatiana's Albanian accent was more conspicuous than ever.

"Got it," 'Lewis' said smiling, obviously finding the situation more amusing than threatening. He grinned broadly as he tugged his T-shirt over his head.

Tatiana grabbed a hand towel and started to wipe the

cum from her pussy and backside. She was in mid-wipe when she heard the front door open.

"Tatiana, you home, sweetheart?" a familiar voice called out.

The workmen glanced at each other and started to snigger. Tatiana raised a finger to her lips. They quietened and watched wide-eyed as she flattened her hair down and teased it into some sort of order. They were still watching as she grabbed a robe from the door and hurriedly belted it around her.

"Hey, babe," Tatiana purred as she emerged into the hallway, carefully closing the door behind her.

She took Eddie's hand in hers and led him to the bedroom, shutting the door with a decisive slam. When she detected the click of the front door as it closed softly, she was on her knees. Tatiana smiled mischievously and began to deep throat her man with great gusto.

FOURTEEN

EDWARD

In the hallway, Edward stood in front of the mirror, carefully knotting his navy blue tie, attempting to get it just so. He was something of an expert, having mastered the art out of necessity at his prep school when he was just six years of age. He was an attractive man; distinguished, some might say, wearing well for a man in his early forties. His dark hair was peppered with grey, and his tailored pinstripe suit looked good on him. Tatiana came at him from behind. She wrapped both arms around his neck affectionately and pressed a kiss to his cheek. The scent of her made him giddy. She was just so goddamn beautiful. She smelled of flowery perfume fused with the powerful aroma of their lovemaking. He wished he could stay home and fuck her all day.

He nuzzled back into her. "I guess I'd better get back." He pulled a long face.

"It's good you pop home, babe," Tatiana cooed in his ear, her accent heavy and sexy on her tongue as she rubbed her smooth naked body against his clothed one. "I miss you so much, Eddie," Tatiana murmured and then started to nibble his earlobe. "Can we go somewhere special for dinner tonight? How about we go to Le Gavroche and then we could go to dance at Tramp? I'll need a new outfit, though." Tatiana giggled and linked her arms around his waist.

Edward forced a smile and pulled her around for a proper hug. She fell into his arms and hugged him back. He was stressed and exhausted and spending money faster than he was making it. He wanted a quiet night at home with Tatiana, not a night on the town, out dancing till the early hours. For God's sake, he had to get up soon after six! And another outfit? He wouldn't mind but each one cost thousands when you totted up the shoes and handbag to match, and then, of course, there was the jewellery. He didn't even want to think about how much he'd spent on jewellery in the last week or so. The Cartier love bangle he'd bought Tatiana as a welcome home gift had set him back more than twenty-six thousand pounds alone.

"I'm not sure, babe. I may have to work late," he lied. "Let's leave it to the weekend, eh?"

Tatiana stuck out her bottom lip, like a sulking toddler. Trying to win her over, Edward kissed the tip of her perfect button nose. "I'll call you when I get back to work and let you know. Okay, babe?"

"Okay, Eddie," Tatiana answered quietly and sullenly. She pulled away from his embrace and flounced into the bedroom. At the door, she blew a perfunctory air kiss.

He blew one back, but by then Tatiana had already shut the door and disappeared behind it. "Speak later, babe," he called through the closed door, knowing full well that she was in a strop. There was no reply.

Edward sighed and collected his briefcase from the side table. He needed more money. It was as simple as that. Thankfully, he might just have found a way to net himself a big windfall. Enough to get him out of trouble for a while. The information he'd stumbled on that morning might be the answer. If he could just connect with the right person to broker the deal, then they'd split the money and his beautiful Tatiana could have all the jewels and outfits she deserved. Edward smiled. Yep, he felt happier now he had a plan of sorts. He got into the lift, nodding civilly to the two workmen loafing around outside the neighbouring penthouse. As the lift doors shut behind him, he wondered what they both found so amusing.

FIFTEEN

THURSDAY 10 JANUARY

SEBASTIAN

Sebastian sat alone, sipping Laurent Perrier rosé. His midnight blue slacks and Ted Baker shirt in various shades of purple and turquoise showed off his magnificent eyes to perfection, though clashed dramatically with the bright sofa on which he sat stiffly, and upright. He leaned over and helped himself to a smoked salmon blini and then wished he hadn't when he realised there were no serviettes. He took out a clean white handkerchief and gave his fingers a brisk wipe. He hoped the smell of fish didn't linger, although it was pretty obvious it did as Abigail's cuddly white pooch, Teddy, immediately jumped up and attempted to lick his fingers. Sebastian stroked Teddy's soft head gently and then lifted him down onto the floor again. Sebastian wondered where everyone was. He knew Abigail's partner had yet to arrive. He guessed the others were in the kitchen, helping out. He'd been told to go and relax, so with Teddy eyeing him, he tried to do just that. Though he wasn't finding it terribly easy.

Sebastian couldn't help but reflect upon the last time he'd sat on Abigail's comfortable lime green sofa.

Tonight, Suzanne was safe and by his side. All was calm and he was looking forward to an evening amongst friends. But only a few months previously when he was sitting on the very same sofa, his head was in a very different place. Back then, he was crazy with worry and in need of Abigail's help to find Suzanne and get her back safely from the violent pimp who'd abducted her. The very same Albanian asshole who was heavily connected with Tatiana Berisha; his provocative new patient and the lover of Suzanne's ex. Sebastian sighed. *Why was everything so fucking complicated?*

He took another sip of champagne. It was his second glass, and it was already beginning to relax him. Sebastian hated keeping secrets; his covert meetings with his therapist, his intent to meet up with his father on their Canadian break, but his main concern was Tatiana. He'd mulled over their brief encounter and decided not to mention her visit until they'd got back from Whistler. *Why worry Suzanne while they were away?* Sebastian hoped he was making the right decision.

Carrying a bottle of Moet, his beautiful lady entered and walked towards him across the lavish drawing room. The room was spacious and as warm as toast. Scented candles flickered everywhere. It smelt like a high-end spa. In the gauzy light, Sebastian's gaze followed Suzanne's every step. She looked radiant; utterly ravishing in a full-length raw silk dress in shimmering ivory. It clung to her torso and then kicked out stylishly around her hips. He knew she wasn't wearing panties, just those sexy hold-up stockings in a neutral tone and high heels that made her legs look even longer and lovelier. They'd made love when he'd collected her, a wonderful quickie on her living room floor, her straddling him, her dress yanked up, her sensational body spasming on top of him, while their taxi waited for them outside. Already he wanted her again. The look in her eyes convinced him the feeling was mutual. Suzanne dazzled him with a smile. He seized her with heavily lashed, big blue eyes that said: 'I love you. I want you. You are mine.' Suzanne got the message loud and clear. She leaned over and kissed him full on the mouth. Her tongue tasted of champagne. She smelt divine; her own wonderful natural scent sweetened with a glaze of Coco Mademoiselle perfume. Sebastian drank her all in.

"Couldn't resist," she giggled.

"You look so hot, baby. How am I going to keep my hands off you all night?"

She took his hand in hers, and her mouth widened into another enormous smile. "Who says you have to?" Soft laughter tinkled from lips painted in baby pink sparkle.

"Suzanne!" Sebastian exclaimed, pretending to be shocked. There was fire in his eyes. "Where's Abigail's new man, then?" he asked, before pressing his lips to Suzanne's knuckles and kissing them.

"He's not that new. She just hasn't introduced him to us yet. He's on his way, apparently," Suzanne replied, sinking down on the sofa.

Sebastian took the bottle from Suzanne and filled a glass for her, tipping the flute expertly at an angle to reduce froth and spillage.

"Thank you, baby." Suzanne smiled and sipped the pink bubbles greedily. "That is so good." She drew her knees up and snuggled in close to him.

"He's had a bit of an emergency, I think. He's a vet. They met when Abi took Teddy in for his injections and they just clicked."

Teddy, hearing his name mentioned, joined them on the sofa, Sebastian's side. Instinctively, Sebastian began to stroke him. "A bit like you and me. Though not saying Rayan's a dog, but you know what I mean."

Suzanne grinned. Her eyes flashed seductively, as if remembering their magic moment. "Indeed, I do."

"What's his story, then? He's not another married one messing her about, is he?"

"No, he's a widow. No children. No complications. He sounds like a really nice guy, actually. I'm glad Abi seems to have found herself a good man at last."

"Good for her. The Three Musketeers all sorted and lucky in love," he joked, and then enfolding Suzanne in his arms, went in for another kiss. After enjoying the taste of her for several seconds, he pulled away breathless. "I'm not joking. I really want to fuck you, Suzanne."

Suzanne smiled sweetly. She kissed him again, this time her tongue dipping into his mouth before she drew back. She licked her lips and stared at Sebastian, throwing down the gauntlet. He slipped a hand under the hem of her dress and squeezed just above her knee. The sheer nylon felt delicious. Their eyes locked and held. Sebastian's fingertips moved in tiny circles on her inner thigh. His touch was light, his breathing shallow. Sexual tension hung in the air.

The magic was broken when the door opened and Ayman and Angie busied into the room carrying trays of decorative and delicious-looking canapés, more champagne and a pile of linen serviettes. Angie was one of Suzanne's closest friends, and Ayman, her younger Egyptian partner, was an incredibly smart city boy. The two couples had met around the same time, and now they often went out as a foursome.

"Here you go." Angie proffered a tray of snacks.

"Thank you," Sebastian said, while still maintaining eye contact with Suzanne. He dragged his eyes away, and then, grinning, he regarded the food on offer. There were open mini burgers piled high with a rich tomatoey relish and a tray of beautifully risen Yorkshire puddings filled with rare roast beef and creamed horseradish.

"They look great," he said as he accepted a mini Yorkshire from Angie who looked totally stunning in a slinky Lipsy pencil dress in white with flashes of bold purple. She was blonde and attractive with slim hips and a big bust, showcased to the max as usual with another of her low-cut frocks. Since her break-up with her husband, she'd had several lovers on the go until she met Ayman, who was more than a decade younger than her. Now the two of them were inseparable. Ayman had moved in with her, within a few weeks of their meeting.

Sebastian popped the warm roast beef canapé into his mouth and ate it in one sumptuous mouthful. Beside him, Suzanne was tucking into one too. Angie offered Sebastian another, and so he repeated the process. "Mmm, that's delicious," he mumbled, still chewing. He swallowed and added: "But if I eat any more, I'll ruin my dinner, and I need to go and wash my hands." He smiled lazily, totally relaxed now. He leaned over and planted a gentle kiss on the bridge of Suzanne's freckled nose, gave her hand a squeeze and then left the room.

★

It was almost nine when Michael finally arrived. By which time the five of them were on their fourth bottle of bubbly and were a little tipsy and very hungry, hanging out in the kitchen drinking and chatting, and being tormented by the wonderful aroma of *duck a l'orange* wafting from the oven. Michael was all apologies as Abigail ushered him into the kitchen. He was carrying a sizeable bouquet of flowers; fragrant, dusky pink roses with gypsophila and greenery wrapped in hot pink tissue paper, plus two bottles of pink champagne.

As Abigail made the introductions, Suzanne leaned her head on Sebastian's shoulder and hugged him one-handed around the waist. Sebastian adored that she was so tactile. He gave Michael the once-over. He was greying at the temples and a fair bit older than Abigail but was smartly dressed and handsome. They looked good together. As Michael explained that his tardiness was due to a tiny tabby kitten called Minnie who'd been hit by a car but would be as good as new in a few days, Sebastian noticed Michael's eyes. They were a similar shade of blue to his own. He liked him at once. Something about him really clicked with Sebastian. He was impressed by his firm handshake and the way he wrapped Abigail in his arms and gave her a huge, genuine hug. Michael's vivid blue eyes lit up when he looked at Abigail. Sebastian swallowed a wide smile. He had never seen Suzanne's girlfriend looking so happy.

"Okay, now Hughie's finally arrived, can you guys all take your seats in the dining room?" Abigail said beaming. As she spoke, she held Michael's hand proudly.

"Hughie?" Suzanne quizzed.

"Just a nickname," Michael replied, his eyes twinkling as he smiled warmly at Suzanne.

"Suzanne, can you grab the two bottles of Chablis in the fridge and the breadbasket? It's over there," Abigail said pointing. "And Angie, can you help me with the starter?"

Soon after, everyone headed to the dining room and dinner was served.

★

After dessert was eaten and the plates and crockery were cleared away, while Abigail and Michael prepared coffee, Suzanne excused herself to go 'powder her nose'. With greedy eyes, Sebastian watched her get up. He observed the sway of her hips, marvelled at the slenderness of her waist and enjoyed her honey blonde hair, free and flowing, as it dusted her bronzed shoulders. *Fuck, he wanted her!* His eyes were still following her as Ayman and Angie got up from the table.

"Just popping out for a smoke," Angie announced, grinning broadly and taking Ayman, and a big fat joint she'd rolled earlier, out into the back garden.

Sebastian smiled back at them, then got up from the table and hurried after Suzanne. He caught up with her just outside the downstairs cloakroom. Silently, he took her hand and followed her in. He shut the door behind them, slid the bolt and then swivelled to face her. Suzanne was all smiles too. He guessed she knew exactly what was about to happen.

"Oh God, Sebastian. You are so bad! What's everyone going to think?"

Sebastian said nothing, just grinned as Suzanne cradled his cheeks and moved in close, teasing his lips with her tongue. Sebastian took in huge mouthfuls of her, kissing her softly while he trailed fingers up and down the outside of her thighs. His fingertips dug into Suzanne's flesh, gently squeezing it through the thin material of her dress. Just touching her, he could feel himself getting hard.

"That you are so fucking sexy that I can't keep my hands off you," Sebastian growled, brushing golden hair off Suzanne's forehead. "Baby, they're outside smoking a joint. They'll be a while," he laughed, and then kissed her mouth hard; an 'I've-got-to-have-you' kind of kiss. Her lips tasted of lemon posset; zingy and fresh. Sebastian took her hand and placed it on his cock. "Look how much I want you, Suzanne."

Grinning wickedly and with hands already fumbling at his belt, Suzanne murmured: "Then you must have me, Sebastian."

Suzanne slipped a hand into the waistband of his briefs and touched him. Groaning, Sebastian sank down on the closed lid of the toilet and watched her unzip him. She knelt before him, took his cock in both hands and then wrapped her soft lips around it. In less than half a minute, he was fully erect.

"We'd better make this quick, baby," he grunted as he helped her up.

Sebastian lifted Suzanne's dress, and facing him, biting her lip in that oh-so-sexy way that drove him absolutely fucking crazy, she steered him to her. Spanning him, she sat down on his cock, moaning as he went into her. It was a mind-blowing, impeccable fit as always. Her hands tangled in his hair, her lips insatiable, she eased herself up and down, fucking him fast and furiously, taking the lead, tightening her pussy around him and sucking him dry. Sebastian was in awe of this beautiful woman. Somehow Suzanne even managed to look amazing making love on the loo.

SIXTEEN

FRIDAY 11 JANUARY

SUZANNE

At a little before ten in the morning, Terminal 5, Heathrow Airport, was full of activity. Flying BA Club World certainly had its advantages, Suzanne noted with a smug smile as she eyeballed the long line waiting to check into economy. In a soft cashmere dress the colour of a brewing thunderstorm, with Sebastian at her side decked out in just about every shade of blue, they made a striking couple. They checked in their suitcases swiftly and took charge of their boarding passes and then survived the rigours of security; separating her iPad, his laptop and their liquids, removing belts and shoes and feeling afterwards as if they needed to get repacked and dressed all over again.

There were no last-minute dramas, and they made it through to departures in record time. Which was fortunate as they were both feeling a little jaded after a late night, fuelled with rich food and an excess of champagne. The dinner party had been a great success. Abi's Michael was an absolute delight and fitted in seamlessly, Suzanne decided. She loved the way that he and Sebastian just seemed to get on. But now she was suffering. Suzanne was hung over and her legs felt heavy. It was as if she was wading through treacle. Although their flight was a day flight to Vancouver and the nine-and-a-half-hour journey would skim only the bright hours of daylight as they passed through several time zones, she was looking forward to getting settled in her seat, cuddling up and having a nap.

Sebastian seemed to be handling the aftermath of their boozy night so much better. *Perhaps he didn't drink that much?* Suzanne wasn't sure but remembered only too well that she'd been very tipsy. Her cheeks flushed as she flashbacked to them sneaking off to the loo for a quickie. *What was she like! Behaving like some bloody nymphomaniac! But who wouldn't?* Suzanne glanced at Sebastian, striding alongside her. His hand clutched in hers felt smooth and reassuring as they weaved through the busy airport. He looked as wonderful as ever; long and lean, blue-eyed and beautiful. Of course, Suzanne noticed the women checking him out, their eyes all over him, some surreptitious, some full-on staring. She loved to look at him too. He was just so gorgeous. Suzanne was getting used to the stares. It often happened when they were out together, though Sebastian barely seemed to notice. Suzanne wasn't jealous. On the contrary, she liked it. She knew Sebastian was all hers; and it made her feel as if she'd won first prize.

After downing hot bitter double espressos in an effort to wake themselves up, they drank mugs of tea and tucked into bacon butties in the business class lounge. Suzanne was feeling slightly more human, as they wandered around aimlessly. Hand in hand, wheeling their matching Louis Vuitton carry-ons, they perused the array of designer shops; their windows expertly dressed and enticing, filled with exorbitantly priced handbags and cut-price winter clothes in the January sales. The couple did little more than window-shop, their efforts half-hearted, neither buying anything aside from reading matter in WH Smith. Before too long, their flight was called and they trundled out to the satellite gate for boarding.

"Why is it every time I fly, the plane is always parked up at the furthest gate? I've never flown from gate one, that's for sure!" Suzanne grumbled, sticking out her bottom lip in a mock pout. She was feeling the discomfort of travelling in high heels.

Sebastian chuckled at her grouchiness and astute observation, his wide grin showing off his perfect teeth. Suzanne wanted to kiss him. She wanted to claim his delicious mouth and run her greedy tongue all over it.

Sebastian raised her hand to his lips and kissed it. "I think your sore head is making you a little bit grumpy today, baby," he teased.

Ten minutes later, they were boarded, and with Suzanne stepping out in front, they made their way to the exclusive upper deck. Flying 'up top' was a new experience for them both. Suzanne was thrilled she'd managed to reserve them double linked seats; a pair from the one set in each row that were specially designed for couples. They faced backwards, side-by-side, and reclined fully flat to fashion a narrow double bed. She'd done her research on the seating plan and made absolutely sure she'd got them when she made the booking. She wanted this trip to be perfect, wanted her and Sebastian to begin their trip in their own little bubble of intimacy and luxury.

Now they were actually on the plane, Suzanne started to feel a bit more like her old self again. She was excited as they located their seats. They were just as advertised: spacious and just right for couples in search of maximum privacy. For once, she considered she'd really enjoy the long-haul flight; eat a late lunch, maybe sample a glass of wine or two, take a nap and watch a movie, all of this in an idyllic cocoon with her wonderful boyfriend. She suppressed a self-satisfied smile and wondered if they'd be able to behave.

Sebastian stowed their hand luggage and coats away in the overhead locker while Suzanne kicked off her patent court shoes and flopped into her seat with a satisfied groan. She began checking out all the little luxuries. There was a proper pillow in a smooth cotton pillowcase; a generous quilted blanket, probably twice the size of the usual scrap of material that barely covers you all over and makes you feel short-changed in the deepest, darkest depths of your airborne slumber; an eye mask; a good selection of Elemis skincare products and a toothbrush. As Sebastian settled beside her, a stewardess leaned into them with a smile and the offer of a glass of champagne. Suzanne and Sebastian exchanged playful glances, and, with barely a second's hesitation, they both took one, eyeing each other as they did, clearly amused by their mutual weakness to resist.

"Hair of the dog!" Suzanne declared and chinked their glasses together. She took a small delicate sip of the effervescent bubbles. "I don't believe it. It's only twelve thirty and we're drinking again."

"Well, we are officially on holiday now," Sebastian laughed, as, glass in hand, he got comfy in his seat beside her. He threaded his fingers through hers and took a quick swig before leaning over and kissing her. Champagne lingered on his breath. He grinned boyishly at her.

Suzanne melted under his blue gaze and kissed him back, notching it up a gear, slipping her tongue into his warm, wet mouth. She was blissfully happy. This was their first real trip away together, and Sebastian had never looked more appealing. She felt dazzled under his intense scrutiny, his eyes flashing like glittering sapphires as they reeled her in. He was just so goddamn handsome. His paisley blue shirt open at the throat, it was close-fitting and hugged his broad shoulders. Suzanne sighed happily and snuggled into him, pecking the underside of his throat, loving the slight roughness of the shadow of bristles on his chin.

Sebastian brushed flaxen hair from her face and studied her for a moment. "Suzanne, this is really amazing. We're going to have a great time. I just know it. Come on. Let's get cosy," he said brightly as he started to unbag his blanket.

Suzanne turned in his embrace, and her heart skipped a beat as he spread it carefully over them both. As his fingers slipped beneath the blanket and settled on her thigh just above her knee, unwanted memories spilled into her head. She coloured up. She didn't want to, but she couldn't help thinking about the plane ride sitting alongside Angelo Azzurro, the total stranger who she had allowed to play with her under a blanket on a flight to Rome. For a moment, she felt soiled, she felt dirty. *How could she let some stranger finger her on a plane?* It seemed like a very long time ago now. It seemed like it happened to someone else. Not her.

"You're not having naughty thoughts, are you, sweetheart?" Sebastian whispered softly in her ear, nibbling her lobe. With light fingertips, he squeezed her, mid-thigh.

"As if!" Suzanne replied and closed her eyes. Her lids were smoky with grey shadow. She inhaled deeply. She adored the feel of his hands on her as always, but as Sebastian touched her, Angelo crawled into her head once more. Suzanne's cheeks flushed at the recollection of her astonishing behaviour.

Sebastian noticed her reddening cheeks and quiet demeanour. "You okay, baby?" he asked, a frown creasing his brow.

"Of course. I'm just still a bit wiped out from last night." Suzanne forced a big smile. It wasn't too difficult. She knew she just needed to put that Albanian asshole out of her mind and enjoy the ride.

SEVENTEEN

FRIDAY 11 JANUARY

SEBASTIAN

A little more than an hour after the wide-bodied, four engine jet broke majestically through the puff of cotton wool cloud and settled at 36,000 feet, lunch was served. Sebastian and Suzanne both selected a starter of Scottish smoked salmon with capers and a horseradish cream. Sebastian followed that with a medium rare seared fillet of beef in a béarnaise sauce. As they tucked into their main course, Suzanne sipped a chilled new world Sauvignon Blanc while Sebastian went for the Châteauneuf-du-Pape. The food and the wine were delicious. The best he'd ever had on a plane. Sebastian couldn't believe how hungry he was. He always felt that way after drinking too much. He chuckled to himself. It had been a pretty crazy night. Good crazy though. He couldn't believe they'd kept a taxi waiting while they'd fucked on the floor of Suzanne's lounge, and then a couple of hours later they were at it again in the loo at Abi's! *That was just mad. Great, but mad!* He grinned over at Suzanne who was picking at her corn-fed chicken in Madeira sauce. She grinned back at him before dabbing her wonderfully kissable mouth with a linen serviette.

"How is it?"

"It's lovely, but I'm still full up from breakfast." Eyeing his clean plate, she added: "You look like you're ravenous."

"Maybe it's got something to do with the company I keep." He shot her a meaningful smile, his eyes suggestive as he downed a mouthful of crimson wine.

Sebastian was stuffed and feeling a little sleepy. He was looking forward to settling down and watching a movie, snuggled up with Suzanne. He decided to eat dessert later. He relocated his dining tray on the side table beside him and fiddled with the chair mechanism until his seat converted into a bed. He watched Suzanne do the same, then adjusted their shared blanket, banded his arms around her waist and spooned into her from behind.

His teeth catching on her collar bone, he whispered: "You know this is just such a great present. No one has ever given me something this wonderful, this thoughtful, ever."

Suzanne pressed back against him, her bottom settling neatly into his groin. "Aw, poor baby, you've obviously been deprived," she teased.

"Can you tell?" Sebastian replied, thankful that her face was partially turned from his. He forced a smile that masked the black memories spinning in his head.

Yes, Sebastian really did consider himself deprived. Of course, he'd grown up in a lovely house and was sent to the best schools. To others, it must have appeared that he was living the privileged middle-class dream. But what a crock of shit! It was all a façade because of his father. The man was nothing more than a vicious drunk who beat the shit out of his wife in front of their child. Bizarrely, at that moment a fleeting memory hit Sebastian. A hazy picture formed. He was very young, maybe three or four years old, and his father was throwing him in the air, the pair of them laughing joyously as his father's strong arms caught him. The startling imagery crowded his head. *Where the hell had that come from?*

Sebastian was momentarily dazed. He absorbed a deep gut-wrenching sigh and lost himself in the softness of Suzanne's golden hair. It smelt of fresh cut flowers. He nuzzled into it and just breathed her in. Calmer now, he made a decision. As soon as it was possible, he'd fire up his laptop and email his father. Set a day and time to meet up while Suzanne was busy with her review. This trip would be great fun, he was sure, but it was all about closure as well. Sebastian was well aware for that to happen he needed to unlock the secrets of his past once and for all.

EIGHTEEN

FRIDAY 11 JANUARY

EDWARD

Edward was delighted it was the weekend. Humming under his breath, he stepped off the train. As he exited Imperial Wharf station to begin the short walk home, the icy early evening cold hit him full-on. Edward thrust his hands deep into the pockets of his cashmere calf-length overcoat and hunched his shoulders as he strode briskly through a scattering of sleet that swirled in the frosty air. He couldn't wait to get home. Every single step brought him nearer to Tatiana. *God, he missed her so much!* He hoped she hadn't planned too much for the weekend. He needed some rest and relaxation. Life with Tatiana was wonderful, but it had to be said, she was extremely high maintenance. Edward smiled to himself as he marched along. Yes, he adored her, but the constant pressure to spend money was incredibly stressful. His cash-flow problem needed sorting, that was for sure.

Maybe a nice Sunday lunch out somewhere special would keep Tatiana happy, he mused to himself, though somehow, he didn't really think it would cut it with her. She was so young, so vibrant, and so full of life. She wanted to be out and about all the time. He managed to put her off clubbing this evening once he'd explained he had an early business meeting in the morning. Didn't think he'd get away with it on Saturday night too. He grinned. If his beautiful, sexy Tatiana wanted to go shopping in Knightsbridge and dance the night away in some exclusive London nightspot in a new outfit he'd bought her, then he'd be proud to be at her side. Once he sorted out this bit of business and had a much freer cash flow, he'd stop worrying about his escalating expenses and be able to enjoy his stunning woman to the max. Yes, if he could just pull this deal together, he'd soon be able to give her the fairytale wedding she craved and deserved.

There was a spring in his step as he turned into Harbour Avenue.

NINETEEN

SUZANNE

The Fairmont Chateau hotel was every bit as impressive as the collection of images the internet had promised. Situated at the base of the Blackcomb mountain range and surrounded by a sprawling forest of imposing pines dusted with shimmering powdery white snow, the majestic hotel resembled a perfect picture postcard. Hundreds of lights shone from its numerous windows and illuminated the dramatic darkening sky. It was a truly spectacular five-star hotel in a truly spectacular setting.

It was a little after five as Suzanne and Sebastian hopped out of the comfortable courtesy car that the hotel had sent to collect them from Vancouver International Airport. A couple of smartly turned out young men, who looked more like college freshers than porters, rushed up and began removing their luggage from the boot, one of them handing Suzanne a ticket. She took it and then grabbed Sebastian's hand, swinging it girlishly in hers. She was so excited! Inhaling deeply, she sucked the exhilarating scent of the mountains and fresh pine into her lungs. The air felt fresh and clean and wholesome.

"Wow, Suzanne, this place is something else!"

Sebastian declared in awe, gazing up at the grandiose hotel a few short steps from where the car had deposited them.

"I know. It looks amazing," Suzanne agreed. "I can't wait to see our room. Come on, let's get checked in." She smiled over her shoulder at the bellboys. "Thank you," she called out, and then she and Sebastian made their way to the arched double entrance doors.

Suzanne had changed into some more suitable footwear and was now sporting a dramatic fluffy Cossack hat that Sebastian had said made her look extremely winsome. His choice of words had made her laugh out loud. There had been a lot of laughter on the flight over. Their journey had been smooth and relaxing. They'd watched a couple of films; a weepy: *I am Sam*, starring the brilliant Sean Penn, followed by *Forrest Gump*, brought to life by the very marvellous Tom Hanks. They'd snoozed a little, chatted and cuddled, ate the exceedingly good fayre on offer washed down with champagne, wine and liqueurs. They'd sensibly balanced the booze with plenty of water and now Suzanne felt refreshed.

With their hands laced together, they crossed the bustling lobby to check in. The double height reception area was vast with exposed beams and large areas of open brickwork. Mocha coloured comfy sofas and winged leather chairs in a similar hue faced coffee tables. Substantial side tables topped with low voltage lamps and enormous vases of fresh flowers succeeded in giving the lofty room an indulgent intimate appeal. The smell was incredible too. The soothing aroma of the floral displays mingled with the scent of wood smoke and spruce and fern.

Suzanne was so happy she felt she must be grinning like an idiot, but she just couldn't wipe the blistering smile from her face. This trip was going to be fabulous. The only dilemma facing them was whether they'd have time to make love before heading off and grabbing their ski gear as they'd planned. They'd managed to control themselves on the plane, but right now Suzanne wanted Sebastian. She wanted to taste him. She wanted to smell him. She wanted to feel his body against hers, skin on skin.

As soon as they were in their room, a Fairmont gold suite, Suzanne gave it the once-over, wandering around, checking out the amenities. Not only was it five-star luxury, but it was warm and cosy as well. There was a gas fire in an creamy marble hearth which had obviously been lit in readiness for their arrival. It faced the oversized bed that was made-up with gold and red covers and fat, plumped-up goose down pillows. A box of handmade chocolates sat on the coverall, and there was champagne on ice in a sterling silver ice bucket. The television was on, tuned into the hotel's own dedicated channel, and an on-screen welcome message awaited them.

"This is so nice, baby!" Sebastian enthused, poking his head into the ensuite. "There's a spa bath too. That's going to be so good after a long day on the slopes."

"God, yes!" Suzanne wandered over to the window. "Sebastian, just come and look at that view!" she added, marvelling at the wonderful panoramic vista; their enormous picture window crammed full of what appeared to be a never-ending range of towering mountains and gigantic evergreens, all iced with pure white snow.

Many of the slopes were lit up and still busy with a jumble of stop-starting ski lifts, each carriage at maximum capacity, suspended on corded cables as they criss-crossed the darkening sky, descending on their final journey for the day. Suzanne drank in the scene and watched the last of the skiers making their way down in random lines, their skis skimming rapidly, the varied colours of their skiwear another flash of brightness against the snowy white canvas.

It had started to snow. A steady stream of crystalline powder twirled dramatically in the breeze as Suzanne stood captivated, watching a million snowflakes floating magically in the air. It reminded her of one of those Christmas movies she'd watched with her boys when they were little. *What was it? Polar Express. That was it! Tom Hanks again, of course.* She'd texted the twins on landing but felt the urge to call them at that moment. But it was far too late. It was the middle of the night back home. First thing in the morning, she'd text and then get her head around the time change and work out a good time to call. Suzanne was loving her new independent life but still missed her boys every single day.

Sebastian came up behind her and wrapped his arms around her tightly, his hands settling around her waist. Suzanne moved easily into his embrace and exhaled with a gentle sigh.

"It's beautiful, Suzanne, just like you." Sebastian's soft lips closed in on the delicate nape of her neck, but her gargantuan furry hat got in the way. She removed it, and giggling like a pair of adolescents, they fell onto the bed as one.

"So, 'Miss Travel Writer', do you fancy trying out this lovely bed?" Sebastian asked huskily as he stared down at her, his eyes the feverish blue of a glacier, his breath hot as it tumbled from his mouth into hers.

Suzanne had no time to answer as Sebastian's mouth swiftly covered hers, sucking away her breath. As they exchanged suffocatingly deep kisses, he rolled her flat on her back and positioned himself directly on top. Face to face, nose to nose, lips to lips. Sebastian's hard cock pressed into Suzanne's sex as his tongue continued to worship her mouth. He tasted of spearmint, clean and fresh. Suzanne couldn't get enough of him. She filled her lungs with his masculine scent as he shrugged the coat from her shoulders. Suzanne wanted nothing more than to feel the warmth of him embedded deep inside her. The only foreplay she needed to make her wet for him was the harmony of his lips on hers. Their shared kisses were intense and hypnotic. Suzanne groaned as he parted her legs manfully.

They struggled with each other's heavy winter clothes, tugging and unzipping until Suzanne was in her undies and Sebastian was shirtless and showing off his masculine chest. Fine black hair curled at the centre of well-defined pecs. Within seconds, his trousers and jockeys were off, and his cock throbbed hot and silky in Suzanne's hand. Sebastian pulled exquisite Rigby and Peller silk panties off to one side, and with a little help from Suzanne, he guided his cock in with one easy shove.

"Aw, baby, I've been wanting to do that ever since they dimmed the lights on the plane," Sebastian growled as he moved inside her, the tip of his cock nudging tantalisingly at her cervix as he gave her every inch.

"Me too, baby." Suzanne let out a satisfied groan. "You really need to fuck me on the plane journey home then," she giggled. Her words were jerky, controlled by the power of her lover's spirited insertions. Suzanne smiled; her face full of mischief as she cupped his face. She kissed him hard, her lips and tongue and teeth feasting on his gloriously sexy mouth. She grabbed a handful of his tousled liquorice hair.

"You are so bad and so fucking wet, Suzanne," he snarled. "That's just a couple of reasons why I love you."

"I love you too, Sebastian, and I adore your cock inside me. It's a perfect fit," Suzanne spat out through gritted teeth. She tightened her sex around his driving cock.

Suzanne wrapped knee-high leather boots around Sebastian's waist and rolled her body back to attain the deepest penetration possible. Sebastian raised himself up on powerful arms and gazed down at her. Suzanne stared back into his eyes as he fucked her. She loved looking at him while they made love. She adored that magical moment when he totally lost it. The expression in his astonishing blue eyes when he climaxed was something of great beauty. She adored it. She adored him.

That moment wasn't long in coming. As Sebastian started his slide to the edge, he grasped Suzanne's hands in his and raised them high above their heads. Their arms fully extended and outstretched, their fingers entwined, their conjoined hands dug hard into the bed with the impetus of their rhythm. Pillows tumbled to the floor with the vigour of their fucking. As Sebastian was getting closer, Suzanne rolled him with force and momentum so that now she was riding on top. Sebastian went with it, still holding onto her hands, still deep inside her as she rose up onto her haunches and rode him like a cowgirl. Suzanne's glassy green eyes held her man's as she fucked him, their bodies slapping noisily together. Perspiration trickled from between Suzanne's breasts onto Sebastian's chest.

"I'm going to cum into you, Suzanne. I just can't stop it now!" Sebastian mouthed, and then his words dried up as his orgasm began to overpower him.

Suzanne felt his entire body tense. With a gravelly roar, Sebastian spurted deep inside her. Now it was her turn to let loose, and, letting go of his hands, she arched backwards and got her positioning just right. Pleasure ripped through her as she quickened her tempo and jerked herself off on him. Suzanne screamed as she succumbed to an orgasm that left her gasping in its wake, its power raising her heaven-bound. As waves of ecstasy engulfed her body, she caught her breath and collapsed forward onto Sebastian. Gorging on his divine, edible mouth, Suzanne's whole body shook and convulsed with unfathomable pleasure.

★

Facing each other, end-to-end in a haze of bubbles, Suzanne and Sebastian luxuriated in the enormous spa bath. Suzanne's hair was scrunched atop her head with wispy strands framing her peachy, heart-shaped face. With little make-up, she looked fresh-faced and girly. Golden freckles danced over her nose. Suzanne draped her legs over Sebastian's as they sipped champagne from crystal flutes and made plans.

"There's no way I'm up to getting our skis this evening. It feels like the middle of the night already."

"That's because it is, I guess," Sebastian laughed.

Suzanne gazed at him. She loved Sebastian's posh accent. He sounded classy and cultured. A collection of airy soapsuds clung to his broad chest. His pectoral muscles skimmed the surface of the water. They were magnificent. His damp hair was slicked back and inky, his eyes sparkled, and, in the bathroom light, their penetrating blueness reminded her of a calm and inviting Caribbean Sea. Suzanne was hooked on his beauty.

"Shall we just get unpacked, order some room service and then get into bed, baby? I'm so tired."

Sebastian looked pleased. "Of course, I'm absolutely shattered too. And that bed looks terribly inviting." He tossed her a lopsided grin.

"Shall we go and get fitted for boots and skis first thing?" Suzanne suggested.

"Yeah. That works for me. That's perfect, baby."

"Let's do it straight after an early breakfast. I'd like to do a bit of a tour of the hotel in the morning, and then I've got this lunch with a couple of the management team. I can do that and write a bit while you explore the slopes, and then we'll meet up back here, late afternoon?"

"That sounds like a plan." Sebastian smiled lazily.

"So, you're happy to amuse yourself without me?"

"Well, not exactly happy," he laughed. "But it's totally fine, sweetheart."

"Be good to get a big chunk of my work out of the way tomorrow; that way, we'll have the whole day together on your birthday. We can do whatever you want then," Suzanne said provocatively, before taking another mouthful of champagne. The froth fizzed up her nose and made her giggle.

Sebastian moved towards her and dried the liquid on her parted lips with his outstretched thumb, slowly and sensually. Suzanne moaned softly and chewed on her bottom lip.

"Perfect," Sebastian whispered, his voice low as he slid his index finger into her mouth.

As Suzanne rolled her tongue around the knuckle of his digit, she felt Sebastian's foot between her legs. She eyeballed him and thrust her sex toward his exploratory toes. Sebastian's eyes held hers as his toes gently opened the folds of her pussy. Suzanne shivered. It felt wonderful.

"How tired are you?" he asked, locating her clitoris with his big toe and rotating it in tiny circles. Sebastian removed his finger from her mouth, and, as he waited for her reply, a hand closed around one of Suzanne's nipples.

"Not tired at all, baby." Suzanne closed her eyes as Sebastian began to play.

TWENTY

TATIANA

Tangled in sheets heavy with the smell of sex, her phone in her hand, Tatiana first checked her social media accounts and then began googling randomly. Eddie had left her in bed and headed out to an early business meeting. Tatiana wondered what kind of business he was conducting on a Saturday morning but wasn't really bothered. She was far more interested in what Kim and Kayne were up to on twitter. And in gearing herself up for a shopping trip to Hatton Garden. She was after a ruby heart pendant to accessorise a sexy new dress she'd recently splashed out on with Eddie's American Express card. Time to get up and get going. Sluggishly, Tatiana climbed out of bed.

Wearing only a minuscule cherry red thong that hugged her slightly protruding hip bones and disappeared into the crack of her bottom, mobile in hand, Tatiana slinked into her dressing room and plonked herself down at the dressing table. She smeared her mouth in her favourite Estee Lauder hydra lustre lipstick and then pursed her full lips to make sure the rich red colour was evenly distributed. Her breasts were

125

bare, her nipples pink and puffy. Mirrored images of her astonishing pulchritude surrounded her. Tatiana admired her reflection. She liked what she saw. She smiled conceitedly.

The second bedroom of the penthouse was almost as big as the master and Tatiana had commandeered it to store her vast collection of clothes and make-up. It had to be done, and there was always the smaller third bedroom if Eddie's boys ever decided to come and stay. Tatiana loved having a dressing room all to herself. Behind her, on the opposite wall, there was a bank of floor-to-ceiling mirrored wardrobes, which housed all her exquisite designer labels: suits, dresses, jackets, shirts, blouses and trousers. Beside the hanging space, there was a shelved section for her sweaters, T-shirts, jeans and gym wear, and another for her handbags. She had day bags and evening bags, clutch and shoulder, from Prada to Mulberry to Louis Vuitton. There was an additional roomy area of storage that featured ten pull-out shoe racks groaning under the weight of Tatiana's exorbitantly priced shoes: Christian Louboutin, Manolo Blahnik, Jimmy Choo, Alexander McQueen. She had them all. Eddie and many of her Dubai clientele had been extremely generous.

The mirrored surface of Tatiana's make-up area was swamped with an overabundance of cosmetics: face creams, toners, cleansers, day creams, night creams, body creams; you name it, she had it. There was make-up from Mac, Clinique, Chanel, Lancôme, YSL, Clarins and Urban Decay. Lined up on a purple velveteen cloth was a collection of pure bristle make-up brushes. Eyeliners, mascaras, lipsticks, lip glosses and eyeshadow palettes littered the top, alongside carefully lined up bottles of perfumes, some in stylish cut glass atomisers in emerald green, mauve and topaz blue. There was a tall mirrored chest of drawers, which acted as a spillover area and was covered with even more cosmetics and toiletries, as well as Tatiana's jewellery box heaving with expensive trinkets. Four of the chest's six deep drawers were home to Tatiana's colourful lingerie sets, heaps upon heaps of expensive bras and panties and tiny thongs in silk and lace, stored alongside fine denier stockings and garter belts. In the bottom two drawers she kept her sex toys.

With a stiff brush, Tatiana began brushing her flowing hair, regimentally, from the crown to the tips. One hundred strokes. Her ebony hair rippled around her bare shoulders, flyaway with static electricity. Eddie had made it very knotty indeed, fucking and licking her and playing around with a vibrator while she writhed on her back in ecstasy. She smirked at her mirror image. Eddie loved to spoil her, both financially and sexually. They messed around for almost half an hour this morning, before he fucked her. She adored the feel of Eddie's tongue when he spread her wide until her clitoris popped right out, like a tasty little bud. When she was open like that and he tormented her with his fingers and tongue, she came like crazy; colossal multiple orgasms taking her one after the other. She giggled. This morning, Eddie had scored a hat-trick, before he penetrated her.

Ready to get dressed for the day now, Tatiana selected her favourite perfume and sprayed herself generously. A couple of squirts on each breast, at the crook of her throat, a quick squirt down her panties and on the insides of both wrists. Satisfied she was suitably coated and smelling wonderful, she slid out the top drawer and her eyes lingered. She was on the lookout for suitable brassiere to match her gauzy thong. She was still deliberating when her mobile rang. *Angelo* flashed up on the screen of her smartphone.

"Shit!" she mouthed out loud. Tatiana held her breath and stared at the ringing phone. Another call from Angelo she just couldn't bring herself to answer. She didn't move.

A few seconds later, her phone rang again. It was her callback message service. She snatched it up hurriedly and answered. She listened, her heartbeat noticeably faster in her chest.

Angelo's voice sounded hard and angry:

"Tatiana, I don't know what the fuck you are playing at, not answering your phone or calling me back. You are seriously taking the piss. I have big money clients of yours waiting for you, so I need to know what time you're back. So, call me. And fucking do it soon. Capiche?"

All of a sudden, Tatiana had lost the sparkle in her silver-flecked green eyes. She shivered and tapped a long red fingernail on the screen to end the call.

TWENTY-ONE

SATURDAY 12 JANUARY

SEBASTIAN

Sebastian woke very early, the hefty eight-hour time change mucking up his body clock. Wrapped in a hotel bathrobe, his hair uncombed, he split the curtains just a few inches and peeked through the gap. He inhaled deeply. It was as if he was trying to breathe in the cool, clear mountain air through the glass. Standing at the window, he took in the breathtaking sky striped with oranges and yellows and stark flashes of crimson. A wonderful daybreak was emerging over the snowy vista. Although the view of the sunrise caressing the mountains was outstanding, Sebastian was struggling to appreciate its natural beauty. Today was the day he'd been hurtling towards for more than two decades. Today he would finally come face-to-face with the father he had tried to forget. He was intensely nervous, and for a split second, as he stood there in the cocoon of their cosy suite, he wondered if he was doing the right thing. Sebastian sighed resignedly. Of course, he had to do it, but his chest was so tight it was like his skin was stretched over a drum.

Turning his attention back to the bed, to Suzanne, partially visible beneath the covers, Sebastian studied her, his dark glower softening as he watched her sleep. Surrounded by golden hair that fanned out all around her, she was on her side, facing the spot he'd recently vacated. Her eyes closed, her face unlined and youthful, she looked truly lovely. Sebastian felt a huge rush of affection for her. She looked so serene. He hated deceiving her, hated himself for being so cowardly, but he just couldn't bring himself to tell her his plans for the day. He'd emailed his father secretly, soon after Suzanne had revealed what she was up to today. He vowed to tell her about it tonight. That was if there was something to tell. If his father turned up and opened up about the past. As soon as they'd been fitted with skis and Suzanne got her ski boots sorted, Sebastian planned to leave her to get on with her work and he'd take a taxi to Vancouver. He'd agreed to meet his father at a restaurant near his home. He was hoping he would make it there by noon or soon after. The plan was to text Donald when he was about half an hour away.

"Morning, baby," Suzanne mumbled on waking. Her eyes heavy with sleep, she rolled over onto her back, gradually focusing on him as he stared down at her. It was as if she'd sensed him watching her.

"Hello, sleepy," Sebastian answered quietly. He sank down beside her on the bed. He swept the hair back from her brow tenderly, and, savouring her sweet, doey-eyed countenance, he leaned in and gave her a soft kiss on the forehead, on each of her closed eyelids and then finally he homed in on her lips. First thing in the morning, she tasted of slumber and sweetness. He loved her sleepy smell.

"What time is it?" Suzanne asked, her lashes all aflutter, her voice throaty.

"It's still pretty early, baby. Do you want a cup of tea?"

"Right now, I just want you," Suzanne murmured, and pushing herself up from the covers, she grinned playfully and began to unbelt his robe. Sebastian watched and said nothing as she cupped his balls and fed his hardening cock into her mouth.

★

They breakfasted in the Wildflower restaurant and hired skis and poles and helmets in the hotel's rental shop. Suzanne selected her ski boots; Salomon, in a cool ice white. Reasonably comfy, she declared once she'd stomped around the shop in them for a few minutes. They signed their hire agreements and then headed to the Fairmont's Portobello Market and fresh bakery for a final pit stop before they parted for the rest of the day. They ordered hot chocolate topped with marshmallows and frothy whipped cream. Suzanne smiled as she spooned cream and marshmallows into her mouth. Sebastian smiled back at her but was itching to get away. He knew it would take him all of two hours to get to West Vancouver.

"We'll need to take our gear to the boot room before we head off," Sebastian said, grimacing slightly as he swallowed the last mouthful of his drink. The undissolved chocolate was thick and dense at the bottom.

"Are you planning on skiing today?" Suzanne asked, dipping a spoon in her mug and giving the remains of her drink a thorough stir.

"Um, no, not this morning. I was thinking of heading into Whistler to take a look around then maybe ski later.

I'm just going to play it by ear while I leave you to get on." He didn't look at her as he spoke.

"Okay, but if you do come back to get into your ski gear, text me and if I can, I'll come and find you and say hello." She drained the last dregs of her mug.

"Sure, baby." Sebastian squeezed Suzanne's hand, his eyes still not connecting with hers. "Right, to work for you then," he breezed as he stood up.

Sebastian wore a smiley face as they headed towards the boot room, but inside he felt his tummy lurch and twist as anxiety twirled in his head. He had no idea whatsoever how the next few hours would pan out.

TWENTY-TWO

SATURDAY 12 JANUARY

SEBASTIAN

Sebastian kissed Suzanne goodbye, planting a shower of soft, warm kisses on her mouth before waving her off from the doorway of their room. With the taste of her on his lips, he watched her power down the corridor looking vivacious and professional in a cream coat dress and high-heeled shoes, her golden hair loose and trailing halfway down her back. Her bottom and shapely legs looked wonderful. Sebastian considered himself a lucky man. For a moment, he wished the day was over, that he'd done what he needed to do and was back with Suzanne taking afternoon tea in front of a roaring log fire. They had agreed to rendezvous back at the hotel somewhere around four or five. He hoped that would give him enough time. Suzanne blew him an air kiss as the lift doors closed in front of her. Sebastian raised a hand as she disappeared from view. He breathed out heavily and then shut the door.

Tension settled in the pit of his stomach like a heavy load. Sebastian glanced at the time on his phone. It was already after ten. He knew he needed to get a move on. From the wardrobe, he grabbed a Ralph Lauren navy

133

blue suit; black label. It was single-breasted and skinny-legged. He stepped out of his jeans and dressed hurriedly in it, teaming the suit with a slate grey cable-knit sweater. He slipped the crew-neck jumper over a tight thermal vest and then buttoned up his jacket. Sebastian realised it would be very cold in the city too. He sat down on the bed and tugged on leather Chelsea boots. Standing again, he knotted a midnight blue cashmere scarf around his throat. He unhooked his leather overcoat from a hanger and checked his gloves were tucked into the pocket before putting it on.

Ready to go, Sebastian checked himself in the mirror, nervously running his fingers through his hair. He looked stylish and smart. He wanted to look good. Wanted to show his father that even without him, he'd made a success of his life.

Ten minutes later, Sebastian was in the back of a cab speeding along Highway 99 towards Vancouver.

TWENTY-THREE

SATURDAY 12 JANUARY

TATIANA

Through oversized picture windows, the capital's dynamic skyline dazzled as its collection of tall buildings hugged the Thames. A cornucopia of luminosities in a dense black sky. The moon was rising, just a tiny slither of burning gold. Tatiana was unmoved by the view as she uncorked a bottle of Burgundy. The cork eased out with a soft plop. She had things on her mind. Angelo was on her case and it worried her. Holding a smeary glass up to the light from the chandelier, she rubbed it with a linen tea towel and then sloshed almost half a bottle into one glass before pouring a smaller helping into another wine balloon. A glass in each hand, supported between her forefinger and middle finger, she padded from the kitchen to the cosy TV room. She was unusually quiet. She handed Eddie the glass filled almost to the brim and then in silence sat down alongside him.

"Thanks, babe," he mumbled, his arm outstretched. He didn't glance at Tatiana as he took the glass from her. Eddie lit up and dragged heavily on a cigarette before he began channel surfing, settling quickly on the Sky News channel.

Tatiana was pleased to be home and back in the warm after spending a breezy hour and a half on some godforsaken rugby field after their shopping trip. When Eddie announced he was going to watch his sons play rugby, she tagged along, of course, even though she considered the game rough and pointless and had absolutely no idea of the rules. Eddie tried to explain the basics, but she really couldn't be bothered with it. The only saving grace was watching dozens of muscular young men running around in shorts, doing what she could only describe as wrestling each other to the ground. Of course, the other advantage of going along was to cause trouble, managing to drop something into the conversation that she hoped would piss off the blonde bitch. Tatiana's cat eyes were full of malice as she got comfy and sipped her wine.

Fresh from her warming shower, Tatiana looked cute in a short robe of ivory satin printed with a wealth of summer flowers in lavender and pinks. Aside from a smear of smoky purple on her lips, she wore no make-up. Her hair was still damp and was the colour of ink. Eddie hadn't showered since they got back and was still dressed in a mauve woollen Tommy Hilfiger shirt teamed with Levi's. He'd unbuttoned the shirt a little, and tufts of thick, silvery hair peeped out over the top button. He'd popped one fastener on his jeans. His socked feet were propped up on the table before him as he lounged. He appeared totally relaxed, and yet, Tatiana sensed that he wasn't.

Undeterred, Tatiana cuddled up next to him, doubling her shapely legs beneath her as she leaned over and took a cigarette from the pack of Camels on the coffee table. Eddie didn't stir beside her. He didn't spring to life in a hurry and light it for her like he usually did. He hadn't even asked her what she'd like to watch on the television, which was downright weird, as Eddie was usually so attentive to her needs. He was distracted today. Even at the match, he'd been constantly checking his phone and sending emails and texts all afternoon. She was the one who usually couldn't leave her phone alone. When Tatiana asked if there was a problem, he'd just mumbled something about some big deal at work. She knew there was no way Eddie was playing around. He was so into her; he'd never choose another woman over her. He loved her. She gave him everything he needed, so of course his mood had to be work-related. Something stressful to do with the business meeting this morning, she decided, and right away put it out of her mind.

Shopping in Hatton Garden and Knightsbridge had been fun, and Eddie had been particularly generous. He'd spent thousands of pounds on her in just a couple of hours. He'd treated her to the wonderful heart-shaped pendant she had her eye on, a multifaceted twinkling ruby on a white gold chain; plus new shoes, high-heeled and strappy and very 'come fuck me'; an amazing new season Mulberry handbag in rose petal pink; as well as two exquisite silk blouses, one in baby pink and another in a whippy coffee cream shade. Eddie's credit card came out without question. He just handed it to her with a smile that said he was somewhere else. But Tatiana didn't press him, especially when he was being so easy with his money. She just kept on collecting the mountain of purchases in their decorative designer gift bags and tried her best not to dwell on her own dilemma.

Tatiana sucked hard on her cigarette and then stubbed out the larger part of it, smoke escaping from her lips and nose as she exhaled deeply. She had her own troubles. She hadn't called or texted Angelo back. She was genuinely too scared. *What the fuck was she going to do? She had no idea what to say. Fuck, he sounded furious with her! How do you tell a man like Angelo Azzurro that you're walking away?* Just going over Angelo's message in her head freaked her out. She really had no idea how to deal with it. If she didn't go back, would he come looking for her? She guessed he probably would. Angelo would never let a woman get one over on him. Anxiety pressed down on her chest. A hard, tight knot formed in her belly. She'd seen Angelo when someone crossed him, and he wasn't nice. Not nice at all. She loved him. He'd been a big part of her life for as long as she could remember, and yet deep down she accepted he was one sick motherfucker. Tatiana felt seriously nauseous. No way did she feel like going out on the town tonight.

"Eddie, do you fancy a quiet night in?" Tatiana asked, all big eyes and teeth. She took his arm and linked it with hers. As she moved closer, she allowed her robe to fall open to reveal smooth young flesh.

For a nanosecond, relief flooded Eddie's face and then his dark eyes lit up with lust as he gawped at her nudity. Tatiana had his full attention. Slipping a hand to her, he gave her exposed thigh a gentle squeeze.

"Great idea, babe. Let's order in a takeaway. What d'you fancy? Chinese? Thai?"

"You!" Tatiana purred in response, turning on her sex goddess persona in an instant.

Eddie smiled at her, desire dripping from his mouth. He wasn't distracted now, Tatiana noted as she ran the point of her tongue along her bottom lip and then conjured up a suitably sassy smile in return. She'd dismiss Angelo from her head and lose herself in sex. She'd make a decision in the morning, sleep on the problem and hope for some divine inspiration. Decision made, she suddenly felt a whole lot better.

Flapping long black lashes, Tatiana leaned in and flicked a viper's tongue into Eddie's waiting mouth. Greedily, he kissed her. She tasted heavy red wine on his lips. Her breath rushed out in whispery gasps as they exchanged sloppy kisses. He touched her breasts and Tatiana began to moan. Her nipples ached and burned as he rubbed them. Still devouring his mouth, she rotated one hundred and eighty degrees until she sat astride him. Bearing down with hungry magenta lips, her robe unbelted and open, she released a carnal growl as Eddie walked his fingers to her. Tatiana was wet and ready. She always was. She groaned louder and more urgently, breathing out hard as Eddie parted her lips. With two fingers tight together, he traced the swell of her clitoris.

Tatiana sat back and watched Eddie play with her. She loved the sight of her shaved pussy swallowing up his thick fingers. Eddie slid two digits deep inside her and jerked them back and forth. She let out a low, soft whinny as he settled on her G-spot. As he fingered her, Tatiana squirmed in ecstasy, her long, wet hair falling decoratively over her breasts.

"Get on your knees," Eddie roared.

Tatiana pushed the coffee table out of the way and then stood and dropped her robe. She did it slowly and seductively, her shoulders thrust back, her back arched. Her nipples were mouthwateringly distended. She knew she looked totally awesome. Naked, she leaned over the low table and thrust her backside into Eddie's face. Tatiana heard him unbuttoning his flies.

"Lick me first," she demanded.

Without answering, Eddie knelt and spread Tatiana's buttocks. She was so wet you could hear the squelch as he pulled her apart. Sinking his teeth into the fleshy part of her bum he nipped her, his sharp teeth running along the curve of her ass. He wriggled his exploratory tongue along the soft folds of her thighs before delving it into her puckered asshole.

"I love it when you rim my ass, Eddie. Stick your tongue all the way in," Tatiana instructed.

Doing as he was told, Eddie lost his tongue in Tatiana's ass. While he orally explored her, his fingers got busy. He found her clit and massaged it. Just the way she liked it. Fast and firm. It felt so fucking good. Tatiana just couldn't stay still. She closed her eyes, threw her head back and was lost in the moment.

"I'm going to fuck your sweet little ass now, babe," Eddie growled through clenched teeth. "You know you want it, don't you?"

Tatiana merely grunted as she felt Eddie roll the head of his cock around her rectum.

"You love my cock in your ass," Eddie barked as he gripped damp strands of hair, and tugging them into a fist, pulled Tatiana round to face him.

Tatiana opened her eyes ever so slightly, and with a vigorous nod, she signalled her approval. Moments later, Eddie was in her ass, riding her hard, very hard, but she could take it. She loved it. Absolutely fucking loved it.

TWENTY-FOUR

SATURDAY 12 JANUARY

SEBASTIAN

For more than an hour, Sebastian sat bolt upright in the back of the roomy taxi; a Lincoln Town car with smooth leather seats and plenty of leg room for his long legs. The comfy sedan felt safe and steady as it motored through breathtaking mountainous scenery, along blacktop roads smothered in condensed snowflakes and slush. The interior smelt vaguely of the alpine world outside, courtesy of a pungent air freshener that dangled on elastic string from the driving mirror.

Sebastian was deep in character, playing the role of an aloof English businessman rather well. After telling his driver where to head for and requesting that he let him know when they were getting close, he managed to discourage any idle chit-chat with a series of curt, monosyllabic replies to all conversations started. He was polite and courteous but made it abundantly clear he simply wasn't up for small talk.

The prospect of meeting up with his father again was truly sinking in. How would he feel when he saw him? Would they make their peace? Would his father be full of remorse and apologise for walking out of his life? He had no idea, but what he was about to do overwhelmed him. He could think of nothing else. Hazy images of his early life freeze-framed in his head, sliding into view, one after the other like a home projector flickering to life in his skull. Mostly dark, painful memories with fleeting glimpses of happy times when he was very small. The blissful recollections confused more than pleased.

Sitting back in his seat, Sebastian steepled his hands on his lap and stared out of the side window as the taxi sped south along Highway 99. Mountain after mountain topped with pillowy white frosting flashed before his eyes, but his head was so full of shadowy memories, the beauty of his surroundings was lost on him. Butterflies danced in his gut. He felt sick to the stomach. His mouth felt like an arid desert. Sebastian swigged from a bottle of water he found in the back pocket of the passenger seat, swallowing almost half of its contents before replacing it where he'd found it. He licked his lips but still had a raging thirst. The tinkling of an incoming WhatsApp message halted his thoughts momentarily. Sebastian slipped his phone from his pocket and read the message from Suzanne as it lit up the screen.

What you up to? All going well here. Miss you so much it hurts! Love you lots! X

Sebastian didn't unlock his phone. He just couldn't bring himself to respond to the cheery message, and he didn't want Suzanne to know that he'd read it. He hoped she wouldn't worry and just presume he was somewhere without Wi-Fi. He'd compose a quick reply soon enough. His heart drumming in his chest, he continued to stare through the glass, not really seeing anything, barely aware that the spectacular mountain scenery had gradually, over the last few miles, transformed into coastal views as the landscape changed and the car journeyed ever nearer to West Vancouver.

The sinewy young man at the wheel turned his head and coughed discreetly. He had straggly, unmanageable hair, powerful grey eyes and a neat goatee. "We're about half an hour away now, sir."

"Great, thank you," Sebastian replied and reigned in a heavy sigh. There was no going back now.

He took off his soft leather gloves, methodically pulling at each finger, one by one. With all his fingers free, he was just about to send a text when a rush of strength gripped him and changed his mind. Before he thought better of it, he tapped the phone icon beside his father's number in his contact list. Sebastian held his breath as the phone rang in his ear.

"Hello, Sebastian."

Sebastian flinched as he heard his father say his name for the first time in many years. It was just two words but was enough to release a crashing wave of pain. His father's voice was deep and low, refined and yet still peppered with that easy-on-the-ear Scottish accent, now noticeably softened with a Canadian twang. He sounded robust and strong.

"Hi," Sebastian answered lamely. His tongue felt thick and coated with something unimaginable.

His father broke the silence growing between them. His voice seemingly unaffected by emotion, he said: "Whereabouts are you?" He sounded like he was arranging to meet a mate down the pub.

"Hang on." Sebastian lowered his phone and addressed the driver. "Where are we now, please?"

"Just passed Britannia Beach, sir. Less than half an hour if the traffic is kind to us."

"Thanks," Sebastian said, and then returning his attention to his father, asked: "Did you get that?"

"Indeed, I did, Sebastian. Right then, I'll see you at the Beach House at somewhere around a quarter past." His demeanour sounded almost jolly.

Sebastian couldn't believe his father sounded so utterly matter-of-fact. He swallowed hard. "Okay, I'll see you there." He had no idea what else to say, so ended the call quickly. He gawped at the phone in his hand, his heart pumping frantically in his chest.

TWENTY-FIVE

SATURDAY 12 JANUARY

ANGELO

The palatial accommodation Angelo Azzurro was spending the night in cost a small fortune. Though, of course, he wasn't paying for it. The magnificent two-bedroom suite nestled between Dubai's magical dune and desert landscape boasted a grand outside terrace and a private infinity pool. It was just one of the advantages of working with obscenely wealthy men. Naturally, Angelo didn't consider himself a pimp. He was a businessman providing a service and an excellent one at that. On this starry night, he was taking a well-earned rest with two of his favourite girls.

Linking his hands behind his head, his black hair damp and combed back from his forehead, Angelo reclined on a lounger beside a pool that was lit up decoratively in the soft moonlight. The aqua waters shimmered as the pool's filter frothed out foam. Angelo found the gentle whisper of the water's flow soothing. Even with the time approaching midnight, it was pleasantly balmy. Stripped to his buttercup yellow swim shorts, he stretched out his long, beautifully sculpted body. His skin was moist from the warmth of the desert and tanned from the heat of the sun.

A few feet from him on a circular double loveseat with a canopy and an oversupply of cushions, two young women were touching each other intimately. Angelo smiled as he watched them. He closed his eyes and lay perfectly still. His heart rate picked up as he savoured the stimulating sounds of their eroticism. He groaned and grabbed his cock through his trunks. Soon he'd be ready to go and fuck them both. He appreciated the steady build-up, loved the show. Angelo expected his girls to warm each other up for him; the boss.

Sammi, a curvy blonde beauty from the rough streets of the Gorbals, Glasgow, was a long way from home but seemed totally at ease in her luxurious surroundings. With her mass of dirty blonde hair fanning out all around her, she lay on her back, nude aside from gold jewellery and high-heeled strappy Louboutins. Soft whimpers escaped from her collagen-enhanced lips. Her body arched in ecstasy under a medley of stars. She looked gorgeous; her tummy toned and flat, her large natural breasts cascading off either side of her torso, her nipples hard and pointed. Jenna, a total babe with hair the colour of straw and the body of a goddess, was bent over Sammi, her tongue buried deep inside her. As she feasted, the Scandinavian beauty's hands roamed up and down Sammi's delicious sinful body, squeezing and stroking, pinching and fondling.

Angelo surveyed the action, flat pewter eyes on Jenna's perfectly round naked ass and on her tidy little cunt winking at him. His cock was growing by the second. He was so fucking hard, he ached. Angelo growled under his breath and gripped his shaft at the base. He shifted his position slightly, so he could view

Sammi's pussy, open and pink, while Jenna worked her with her tongue and fingers. *What a fucking beautiful sight.* He couldn't take it much longer. He had to have them. Yes. He'd fuck them both. Jenna in the ass and Sammi in that incredibly hot pussy. Time to make his move.

Standing tall, Angelo kicked off his shorts. His cock upright and tight to his belly, he rolled his fingertips around the engorged head, teasing the tight foreskin as he moved towards the girls. "Who's going to be the first to suck on this 'bad boy'?" he asked, grinning broadly, his Eastern European accent sounding gangster as he joined the girls on the daybed.

Jenna looked up at him with dreamy hazel eyes. Her fingers stayed on Sammi's pussy, caressing her unhurriedly as she watched Angelo. Sammi stared up at him too, her breathing tight. Angelo made room for himself and knelt beside the girls. He lifted Jenna's chin and teased her with his cock, waving it around her mouth, dick slapping her sweet young face. It was heart-shaped with a dusting of dotted freckles. Her teeth were so white and perfect; she could be the star of a toothpaste commercial, rather than a whore. Although Jenna was only nineteen, she was already a great cocksucker. With a groan, Angelo thrust himself between her full pouty lips. Relaxing back on his haunches, he felt her hands and lips on him. He closed his eyes momentarily. As he fucked her mouth, he grabbed hold of one of Sammi's tits and squeezed it hard.

Manoeuvring themselves into a comfy ménage à trois, the threesome got settled. Angelo lolled back on a mound of pillows, his legs flat and splayed out before him, his massive erection the centre of attention, as both

147

girls, on their knees, went to work on him, sharing his cock between them, all hands and lips and teeth. He grabbed handfuls of Sammi's hair and seized Jenna's ass, his punishing fingers leaving red imprints on her smooth fleshy buttocks. From the rear, he worked a finger into Jenna's cunt. She felt warm and tight.

Angelo was on the edge of cumming. It wouldn't take him long. He'd let the whores work their magic and make him erupt like Vesuvius, then he'd take them inside, tie them up and ride them. Hard. Bite them and beat them. Get the riding crop out. He knew he'd have to rein it in a bit. He mustn't get carried away. He couldn't afford to mark their flawless young bodies. Most of his clients wouldn't want that. They expected perfection and paid top dollar for the privilege. But he'd have his fun, nevertheless. He'd chop out some coke to loosen them all up. But first, he needed to call that bitch Tatiana again. *Why the fuck wasn't she responding to his calls and messages?* Angelo clenched his teeth together as aggression took over. Scowling, he exhaled harshly from both nostrils and controlled the anger that invaded his pleasure. A few more slithers of tongue on his shaft was all it took to get it back. He erased the Albanian bitch from his mind and let his orgasm build, once more. His handsome face creased into a self-satisfied smile as he felt his sap rise.

TWENTY-SIX

SATURDAY 12 JANUARY

SUZANNE

Suzanne was making good progress, though she hadn't yet made it to lunchtime and her feet were already killing her. The hotel was huge. She really felt its size taking its toll as she strolled around in high heels. But, she had to look the part. Suzanne popped her head into the various dining options, some that were already open and doing business and others that were getting prepared for the lunchtime service. She had a small Dictaphone tucked into her handbag which she spoke into as she went along. She chatted with staff in several of the restaurants. They seemed friendly and accommodating, obviously well-trained to give first-class customer service. Suzanne grinned; it really wasn't going to be difficult to give the hotel a glowing review.

Suzanne pushed her hair off her face and tucked it behind her ears. The action made her think of Sebastian, who was always sweeping wisps of hair away with his beautiful, soft hands, sliding it behind her ears, and then, just gazing tenderly into her eyes. When he did that, he made her feel like they were the only two people in the world. Like nothing else mattered. She adored the intimacy that simple act triggered. For a few seconds, Sebastian crowded all other thoughts from her head. As she pictured his marine blue eyes fixed on hers, her smile grew wide. She wondered what he was up to right now. She'd sent him a WhatsApp a while ago, but he hadn't replied. As the message hadn't been read, Suzanne wasn't unduly worried; she just assumed he was somewhere without Wi-Fi. She made up her mind that if she hadn't heard back from him soon, she'd text him or perhaps give him a quick call. But first she planned to book them somewhere special for dinner.

After making a reservation for eight o'clock in the Grill Room, which she was reliably informed was the Fairmont's flagship restaurant, Suzanne began exploring the selection of shops lined up in the hotel lobby. Alongside the ski hire shop with which she'd already had dealings, there was a gift shop, a skiwear shop, full of the hottest brands, and an impressive designer clothes shop. Suzanne decided she'd return later with Sebastian to have a good look around. Some of the clothes looked fabulous. She made a mental note to treat herself.

Keen to investigate what she considered to be one of the hotel's most unique facilities, an on-site wedding chapel, Suzanne made her way to the lift, calculating that she had plenty of time to check it out before her scheduled lunch meeting. Even though she'd eaten plenty at breakfast, she was still looking forward to a sit-down and some top-class cuisine for lunch. She'd probably have to give afternoon tea a miss, though, she decided. She hoped Sebastian would be back by then and they could put their time to better use. She longed to grab an hour or two in bed with him before dinner.

Still with thoughts of lovemaking uppermost in her mind, Suzanne took the elevator to the rooftop chapel. The wonderful wedding venue was situated on the woodland terrace; a beautiful glass room surrounded on every side with towering evergreens blanketed in fluffy white snow. The landscape was so bright you needed shades. Although the blazing sun was high in a perfect cerulean blue sky, Suzanne thought it would still be pretty chilly out. She didn't have a coat with her, so didn't venture outside. Instead, she stood and took in the marvellous views of British Columbia, through gleaming panoramic windows.

Smartly dressed hotel staff bustled around her setting up for someone's pending nuptials. An amazing setting for some lucky couple's romantic occasion, Suzanne mused as she got totally caught up in the sheer romance of it all. She couldn't help daydreaming that maybe one day, she and Sebastian might tie the knot somewhere equally romantic, then giggled, chastising herself for thinking that far ahead. *For heaven's sake, I'm still married to Edward, and I've only known him a matter of months!* But deep down, Suzanne really hoped it was a possibility. She couldn't bear to think of life without Sebastian.

A strikingly pretty blonde in her early twenties spotted Suzanne and hurried over, all smiles. She had a cherubic face with huge blue eyes and peaches and cream skin. Once Suzanne introduced herself and revealed she was writing an article about the hotel, it opened the floodgates for a wealth of information on the various wedding services offered at the Fairmont. Suzanne recorded snippets of their conversation and slipped several leaflets into her handbag before expressing her thanks and then heading back to the lift.

Suzanne took her phone out of her bag. No response from Sebastian. She tapped shell pink nails on her phone nervously. *That wasn't like him at all.* She wondered if he was currently hurtling down a mountain at great speed. She checked her message to see if it had been received. It had, but hadn't been opened. Suzanne decided to give it a bit longer, and if he still hadn't got back to her, she'd send a text.

With less than an hour to go before the lunch meeting, Suzanne headed to the spa to check out the treatment list and book herself in for a couple. Complimentary, of course! As she waited for the lift, she suddenly remembered she needed to talk to someone urgently about getting a birthday cake made. Sebastian's birthday was only two days away, so she would need to bring the subject up over lunch.

Back in the grand lobby, Suzanne did a quick calculation in her head. It would be a little after eight in the evening back home, a perfect time to catch her boys, she hoped. The spa could wait for a few minutes. She selected Rayan's number as he was the one most likely to answer his phone, and while she waited for the call to connect, she spotted a vacant sofa and grabbed a seat, immediately enjoying the sensation of resting her aching feet. She let out a little groan of satisfaction.

Rayan picked up after a couple of rings. "Hey, Mum! What's up?"

"Hi, love, just checking in to see how you both are."

"We're all good, thanks. Just getting ready to go out with the guys. Christian's in the shower. So, how's Whistler?"

"It's absolutely breathtakingly beautiful. And the hotel is amazing. We'll all have to come here skiing next year."

"Yeah, that would be very cool."

"How did your match go?"

"Great. We won. And Christian scored two tries!"

"Fantastic! Shame I missed it then."

"It was weird, though, because Dad turned up."

"Well, that's nice. He probably came because he knew he wouldn't bump into me," Suzanne chuckled ironically.

"Yeah, maybe." He waited a beat. "You'll never guess who he had with him."

"Who?"

"Tatiana."

Suzanne was gobsmacked. Totally lost for words for a moment. "Oh my God! Is she back on the scene then?"

"I don't know, Mum, but it looks that way."

"Oh, for God's sake, your father is such a bloody idiot! Were you speaking with her?"

"For a bit, yeah. I thought you might have known because she made a point of telling me that Sebastian is treating her for some old skiing injury. Like the two of us were all buddy-buddy because of us both being his patients, kind of thing."

"What?" Suzanne's mouth fell open in shock. She was speechless again while she digested the information. She found her voice. "That's the first I've heard of it." She really couldn't believe what she was hearing.

"I've no idea if it's true, but… Oh, hang on, here's Christian; the hero of the day," Rayan laughed. "I'll pass the phone over. Bye, Mum, have a great time."

After that unexpected revelation, Suzanne wondered if she could. She felt sick to her stomach; felt that something was terribly wrong. "Bye, love. Be careful. Hope you have a good night," she mumbled as brightly as she could muster.

Suzanne had a scant conversation with Christian, but her mind was focused on other things. Her heart thumped in her chest, and a debilitating sinking sensation raged in her tummy. She couldn't believe that Sebastian would keep a secret like that unless there was a good reason. She had no idea what that reason might be. None whatsoever. All she knew was that Tatiana was gorgeous and young and manipulative, and she'd stolen her husband. Fortunately, her son was fresh out of the shower, dripping wet and wrapped in a towel, so was keen to keep their chat brief too. With her mind whirring with black thoughts and presumptions, Suzanne managed to congratulate Christian on his performance and told him she was so sorry that she hadn't been there to celebrate their victory. But all she could think of while they were talking was that Tatiana was back and Sebastian was keeping secrets. *What the hell was going on? If it was all so innocent, why the fuck hadn't he told her? Fuck texting!* Suzanne decided she needed to call Sebastian straight away.

TWENTY-SEVEN

SEBASTIAN

The Beach House restaurant was bathed in flawless winter sunlight. There wasn't a cloud in the sky as the silver Town car slowed to a halt in the car park. Sebastian glanced around to make sure he had everything. His heart was racing. Reaching over the gap between the two front seats, he paid and tipped the driver, instructing him not to wait. Sebastian had been assured that booking a taxi back to Whistler wouldn't be a problem. He'd worry about that later. He was trying to remain normal and calm, but felt anything but.

Sebastian slipped his gloves on and slid out of the heat of the car. The cold surprised him. An icy wind came off the water, the frigid air making his breath seep out in smoky wafts. Sebastian fastened his coat almost all the way to his throat and knotted his scarf around on top and tucked it in. Wrapped up to the max, he didn't look back as he strode briskly towards the restaurant. When he was just a few feet from the car and he sensed it steadily reversing out of the parking space directly behind him, Sebastian's phone rang in his pocket. Recoiling, he stared at the display. It was Suzanne. He swore under his breath. He knew she'd worry if he didn't answer, but he really couldn't right now. He'd text her as soon as he could, he decided, which made him feel a little less guilty about his decision not to take her call. He'd never done that before. But today he felt he had no choice.

As he let his mobile ring out, he saw him. Sebastian's blue eyes misted as he focused on the familiar man sitting at an outside table, wrapped in a dark heavy parka complete with a sizeable furry collar. There was a patio heater beside him and a pint of beer on the table in front of him. Even at some distance, Sebastian could see that he'd hardly changed at all. His hair was greyer and thinner, and was clipped short, but aside from that, little about his father's appearance had altered. He still looked exactly like the big man Sebastian remembered. He recognised his son at a distance too, as almost immediately Donald Black raised his hand in greeting. Sebastian lifted a hand in return and then wiped away the wetness filling his eyes. He wasn't crying; it was just the cold making his eyes run. Sebastian felt his stomach cramp, as head down against the bracing ocean breeze he made his way to the outside seating area to join the father he hadn't seen for twenty years. All good intentions of replying to Suzanne at some point soon flew out of his head.

Donald Black stood to greet Sebastian and held out his hand. Right away, Sebastian noticed that he was now the taller man. He shook his father's hand briefly but pulled away as soon as was polite. His emotions were in tatters whereas his father seemed perfectly at ease.

"Good to see you, Sebastian," Donald said, condensation pouring from his mouth as he spoke.

"What are you drinking? A whisky to warm you up, perhaps?"

"No, thank you. I don't drink whisky," Sebastian answered, trying not to allow any sarcasm to creep into his reply. He didn't want to get off on the wrong foot, but his father's suggestion only served to reinforce the fact that he knew absolutely nothing about the man his son had become.

"Let's go to the bar then, shall we? And you can have a look, see what you fancy," Donald Black suggested chummily.

Sebastian said nothing as Donald ushered him ahead. Together they walked silently into the heart of the restaurant's comfortable interior.

As the two men lined up side by side at the bar, Sebastian heard his phone ring again. Feeling extremely torn, he groped in his pocket and switched it to silent mode. After dealing with the intrusion swiftly, the quietness and disconnection between father and son were excruciating. Sebastian was starting to feel really hot, and so he took off his coat and lay it on the bar stool beside him. He forced a smile and made eye contact with Donald. With very little conversation, Sebastian selected and ordered a glass of Malbec, a large one, even though it was pretty early. He needed a drink. He hoped it would calm him while he struggled to get some answers. When both men were sitting on stools at the bar counter with drinks in their hands, Donald broke the silence.

"I'm guessing you're here because your mother still hasn't told you?"

Sebastian was caught totally off guard. "Hasn't told me what?" he asked quickly.

"Of course, she hasn't. Why would she?" Donald Black added disdainfully. He rolled his eyes. "Well, there's no easy way to say this, Sebastian." He paused for what seemed like a lifetime and then dropped the bombshell: "I'm not your father."

Sebastian was glad that he was sitting down as he feared his legs may have given way beneath him. He certainly hadn't been expecting that.

"What do you mean?" he managed to utter.

"I mean exactly what I've just said," Donald Black replied wearily. He continued: "Your mother was a slut, Sebastian. A pretty little blue-eyed whore." Donald sipped his beer and looked at Sebastian pointedly, his eyes cold.

"What? What are you saying? You have to explain! You really do!" Sebastian kept his voice low but sounded desperate.

"Your mother had sex with another man, fell pregnant and managed to convince me the baby, you, were mine. I didn't need much convincing as we were in love. Or so I thought. I only discovered the truth when you were nearly five years old. We'd been trying for another baby for a while, and then when that didn't work out, I had some tests. That's when I discovered I was infertile and the cheating bitch had been lying to me for years."

Sebastian felt his stomach drop like a stone. Nausea gripped him. Donald Black's shocking words reverberated in his head, drowning out the background noise of a sports match on the bar's television up above them. Sebastian was relieved there was no one near enough to overhear their conversation. Lost for words, he put his head in his hands. After a few seconds, he faced Donald again.

The older man's face fixed with a hard scowl. It was obvious to see that blind hatred and bitter resentment still lived in his heart. He continued louder now: "The whoring bitch couldn't explain that away, no matter how hard she tried!"

After that outburst, the barman moved a little closer and began to wipe down the already spotlessly clean bar top beside them. Sebastian was past caring. He hated hearing his mother being referred to as a bitch and a whore, but he struggled to find the words to defend her while he processed the information. He knew he was only listening to one side of the story, and the man beside him was not a man he trusted. He was a man who had abandoned him with no explanation whatsoever and hadn't been in touch for twenty years. On the other hand, his mother had always been there for him. He adored his sweet-natured, capable mother, who seemed to have tried her best for him all his life.

Sebastian sat in silence, trying to make some sense of what he'd been told. In his head, everything began to slip into place. Good times with his father when he was a little boy and then everything going horribly wrong; the never-ending rows, the bewildering ugly violence and, of course, being shipped off to boarding school at the earliest opportunity.

Shrugging off the stares of the bartender, Sebastian finally spoke, his voice angry, but the volume controlled. "So, why did you stay so long? You stayed together for years after that. And from what I can remember, you beat her up on a regular basis. You were drunk all the time, shouting and hitting her, blacking out, supposedly having no recollection of the damage you'd inflicted. It was a fucking nightmare. Even if what you say is true, she didn't deserve that!"

"You were just a kid. It wasn't like that. Your memory is flawed, or she's been filling your head with lies, son."

"I'm not your fucking son, though, am I?" Sebastian rounded on him furiously.

"I tried to do the right thing by you, Sebastian, I really did. For almost five years I watched you grow up believing you were my son, and I loved you more than you'll ever know. But when I found out you weren't mine, you were nothing to do with me at all, there was an anger raging inside me that I just couldn't control. It was like a bereavement; losing you like that. As soon as you went off to boarding school, I moved out. Moved to an apartment in London. I just came back to Surrey when you were on school holidays and turned up with Gloria playing happy families for sports matches and parents' meetings." When he spat out Sebastian's mother's name, there was hatred on his tongue. Donald Black huffed and added bitterly: "Parents' evening. I wasn't even a fucking parent!"

Sebastian said nothing. He really had no idea what to say.

"I pretended we were still together for your sake, but in hindsight I realised that was a big mistake. I know now I should have walked away then, but I was trying to raise you to manhood. I saw that as my duty even though you were another man's son."

Tears were back in Sebastian's eyes and this time they were flowing liberally. He tried to blink them away but was fighting an impossible battle. Salty tears dropped on his top lip and he licked them up before saying: "So, who is my father?" His voice was full of pain.

Donald Black answered glibly: "I've absolutely no idea, Sebastian. Your mother would never tell me who her secret lover was. You're gonna have to address that question to her."

It seemed as if that was all Donald Black wanted to say on the matter. He sipped his beer and fell silent. Neither man spoke for what seemed to Sebastian to be minutes rather than seconds.

"Now that's all out in the open would you like another drink or something to eat?" said the stranger who Sebastian had for almost thirty-seven years of his life considered to be his father.

Sebastian shook his head. "I don't think so."

Donald Black downed the remainder of his beer. "I think it's best I leave you to digest this, and then I suggest you ask your mother to fill you in. For your sake, I hope she'll be more honest with you than she ever was with me."

He touched Sebastian gently on the shoulder. Sebastian pulled away instinctively, uncomfortable by the contact. He felt bile rise in his throat. He knew that there was every chance he'd throw up. He swallowed hard, breathed in through his nose and out through his mouth.

"It's been good to see you, Sebastian. I'm glad you've grown up to be a success as a man. I really am."

Sebastian remained silent. And with great sadness in his eyes, and his breakfast churning in his stomach, he watched Donald Black take some notes from his pocket

161

and lay them on the bar. Sebastian hung his head as the man who he felt he never really knew, and would surely never know now, walked calmly out of the Beach House and out of his life forever.

TWENTY-EIGHT

SUZANNE

Five times Suzanne called Sebastian's mobile and five times it just rang and rang. She willed him to pick up, but he never did. Each time when his phone switched to voicemail, she left a message, her voice becoming more and more distraught with every unanswered call. Her head was spinning. Tears dribbled down her cheeks. Anxiety gnawed at her core like an unwanted visitor. *What the hell was he up to? Where was he? They always kept in touch – almost obsessively so.* Suzanne was exasperated now. She needed to speak to him urgently about Tatiana. *For fuck's sake! Surely that woman hadn't got her claws into him too?* She had to discover the truth before she went to lunch. *How the hell would she get through it with this playing on her mind?* There was a plummeting sensation in her belly as she recalled how vague Sebastian had sounded when she'd asked him his plans for the day.

For what seemed like an age, but was in reality only a couple of minutes, Suzanne considered the possibility that Sebastian might have had some kind of skiing accident, but then her logic kicked in and she hurried

163

to the boot room, her heart thumping so hard she started to hyperventilate. She discovered all his ski gear stored neatly away as they'd left it a few of hours earlier. But still it didn't quieten her racing heart. The idea that he was still in their room taking a nap, or more likely he had just left his phone there, leapt into her head. She ran to their suite, bustling past groups of people on her way, pacing nervously in the lift amongst others who looked at her suspiciously. Suzanne blanked them. She didn't care. When she checked the suite, there was no sign of him. Suzanne called his mobile once more, just in case. It rang out somewhere else and then went to voicemail. This time she didn't bother leaving a message.

Suzanne flung herself face down on the bed. Her chest was so tight it was as if she couldn't catch her breath. She gulped in a lungful of air and then punched the pillows with all her might, scattering them. It didn't help. She just felt so incredibly frustrated. She knew she was probably overreacting, but somehow, she couldn't help it. She just couldn't understand it. She and Sebastian were always in touch. An inner voice lectured her to calm down, to get a grip. She had this lunch to go to, but in her current agitated state, she had no idea how she would carry it off. She was absolutely fuming at what she had learned about Tatiana, but surely there had to be a reasonable explanation? Perhaps Rayan had somehow got it wrong? But even as she told herself that, she didn't believe it for a minute.

He must have lost his phone. That was the only explanation Suzanne could think of that worked. If the conversation with Rayan hadn't happened, Suzanne would have been able to console herself with that supposition, but the nugget of info that the Albanian bitch was being secretly treated by her lover niggled away at her brain like an insect crawling inside and setting up home. She felt sick. *How the hell was she going to act like a professional and smile her way through lunch?* She checked her Cartier. *Fuck! Time to go.*

Suzanne got up and rushed into the bathroom. She used a cotton bud to clean up her panda eyes and a tissue to blow her nose. She fluffed up her hair and reapplied an outline of lip pencil and filled in the gaps with lip gloss. Suzanne stared at her reflection in the mirror. Thankfully, she looked okay. Fortunately, the crippling anxiety etched into her pretty green eyes didn't show.

Suzanne decided she'd leave Sebastian a note, just in case he got back before her. She grabbed the pad from his side of the bed. Just as she was about to pen him a message, she read what was written on the top sheet in Sebastian's hand:

The Beach House, 150, 25th Street, West Vancouver, BC. V7V 4Y8

"What the fuck?" Suzanne blurted out loud.

Surely, he's not in Vancouver? Why would he be there? Suzanne was totally confused. She dismissed the idea that Sebastian was in Vancouver. That was just too mad. She had no idea why he would write down that address, but there was no time to wonder about it now. She had to get her head together and get to lunch. She couldn't let Uncle Jack down. She ripped the top page of the pad off, dropped it on the side and then scribbled on the next sheet in capitals:

WHERE ARE YOU, SEBASTIAN? CALL ME, BABY, PLEASE!

Suzanne placed the note dead centre on the bed and then grabbed her bag and left the room. If she was quick, she'd just about make it on time.

TWENTY-NINE

SEBASTIAN

As soon as Donald Black was gone, Sebastian signalled to the bartender for another glass of wine. Once he was served, he found himself a high table for two, as far away from the nosy barman as possible. Furthest from the dramatic ocean views and tucked away in a small, moodily lit alcove, Sebastian dragged a leggy stool out with one foot, and sat, tucking his long legs up on the footboard. He rested his elbows on the highly polished table. His glass in his eyeline, Sebastian's shoulders slumped and he exhaled loudly. He lowered his head and cupped the crown in both hands. He stayed in that position for several moments, battling to control his breathing. Sebastian feared he might have a panic attack. He remembered having them when he was a little boy, his mother taking care of him. Her eyes full of concern and love as she calmed her child and stroked his forehead.

Sebastian was in a world of his own as he glanced up at his surroundings. The place was filling up as singletons, couples and groups drifted in. The interior had a dark, old-fashioned feel. Much of the décor was formed out of deep rich mahogany. The presence of so much wood

167

reminded him of the boat he owned, moored on the Thames. The place where he first made love to Suzanne. Guilt tugged at his heart when he thought of his beautiful girlfriend, but still he didn't reach for his phone. Instead, he continued gazing around aimlessly. There were tall built-in shelves, cubby holes galore, recessed lighting and a large flatscreen above the bar. American football was playing with the sound turned down low. Sebastian didn't look at it. He wasn't interested. He felt numb, totally numb. He drank more wine. There was a bitter taste in his mouth. His tongue tasted iron, but the wine slipped down his throat like sweet nectar. He knew he must call his mother. It was evening back home. He hoped she was home alone. He didn't want to confront her while she had company.

Sebastian took another large glug, finishing his drink in one greedy swallow. He wiped his mouth with the back of his hand and just sat licking the perfect bow of his lips. He caught the eye of a pretty young waitress and ordered himself a bottle. *Fuck it!* He didn't care. He'd come all this way for some answers and he'd certainly got them. But not what he'd been expecting at all. He couldn't believe his mother hadn't told him the truth. Couldn't believe she'd lied to him all this time. *Why the hell hadn't she told him when his so-called 'father' left for good all those years ago?* The answer was simple, of course: because she was ashamed. Ashamed of living a lie for so long. Worried her son would hate her for what she'd done. He didn't hate her. He loved her dearly, but he was absolutely furious with her right now.

Sebastian took out his phone. There were six missed calls from Suzanne. He loved her more than anything, but he couldn't deal with her right now. He'd call his mother and then send Suzanne a text. Make up some excuse for not being in touch. His heart beating frantically, he called his mother's mobile. She answered after a couple of rings.

"Seb, darling, how are you? Are you having a good time?"

Sebastian swallowed hard. "No, not really, Mum," he replied shortly.

The young woman was now by his side with his open bottle of wine, preparing to pour. In her mid-twenties, she had baby blonde hair cut in a feathery urchin style that framed chocolate brown eyes. She was cute, though Sebastian didn't really notice.

"Hang on a minute," he said to his mother and then gestured to the waitress that he'd pour his own wine. He tipped a large helping of the maroon liquid into his glass, sipping it as he watched the waitress take her leave. Only then did he return his attention to the phone and his mother.

"No, I'm not having a good time, Mum," he finally replied, resentment screaming from every pore. "I'm in a bar in Vancouver where I've just been having a chat with a stranger, who for the last thirty-seven years I believed was my father. And I've just been told categorically that he's not!"

There was an agonising silence.

Eventually, after many seconds of nothingness, Sebastian spoke again. "Mum, are you there?"

He heard a crescendo of tears. His mother was weeping softly into the phone. He waited silently as she struggled to compose herself.

Sounding like a cried-out toddler, Gloria gulped: "I'm so sorry, Sebastian. I should have told you, but I never felt the time was right."

"I'm sorry too, but I am so bloody angry." Sebastian raised his voice though he was really trying not to. "Why couldn't you have told me? Maybe not when he was still around and I was a kid, but why didn't you tell me once he'd left? Why did you leave me thinking I had a father who abandoned me and didn't want me? It's messed with my head for years. You know that, Mum. All that bloody therapy. How could you do that?"

"I'm so sorry, my love. I really am." There was a pause before she continued falteringly. "It's a very long story, Seb, and I'm sure Donald has only told you his side of the story. Painted me as a total slut. What happened with your father…"

"He's not my fucking father, though, is he?" Sebastian interjected angrily.

Gloria started to weep again. "No, he's not. I'm so sorry, Sebastian," she grizzled. Her voice grew weak.

"Please just tell me, Mum," Sebastian begged, and hugged the phone tight to his ear.

Gloria seemed to compose herself, though when she spoke, her voice was heavy with anguish. "It was all right for him to be running around with all kinds of women and prostitutes too, and then one night, after a terrible argument, I took comfort in the arms of another man. Well, he was no more than a boy really. Eighteen years old and soon to head off to university. When I found out I was pregnant, I just buried my head in the sand and presumed you were Donald's. When I told him I was pregnant, he told me over and over again how sorry he was for his womanising. Promised me that it wouldn't happen again, and we got married soon after. Everything was fine for a while. He was a good father and absolutely adored you, Sebastian." Gloria went quiet.

"Yeah, adored me until he found out I wasn't his son, of course!" Sebastian spat out scornfully. He didn't want to hurt his mother, but he just couldn't help himself. Reeling in his bitterness, he added quietly: "So, who is my father, Mum? Please! I need to know."

There was a long pause before his mother spoke. "His name was Micky. Micky Hewkin. He lived locally and worked part-time at the hotel I managed. Honestly, I've no idea where he is now, and I've never tried to contact him. Sebastian, please, let's talk about this when you get back. I promise I'll help you track him down if you decide that's what you really want to do."

Sebastian breathed out hard. Under the table, he jiggled his legs restlessly. He drained his glass before he spoke.

"Yes, you're right. I have only heard his side of the story. But I need to track down my father. My real father. And you need to help me, Mum, okay?"

"Okay," Gloria replied shakily. "We'll talk about this as soon as you're back."

"Okay. Love you, Mum."

Sebastian disconnected before Gloria had time to reply. He poured himself another enormous glass of wine, his face a mask of misery, his heart thumping.

THIRTY

TATIANA

A quiet Saturday evening at home with her lover should have been relaxing, and yet Tatiana wasn't relaxed at all. She felt uneasy, every nerve in her body stretched taut with tension. The takeaway they'd ordered from *Just Eat* was fine, but she had no appetite and had only picked at one slice of her pepperoni and hot chilli pizza. It sat congealing, still in its box. In the comfortable TV room, with the drapes pulled, they'd had sex twice in quick succession. Eddie had made her body tremble, and she'd erupted like a fountain. Orgasms usually made Tatiana feel amazing, but tonight even good sex hadn't cleared her head.

Still damp from their lovemaking exertions, they'd snuggled up on the chaise sofa under a chenille blanket and watched a movie, *The Wolf of Wall Street*, though Tatiana couldn't concentrate on the plot at all. She wrapped herself around Eddie and stared vacuously at the manic, drug-fuelled goings-on onscreen, stirring only occasionally to smoke or sip red wine. Tatiana was restless. Unsure of her next move. Angelo's angry words rang in her head, no matter how hard she struggled to expel them.

With Eddie in his office on a late night business call, Tatiana lay, covered up, stretched out on the couch. She toyed with her phone. With her heart pounding against her ribs, she listened to Angelo's message one more time:

"Tatiana, I don't know what the fuck you are playing at, not answering your phone or calling me back. You are seriously taking the piss. I have big money clients of yours waiting for you, so I need to know what time you're back. So, call me. And fucking do it soon. Capiche?"

Even with the volume low, the venomous tone of Angelo's barked words gave Tatiana the chills. She sat up and lit up, and puffed on her cigarette nervously. Trying to take her mind off Angelo, she browsed social media. She flicked through her Facebook news feed and scrolled through a host of largely pointless postings, video clips and photographs. She spied an advertisement for *Secret Escapes*, the discount holiday site, and a germ of an idea sneaked into her brain. As the plan formulated, Tatiana started to feel calmer. It was all so simple. Just lie. All she needed to do was text Angelo and reassure him she'd be back on the 16th. And when she was supposed to be returning to Dubai, just fly off somewhere else. That would get him off her back. And, if he did come looking for her, she'd be long gone. Surely, he'd get the message? With a smug smile, Tatiana composed a text. Even though they were both Albanian, they always communicated in English.

So sorry, Angel! I haven't been ignoring you. I lost my phone. I have it now, but too late to call. My flight gets in at 8pm Dubai time on the 16th. Can't wait to see you! Big wet kiss, darling!

Tatiana added a multitude of emoji motifs of aeroplanes and sunshine and sticky lipsticky kisses and then pressed send. Now all she had to do was convince Eddie to take her away on holiday. Where did she fancy? Tatiana had always dreamt of going to the Maldives; the group of paradise islands in the Indian Ocean boasting powder white sand and astonishingly beautiful turquoise seas. The island listed on the website looked like utter heaven. It shouldn't be too difficult to arrange, surely? Eddie seemed so stressed. Like he needed a break. Tatiana heard him in the office, still talking on the phone. So, feeling like her batteries were recharged, she discarded the blanket and sprang up with renewed vigour. She took a large swig of wine and a deep drag on her Camel Blue. She crushed much of her cigarette out in the ashtray, and then draping her scant robe around her bare shoulders, she tiptoed to the office. The door was closed. Putting her ear to the door, she listened through it. Eddie sounded agitated.

"Look, Rick, just keep it together and it's going to be fine. There's no connection between us, so there's really not going to be a problem."

Tatiana knocked softly and poked her head around the door. Eddie was sitting behind his desk, talking into his mobile. The masculine room was shrouded in darkness, with only a single desk lamp lighting the room. Eddie smiled awkwardly over at her and gestured for Tatiana to enter. As she passed into the room, she dropped her short wrap to the floor. Swishing her mane of wonderful hair, she strolled towards him nude and delicious, swaying her hips, loving the drama of her entrance. She knew she looked awesome. Eddie said nothing, but his eyes were all over her now. Tatiana presumed whoever was on the other end of the phone was doing all the talking. She had no idea who Rick was but knew their conversation would soon need to be cut short. Eddie remained silent and watched attentively as, with the grace of a lynx, Tatiana hopped up onto the desk. Knees up, she swivelled to face him.

"Look, it's going to be fine. You've just got to stop calling me every five minutes. We need to keep our distance until this is done. Okay?"

As Eddie spoke into the phone, he continued to stare at Tatiana as if hypnotised by her allure. With her eyes fixed firmly on his, she inserted a forefinger into her mouth and sucked on it greedily. Rolling her tongue around the knuckle, saliva dripped from her lips. Still sucking, she swept papers out of her way. Once she'd made a clear space, Tatiana lay down on her back and positioned herself decoratively across the width of the desk. She raised and opened her knees. Bottom-shuffling, she aimed her pussy at Eddie. He licked his lips and groaned.

Grinning naughtily, Tatiana pushed her finger into Eddie's mouth. She allowed him to suck on it for just a few seconds before she trailed it over her tummy to her pussy. Unbearably slowly. Still holding his gaze, she slotted the finger in her pussy, moaning dramatically as it disappeared inside her. Eddie's nostrils flared. He inhaled deeply and made a big show as he breathed her in. She knew she had him hooked. He could no longer concentrate on his call. Eddie tried to talk into the phone, but when he did, his words came out all croaky.

"Rick, I've got to go," he blustered, and then hung up. He moved in close. "Babe, I gotta taste you."

Tatiana had Eddie right where she wanted him. Before the week was up, they'd be flying out to some sun and five-star luxury in the Maldives. She'd have her consultation with Sebastian on the 17th, stir up trouble for the blonde bitch and then fly out first thing on the 18th. Fuck her and fuck Angelo Azzurro. He didn't own her. Her haughty green eyes flashed with victory. Yes, it would all work perfectly. A delicious shiver moved through Tatiana as she sensed the heat of Eddie's tongue. She closed her eyes and hummed as Eddie found her sweetspot. As he lapped at her clit, he slipped a finger into her ass.

THIRTY-ONE

SUZANNE

Many hours had passed since Suzanne had last spoken to Sebastian. Although she was desperately worried something terrible had happened to him, somehow her professionalism kicked in. At lunch while she sat smiling in company, a throbbing headache gnawed at her temples and she felt utterly sick to the stomach. Suzanne struggled to keep everything under control with a smile painted on her face that masked her misery. She sipped at iced cucumber water and moved her perfectly cooked medium rib-eye steak and chopped salad around her plate, but ate very little. She checked her muted phone as often as she could without it seeming bad-mannered. She received no calls and no messages. Not one.

The threesome had met up in a large private dining room which had a phenomenal view over the snowy massif. Sean, the only male amongst them, introduced himself as a general manager. Suzanne didn't really process what part of the hotel services Sean was actually a general manager of. She was having trouble concentrating. Mid-thirties and overweight, his brown suit too tight around his girth, his buttons battling

177

under the strain, Sean had a sunny smile and an air of efficiency about him. As they took their seats, at a table that would comfortably seat a dozen, Sean introduced Stacey-Lou, his assistant. She had pale beige hair that fell to her shoulders in waves. Young and keen, she looked stunning in a figure-hugging cable-knit dress the colour of her smoky grey eyes.

Although Suzanne wanted to be anywhere but surviving a business lunch where she needed to be on top form, in an odd way, she was glad of the enforced distraction. It passed the time. It took her mind off Sebastian, just a little. The service was excellent, and Sean and Stacey-Lou were lovely people. Both seemed genuinely proud of the Fairmont. Suzanne was relieved she'd already prepared a comprehensive list of questions. It made her task so much easier with the uneasiness and uncertainty of Sebastian's whereabouts crowding her head. Behind a veneer of bonhomie, she got through it. She read from her list and used the Dictaphone to record everything. Sean and Stacey-Lou seemed in no great hurry to wrap up their meeting, so it was almost two thirty when she expressed her gratitude for their time and made her way out of the restaurant.

The moment she was on her own, Suzanne took her phone from her bag and checked it again. There was a new message from Abi and a couple of Facebook notifications, but that was it. Nothing at all from Sebastian. Stifling a sob, she stepped into the ascending lift. She wasn't alone, so she dipped her head and fought back the tears that bubbled like miniscule effervescent spheres balancing precariously on her long lashes. Standing with her head bowed amongst three strangers,

Suzanne switched her ringer back on. She was so frustrated she wanted to scream. Her heart ached for him. *Where was he? Why hadn't he been in touch? And what the hell was going on with him and that fucking bitch, Tatiana?*

Suzanne felt so alone. She had absolutely no idea what to do. So, she did the only thing she could do and that was to call Sebastian again. As she stepped out of the elevator, she tried his number. She waited with bated breath as his phone rang and rang. He didn't pick up. There was no warm 'Hello, baby' at the conclusion, only the generic recorded message she'd heard too many times already. Suzanne began to cry. With tears trickling down her face, she fumbled with the pass key to their suite.

Once the door was closed behind her, with firm fingertips, Suzanne brushed away tears that cascaded down her face. It was like she was punishing herself for being so weak. She slumped against the door and sank to the floor. With her knees tucked into her chest, Suzanne curled herself into a ball and rocked. It calmed her. She knew she needed to get a grip. Sebastian would call her soon, explain, and everything would be okay. She had to hold on to that. She just had to be patient. Unfortunately, patience had never been Suzanne's virtue.

THIRTY-TWO

SATURDAY 12 JANUARY

SEBASTIAN

The bar was quieter now, the restaurant section populated with just a handful of stragglers spread around the L-shaped expanse. Sebastian noticed an elderly couple tucked away in a corner eating enormous burgers, and a family of six, complete with a couple of sulky teenagers glued to their phones. A trio of lone drinkers sat hunched over the deep redwood bar. With frothy topped jugs of beer in their hands, they talked in loud, brash voices and discussed the news items that filled the TV screen above them. Guys just hanging, just chilling. Sebastian was in a totally different frame of mind. In another world. He hadn't budged from his seat in hours except to take himself off to the restrooms to pee, which proved extraordinarily tricky. As soon as he got up off his barstool, he realised how wobbly he felt and was relieved when he'd made it back to his seat. Once he was seated again, he topped up his glass.

Even though he was seriously smashed, Sebastian had no intention of stopping drinking. The booze numbed the pain, soothed the emptiness and confusion penetrating his soul. He had a father out there somewhere. A father he didn't know and who didn't know him. A fiery determination clamped his heart. He'd track him down. He had to.

Sebastian gazed around at his surroundings as if he was taking it all in for the first time. Everything around him was beginning to look just a tiny bit blurred. It was getting late. The lunch crowd had come and gone with the sunshine, and now outside on the waterfront, everything was veiled in darkness as dusk moved in and the shadows lengthened. Icy cold air seemed to hover over the shimmering black water. In the warmth and snugness of the bar, Sebastian had whiled away the entire afternoon. He had just sat and drank wine. Glass after glass, and then bottle after bottle.

"How you doing there?" A soft voice invaded his space.

Sebastian glanced up to meet the deep, dark eyes of the waitress that had been serving him all afternoon. Her lashes were long, and he noticed, for the first time, that her eyes were very pretty.

"I'm just dandy!" he replied, a touch sarcastically. Try as he might, Sebastian couldn't quite conjure up a captivating smile to dampen his sarcasm. "I'll have another bottle of your finest Malbec," he added, though he was well aware that some of his words weren't coming out quite right. As he spoke, he tipped the remains of the bottle into his glass.

"Maybe you'd prefer a coffee instead, sir?" the waitress suggested smoothly as she moved in tight to his table.

Sebastian sighed heavily and chuckled to himself. "Yes, maybe you're right." He swished the last of the

181

maroon liquid around the circumference of his glass before necking it. He licked his lips and then peered at the name tag pinned to the left side of the young woman's chest. "Taylor," he said. "Can I call you Taylor?"

"Of course, sir." Taylor grabbed the empty bottle by the neck and waited.

"I've had a bit of a shock today, Taylor. A bloody awful shock." Sebastian was slurring his words.

"Well, that's a real shame, sir," Taylor replied soothingly, her accent warm and rich like honey. "Maybe you should forget the coffee and get yourself home. Are you staying locally? I could call you a cab."

"You can call me Sebastian," Sebastian replied, and then grinned boyishly at her, clearly amused by his own corny joke. He offered her a hand and said: "Sebastian Black. Nice to meet you, Taylor."

Taylor took his hand and shook it. She smiled kindly, and when she did, her eyes lit up her face. She was very attractive in a tired kind of way.

After a few seconds' consideration, Sebastian mumbled: "I think you're probably right. I should go home, but it's a bloody long way back to Whistler." He didn't stir. "Yes, I'll go back to the Fairmont," he repeated, as if he was talking himself into it. "I'd better have the bill then, please."

Taylor nodded and ripped off a page from her pad and handed it to him. Bleary-eyed, Sebastian grappled for his wallet while he peered at it. The bill came to one hundred and forty dollars. He couldn't believe he'd drunk a hundred and forty dollars' worth of wine. All by himself. That was not good. Not good at all. Looking bemused, he took out a hundred-dollar bill and then added four twenties. He stood. He was very unsteady on his feet, but he was totally expecting that. Sebastian gripped the table to stabilise himself.

"That's for looking after me so well, Taylor," Sebastian slurred as he placed the dollar bills on the table top. He slid his wallet back into his pocket. Finally, he managed that winning smile.

"Thank you, Sebastian," Taylor grinned. Even when she was smiling, Sebastian thought she still looked a little sad. She picked up the notes and then looking concerned, added: "You sure you're going to be okay? Shall I get you that cab? It's no trouble, really."

"No, no, don't you worry about me. I'll be just fine." His smile was mesmerising now, his eyes flashing indigo, his teeth sharp and devilishly white. Even drunk, Sebastian was drop-dead gorgeous. "I think I just need some air. I'm going to take a little walk."

While Taylor looked on, Sebastian punched his arms into his overcoat. He wrapped his scarf around his neck and then struggled to free up his mouth. Fumbling with his gloves, he dropped one to the floor, swaying precariously as he retrieved it. Taylor took hold of his arm to steady him. He accepted her help, trying to make light of it. "I'm not drunk, you know!" he announced.

"Of course not, Sebastian," Taylor replied knowingly, suppressing a bittersweet smile as she watched him struggle.

When Sebastian was fully ready, he raised a hand in farewell, and on shaky legs, he made his way to the exit.

"You take care, Sebastian," Taylor called after him as she watched the very beautiful, very drunk man head out into the bitterly cold night air. She slipped two twenty dollar bills into her apron pocket, cleared and wiped down the table and then made her way back to the bar. She smiled broadly when she registered it was just after six thirty and she had less than half an hour of her shift to go.

THIRTY-THREE

SATURDAY 12 JANUARY

SUZANNE

Outside, the temperature was tumbling. Wearing one of Sebastian's sweaters over her bra and knickers, Suzanne stood at the window and stared out. Particles of pure virgin snow swirled in the blue-black moonlit sky, smashing against the glass and dissolving into a mush that trickled slowly downwards. Suzanne watched their languid descent. She was a wreck. She couldn't sit still. The suite was warm. The heat turned up full, it was like a sauna. Suzanne spun around and started to pace, wandering around nervously, marching back and forth many times. The TV was on, but muted. Just a collection of images lighting up the screen. It didn't hold her interest. She couldn't concentrate on anything other than Sebastian.

Suzanne sighed heavily, and, looking like she had the weight of the world on her shoulders, she flopped down on the bed. She was drained and exhausted, her tummy a collection of knots, her head thumping. The scent of Sebastian permeated the pillar-box red jumper that clung to her. Wearing his clothes and inhaling his familiar aroma reminded her of the man she loved, with every sharp intake of breath. She lifted an arm to her face and took a deep breath. A sharp pain invaded her heart, grabbed it and ripped it in two, and yet his jumper on her skin made her feel close to him. She missed him terribly.

They'd had no contact for almost nine hours, and Suzanne felt empty. She felt numb. *This wasn't how it was supposed to be. This trip was supposed to be wonderful. What the hell had happened to him? Where was Sebastian and why hadn't he been in touch? They talked all the time; this just wasn't the way it was with them!* Everything had been perfect this morning, but now Suzanne was enduring a nightmare day that was stretching into a nightmare evening.

Suzanne was angry. She couldn't get the Albanian bitch out of her head. *What the hell was going on there? What was she up to?* Suzanne needed answers. She loved to get situations explained and sorted and tucked neatly away in little boxes in her brain. The only rational explanation Suzanne could come up with was that Tatiana had consulted Sebastian in the last few days or so, and for some reason or other he hadn't mentioned it to her yet. Maybe it was simply because he didn't want to ruin their trip. That scenario seemed reasonable enough. That was definitely the kind of thing Sebastian would do, Suzanne reassured herself, but then that didn't explain why he'd gone AWOL today. No matter how many times Suzanne tried to placate herself by explaining his mysterious disappearance away, the fact remained that they'd planned to meet up hours ago and he hadn't turned up and hadn't called to explain why. There had been no word from him since they parted company at around ten o'clock. He could so easily have called the hotel if he'd lost his mobile. *They had payphones in Canada, for God's sake! So, where the hell was he?*

Sitting propped up on the bed, on misshapen pillows she'd battered in frustration, Suzanne tucked her knees inside the jumper and hugged them to her chest. Her face was wet and puffy from crying, black make-up smears ringed her eyes, and her golden hair was an untidy mess. She felt she had no one to turn to. It was the dead of night back home, and anyway, she wouldn't bother her friends. She'd considered calling the Whistler police but didn't want to make a fool of herself. They'd just think she was some dumbass English woman whose boyfriend hadn't called her all day, so she wants to put out an APB. She could see them in her mind's eye, sniggering at her. No, she'd just have to sit it out and wait for news. Which in her heart of hearts she acknowledged would come eventually. She just needed to remain optimistic and be patient, she told herself for the hundredth time. Suzanne lay back, gripped her phone and stared at the screen willing something to happen; a call, a text, anything!

Suzanne watched the numerals on her iPhone change from 18.39 to 18.40. She sighed. They had dinner reservations at eight. She knew it was very unlikely they'd be dining out together tonight. And she'd been so distracted over lunch that she'd forgotten to order Sebastian's birthday cake. Not that it mattered. Suzanne had no idea where he was and if he'd be back with her for his birthday. The very idea that that was a possibility made her sick to the stomach. Suzanne emitted a whimper of excruciating anguish as she pictured Sebastian lying somewhere hurt, or even worse. She just couldn't go there. She couldn't think about that at all. Hot tears tumbled from her eyes.

All of a sudden, there was a hot rush in her belly. Bile burned her throat and she started to retch. Suzanne hurried to the bathroom. She sank to her knees and hugged the loo. Not a second too soon. A gush of vomit sprayed forth from her mouth in a multicoloured torrent. The vivid puke just kept on coming. Finally, when Suzanne had emptied the entire contents of her stomach, she lay down on the warm tiled floor and gasped for breath.

THIRTY-FOUR

SATURDAY 12 JANUARY

SEBASTIAN

As soon as the sub-zero night air hit him, Sebastian knew he was in trouble. Serious fucking trouble. He realised at once that taking a walk to sober himself up was a very bad idea. He should have let that nice waitress call him a cab. What was her name? His head was so fuzzy he couldn't recall. He needed to focus. If he could just hold it together, he'd be able to find somewhere to sit down and then give Suzanne a call. Tell her he was on his way back. He knew she'd be going out of her mind with worry, and the thought cut him to the bone. He'd been selfish and cruel, spending an afternoon getting smashed, drowning his sorrows, knowing full well she'd be worried sick. It made him feel like an absolute shit. As he lurched through the parking lot, tears began to spill from his eyes. Sebastian's heart ached. He needed Suzanne. He wanted her to take him in her arms, hold him tight and make everything all right.

The large car park was pretty deserted aside from a dozen or so cars and a grimy white pick-up truck parked up in the furthest corner by the waterfront. A thick white frost coated every windscreen, the sharp iciness sparkling like crystals. Numbed by the alcohol, Sebastian barely felt the intense cold. He heard a lone dog howling in the background. He wondered what kind of dog it was. It sounded huge, like a wolf, like something from a horror movie. *An American Werewolf in London* sprang bizarrely into his mind as he staggered about without direction, just hoping to stay upright while he got his bearings.

Rummaging in his coat pocket, Sebastian took out his phone. He gazed at it, trying desperately to focus. Message after message filled the screen. Sebastian took off his gloves and unlocked the phone. He scrolled up and the messages just kept coming. There were forty missed calls as well. Most of them from Suzanne or his callback service and even some from his mother. He knew he had to call Suzanne. Soon. He didn't want to prolong her agony for one more second. He saw a small saloon car maybe ten metres up ahead in the gloom of nightfall. The night was as black as pitch. Its murkiness felt like it was closing in on him. The ground beneath his feet reminded him of an ice rink, but if he could just get to that shiny red car and lean on it, he reckoned he'd be steady enough to make the call.

It was no distance at all, but Sebastian's legs were rubbery beneath him, his knees and ankles bendy with a will of their own. Sebastian couldn't ever remember feeling this drunk. He breathed out hard and fast; a swift series of pants just as he did when he was working out at the gym. It didn't help. In fact, it made him feel worse. Stumbling, his arms outstretched before him, he set off at a faltering pace on the precariously icy ground. His sole purpose was to make it to that first car. Step by tiny step, he tottered towards it, his body uncoordinated. Two steps forward, then one step back.

After what seemed like an eternity, Sebastian was getting close. He was within touching distance. His body arched awkwardly as he reached out and touched the car. It was tacky with ice. His fingertips made contact with the boot, but he was too far away from it for it to support him. Sebastian sensed right away he was going down. He watched in slow motion as his phone slipped from his hand and smashed on the ground beside him. He followed it with his eyes and then his body, as his feet slid from under him. Sebastian went down like a lead weight, a mass of ungraceful limbs. Fortunately, in a moment of clarity and self-preservation, he remembered to lift his head just enough, so he didn't smack it on the hard, unforgiving tarmac. Sebastian groaned and stared up at the heavens. He was so out of it he couldn't tell if the shower of twinkling stars were scattered in the ebony sky or just floating around in his head.

★

Sebastian had no idea how much later it was when he felt the presence of someone kneeling over him. Everything hurt like crazy, and he was shivering uncontrollably. His ears felt numb. He couldn't feel his feet at all. His fingers were stiff and excruciatingly painful. The celestial body floating above him brought him warmth. It was like there was an angel looking down on him.

"Are you okay, Sebastian?" a woman's voice asked.

Sebastian recognised the voice but couldn't quite place it. He opened his eyes for the first time in a while, and there was Taylor. Her name came to him in a fog. She stared down at him, concern written all over her lovely face.

His teeth were chattering. He tried to answer, but everything was just too much effort and nothing intelligible came out.

Taylor's warm breath caressed his frozen cheeks as her arms surrounded him. She was stronger than she looked. She was lifting him from the ground. The heat of her body against his felt good.

"Can you stand?"

A dense mist poured from Taylor's lips. Sebastian watched in awe. Everything was surreal. He was near to passing out, he was sure.

"Don't know," he mumbled.

Sebastian felt strong hands pulling him up, taking his weight, as deftly, Taylor opened the passenger door of the small red car. Puffing and panting from her exertions, she managed to bundle him into the front seat.

"I'll take you to mine. I only live a few blocks away. You can warm up and sober up and then I'll get you that cab." Taylor was out of breath. She stooped and picked up Sebastian's phone from the ground. She noticed the screen was badly damaged. "Don't think this will be much good to you now, but we'll take it with us anyway," Taylor said kindly as she leaned over and tucked it into Sebastian's coat pocket before fastening his seat belt around him.

Sebastian said nothing. He was drifting now. Everything was just too much effort. He smelt Taylor's perfume; it was floral and sugary. He dropped his head onto his chest. He sensed spittle running down his chin. His eyes felt heavy. As the passenger door clicked shut, Sebastian felt warmth seep into his bones, and then he went out like a light.

THIRTY-FIVE

SATURDAY 12 JANUARY

SUZANNE

Suzanne woke up. She was disorientated. Her throat was sore from retching, and the vile taste of sick clung to her mouth. She sat bolt upright and groped around in the darkness for her phone on the bed beside her. She had no idea of the time. The phone's digital readout told her it was 22.10. She switched on the bedside light and released a cry of deepest torment as she took in the time. A whole twelve hours had passed and still there was no word from Sebastian. A horrible sinking sensation attacked her stomach. It was like a physical pain. Something serious must have happened. There was no other explanation. Nothing else worked. *Please let him be okay!* Suzanne screamed silently as she threw back the covers and climbed out of bed. She didn't even remember getting into bed or switching off the lights. She hugged Sebastian's jumper to her, and a single tear journeyed leisurely down her right cheek. She caught it with her tongue as she padded sluggishly to the bathroom.

Suzanne splashed icy cold water on her face. She cupped her hands together and filled them with the cooling water. She took several gulps to try and erase the taste of puke. It didn't work, so she cleaned her teeth, brushing them much harder than normal which made her gums bleed. Taking a second, she eyed herself in the bathroom mirror. The light wasn't particularly flattering, but any way you looked at it, she looked awful; puffy eyes, black smears of eyeliner and flakes of dried mascara streaking her cheekbones, her hair a frizzy blonde mess. Suzanne decided she looked just like she felt. Like utter shit.

Patting her face dry with a soothing warm towel from the heated rail, Suzanne returned to the bedroom. Her heart was beating wildly. It thundered in her ears. It seemed so loud it was the only sound she could hear. Before she'd fallen asleep, she'd called reception and had been told by a jolly sounding Canadian that she had no messages. Not what she wanted to hear. Total radio silence. There was no doubt in Suzanne's mind that something awful had happened to Sebastian. She had absolutely no idea what to do next. All she could think of was to call him. Perched on the end of the bed, her heart in her mouth, she tried again. This time when the phone connected, it no longer rang; it went straight to answerphone. *Had he switched it off or was it just out of battery?* Probably out of battery, Suzanne decided, and then still gripping her phone, she made a snap decision. She needed to call Gloria. *She needed to talk to someone, for God's sake!* Gloria might be calm, might tell her what to do. Anyway, she needed to know. Her son was missing.

It took Suzanne far too long to work out the time difference. Her brain was on go-slow. She just couldn't focus. More than half a minute passed before she calculated it would be a quarter past six in the morning in England. No wonder she felt listless. She knew Gloria was an early riser, but it was a bit of a stretch on a Sunday; but Suzanne felt she had little choice. Pacing the room, she called Sebastian's mother. It rang and rang and then finally it was answered.

"Hello, Suzanne?" Gloria's voice was quizzical, soft and furry with slumber.

"Gloria, I'm so sorry to wake you but I think something's happened to Sebastian."

Gloria woke up quickly. "What do you mean?"

Suzanne started to cry. "Sebastian's missing. He left me this morning at ten. More than twelve hours ago now, and I haven't heard from him since. I was working, and we planned to meet up this afternoon, but he never showed, and he hasn't been answering his phone all day. Oh, Gloria, I'm worried sick!"

"Oh, Suzanne!" Gloria groaned. "Look, I'm sure he's okay. He called me last night."

Suzanne felt a shot of relief seep into her veins. "Did he? Why? What's happened?"

"Look, I'm sure he's fine. He's had a bit of a shock, that's all."

"What do you mean; a shock?"

"Oh, Suzanne. I'm so sorry!"

"Just tell me, Gloria, please. Where is he? Is he okay?"

"Look, I'm sure he's fine." A deep, heavy sigh passed down the line. "Seb was in Vancouver, I think. That's where his father lives. He hasn't seen him for years, but I guess he couldn't resist the temptation while he was there. He met up with him, and I'm afraid he told him something he didn't want to hear."

"What? What did he tell him?"

"He told him that he's not his biological father."

"Oh my God!"

"When Seb called me, he was so angry with me, Suzanne." Gloria started to cry.

"It's okay, Gloria," Suzanne said supportively. She felt better. A whole lot better somehow, knowing there was a reason behind Sebastian 'going dark'. "What time did he call?"

"It was about nine o'clock last night, I think." She paused and totted up the time. "About nine hours ago now. And you haven't heard from him in twelve hours?"

"No."

"Suzanne, I'm sure he's okay. I think maybe he needs to be alone for a while. He called me to ask me who his real father was. He was so angry with me for not telling him. I think he'd been drinking a lot too."

"Maybe he's drunk and passed out somewhere?" A deep sob wedged in Suzanne's throat. Tears pricked at her eyes and she sniffed hard.

"He'll be fine, Suzanne. I expect he's checked into a local hotel to sleep it off."

"Yes, maybe," Suzanne agreed a little uncertainly. She contemplated her lover's mental state and attempted to remain positive. But she still found it hard to believe that he would have checked into a hotel without telling her. Suzanne tried to walk in Sebastian's shoes. Finding out his father wasn't his father must have knocked him sideways. It didn't bear thinking about. She didn't feel good asking, but she couldn't help it. "Gloria," Suzanne hesitated before continuing, "who is Sebastian's real dad?"

Gloria sighed heavily. "I haven't seen him in years. It was just a one-off thing that happened a very long time ago. But I promised to help Sebastian find him."

"D'you think you will be able to find him?"

"Maybe, I just don't know. He had a pretty unusual name, so yes, I think it's possible."

"Okay. Right." Suzanne fell silent for a few seconds while she digested the information, and then with her voice breaking, added: "Where do you think Sebastian is now? It's getting late. I'm so worried something bad has happened to him."

"I don't know, Suzanne. I really don't."

All of a sudden, Suzanne had a moment of divine inspiration. "Gloria, I think I know where he went today." She scrabbled for the piece of paper on the bedside table. She found it swiftly and in a strong voice read aloud: "The Beach House, 150, 25th Street, West Vancouver. He wrote this down on a pad and left it by the bed. I bet he met him there."

"Yes, I bet he did. Give them a call. Maybe he'll still be there."

"Okay, I'll do it right away and call you back."

Suzanne disconnected. Hastily, she googled the Beach House in West Vancouver. She was all fingers and thumbs. Once she'd located the bar's website, she hit the phone icon. It rang for several seconds and then the phone was answered. The background was filled with noisy chatter. It sounded busy.

"Hi there," Suzanne started, her heart in her mouth. "I'm trying to reach my boyfriend; he was at the bar earlier today. I just wanted to check if he'd left yet." Suzanne sounded calm, but inside she was crumbling into tiny pieces.

"Lady, we get a lot of customers in here. But is he English, like you?"

"Yes, he's English. Tall with black hair."

The bartender chuckled. "Oh yeah, I remember him. He was absolutely hammered, ma'am. Left about six, I think. He was so drunk, he could barely walk."

Suzanne opened her mouth to thank him, but no words came out.

THIRTY-SIX

SUNDAY 13 JANUARY

ANGELO

The sun was up, its golden rays streaming into the luxurious boudoir. The state-of-the-art air conditioner toiled noiselessly, keeping the place at a perfect temperature. It was a spectacular room, four times the size of a normal bedroom, warm with the electric colours of a glorious dawn. It was laden with the finest European furniture, flamboyant gold-plated trinkets, statues and objets d'art. A massive sunken bath graced one corner; creamy marble, surrounded in tinted mirrored glass. Dozens of cut white roses were positioned in tall crystal vases around the room. The place smelled of rose petals and sex.

Angelo lay between the girls, a tangle of naked limbs and late night lust rolling over into the morning. Jenna's bare leg was scissored over Angelo's. It was smooth and long and tanned. He gripped her thigh and lifted it. Jenna mewled softly and rolled away from him, curling herself into a tight ball, one abrupt ladylike snore erupting as she got settled and slumbered on. Angelo reached over her and grabbed his phone from the side table. He opened Tatiana's text and reread it. He frowned. Something just didn't sit right with it. He had a sixth sense with women. Could tell when they were spinning him a line. Tatiana was addicted to her phone. She never put it down. If she had lost it, she'd have been making much more of a meal of it; that was for sure. Nah, something wasn't right, something was definitely going on with that little bitch, and he didn't like it at all.

He lay back on the pillow, his jaw set hard, his dark eyes brooding. He sighed. Sammi's beautiful breasts were on view, peeping out from under the covers, an easy distraction; big and soft and moreish. And they were within grabbing distance. Angelo could never resist temptation. He licked his lips. Touching a snoozing nipple, he rolled the flat of his hand over it unhurriedly, watching entranced as it puckered to life beneath his palm. All pink and pretty and firm. Sammi released a drowsy moan of pleasure. Angelo wasn't scowling now. Desire flashed in his cold grey eyes.

Angelo bowed his head to Sammi's breast and flicked his tongue over her aureole. Dripping spittle, he teased it with a series of savage nips. He delved beneath the sheets and rested a firm hand on her tummy, grasping handfuls of her warm flesh. Sammi opened her mouth and groaned as Angelo snuck a finger into her pierced bellybutton and toyed with the tiny pink gem.

Sammi had her eyes tightly closed, but Angelo knew full well she was awake. Beneath the covers, she parted her thighs accommodatingly, and a sleepy smile brightened her face. Angelo latched onto a nipple. His sharp teeth glided up and down the length, biting and sucking. When he clamped his teeth tight together, Sammi squealed in pain and opened her eyes. She locked

201

eyes with Angelo. He flashed her a dangerous smile. Dopamine swamped his brain. Growling softly through clenched teeth, Angelo continued to chew her nipples. He made first contact with her sex, cupping it, savouring the fiery heat of her mound in his hand. Angelo took what he wanted, when he wanted. He said nothing. He had his mouth full.

Sammi let out an expectant groan, and Angelo silenced her with a forceful kiss that told her in no uncertain terms who was in control. He'd finger her when he was good and ready. He trailed a pointy tongue around her teeth, his saliva mixing with hers as he stroked the smooth arc of her shaved pussy. She was wet and warm. Just the way he liked his cunt. Angelo rolled back the covers. His fingers travelled lower, spreading damp lips. He pushed a finger inside and then another alongside it. He hooked them upwards and worked Sammi's G-spot. A throaty purr burst from her lips. Angelo watched her pleasure. As Sammi tightened her sex around his digits, he jerked his fingers inside her a few seconds more and then withdrew. Angelo wanted to concentrate on her clitoris. He gazed down at his nimble fingers, admiring his handiwork as Sammi squirmed beside him. He popped her clit from its hood, skimming it mellifluously from side to side with fast fingertips.

"Oh, baby!" Sammi snarled, biting her bottom lip. Her eyes blinking in the bright sunlight, she spread her legs wide and raised her hips from the bed.

Inches away from the escalating passion, Jenna remained spark out, snuffling softly. Snorting cocaine and drinking champagne all night long had taken its toll on her.

"Do you want me to fuck you?" Angelo's voice was gruff.

"What do you think?" Sammi breathed, wide awake now.

Angelo had her exactly where he wanted. He ceased with the frenetic fingering. Caressing the soft skin of her belly, he said: "You need to tell me something first, Bella." His words were a seductive whisper.

"Okay," Sammi murmured.

"Have you spoken with Tatiana since she's been away?"

Sammi wasn't expecting that. She hesitated for a moment and then said: "I haven't spoken to her, but she texts me all the time."

Sammi looked up at Angelo quizzically. She took hold of his hand and placed it back on her pussy. Angelo allowed it to remain there. He held her sex, his fingers immobile as he asked: "And what does she say in her texts?"

Sammi thought for a minute. "Just that she's having a good time. Enjoying the London life."

"Anything else?" Angelo asked as he squeezed a handful of her, dropping a forefinger lower, resting it tantalisingly on the upper tip of her clit.

Sammi was eager to please and keen to get back to where they were. She whimpered softly and said: "You are such a tease, Angel. Tatiana mentioned she's been seeing that guy, Eddie, again. Says she's staying at his Chelsea harbour penthouse, and he's spending a fortune on her."

"Is he indeed?" Angelo said, his voice detached and cold as if his veins were filled with ice. His brain whirred with dark thoughts. He'd got exactly what he wanted, and now it was time for some fun. His eyes fixed on Sammi, he barked: "Suck my cock, babe, and then I'm going to fuck you."

Sammi grinned up at him, and then, giggling girlishly, she slithered beneath the finest Egyptian cotton bedclothes and went to work.

THIRTY-SEVEN

SUNDAY 13 JANUARY

SEBASTIAN

Sebastian awoke with a raging thirst, his mouth as dry as sandpaper. He opened his eyes hesitantly. *Fuck! He had the headache from hell.* The small room was cloaked in darkness and seemed to be shifting slightly. The place was shadowy and unfamiliar, but warm. *Thank God!* Sebastian recalled waking in the night, his whole body shaking with the cold. He had no idea whatsoever where he was. *Shit, that was scary!* His heart beating wildly, Sebastian sensed a panic attack creeping up on him. He stayed as still as a statue and battled to control his breathing. He held it together and the moment passed. Breathing evenly, his eyes slowly became accustomed to the blackness all around him. He processed that he was in a compact bedroom painted some kind of dark colour; but without the luxury of light, everything appeared to be in various shades of grey. Sebastian groaned. His head hurt like crazy. It was as if a heavy metal band were playing a gig in his skull, the bass turned up to the max in the mix.

Sebastian felt like shit. His neck was stiff and tender, his movement restricted, and he could feel a dull thudding pain in his left shoulder. In fact, he soon became aware that he ached more or less all over. As if in slow motion, Sebastian turned his head ninety degrees to the right and almost jumped from his skin. There was a young woman next to him in the compact double bed. His heart roared in his chest, hammering away against his breastbone. Utter panic set in as he inched away, taking it as slowly as possible for fear of waking her. He gasped as he noticed the woman's shoulders were bare. He couldn't take his eyes off her. Sleeping soundly on her back, her delicate collarbone rose and fell as she took each breath. Sebastian was terrified that his sleeping partner might be naked beneath the covers. He daren't look. He exhaled quietly and wondered how he'd got it all so wrong. Why couldn't he have woken up with Suzanne, with the events of yesterday just a bad dream? But no, the nightmare continued.

Catching his breath, Sebastian stared at the woman beside him. In the dim light, her youthful face was tranquil with sleep. Her short, feathery hair surrounded her pixie face and resembled a pale yellow halo. Her breathing was soft and regular. Stark realisation dawned on him. It was the waitress from the Beach House. He couldn't recall her name. He tried to envisage the name tag she wore on her chest. A split second later, it came to him; Taylor. Cautiously, Sebastian felt his hips beneath the bedclothes and was hugely grateful to confirm that he was still wearing his boxers. For some reason, he felt the need to place both hands on his cock and hug himself there. As he did, he blew out a measured sigh of relief.

As he lay rigidly in the darkness, Sebastian tried to come to terms with the fact that he'd suffered an alcoholic blackout. Even though it was a first, he knew all about being in blackout. He remembered only too vividly those mumbled morning apologies that always followed a crazy night when his father was drinking and out of control. Daddy's view seeming to be that as he had no recollection of the events, it was totally excusable. Maybe he truly believed that. Maybe he thought that by offering a begrudging apology, Mummy's black eyes and broken bones would miraculously heal. *Was he fucking crazy?* Even after thirty years, Sebastian sometimes still felt like that frightened little boy cowering in a corner, watching the ugly violence and trying to make himself small. Oh yes, he certainly knew all about alcoholic blackouts with his psychotic father. Or the man he believed was his father. *Fuck, what a bombshell! That wasn't the closure he'd been seeking.*

Sebastian felt wretched. He felt ashamed that he'd got so smashed he'd suffered a blackout and didn't have a clue what had happened during those many lost hours. He racked his muddled brain, but his head was an empty vessel impaired by the huge amounts of alcohol he'd put away. He remembered his father not being his father, his angry conversation with his mother, and then all he recalled after that was drinking lots and lots of red wine. Somehow, he knew he hadn't contacted Suzanne, and that realisation pierced his heart. He knew she'd be frantic. But more pressing even than Suzanne's emotional state was the fact he had no idea if he'd slept with the woman sleeping so soundly beside him. Surely, he hadn't slept with Taylor, as in actually having sex? He was way too drunk to be capable, surely? And he wouldn't do that, would he? For God's sake, he was head over heels in love with Suzanne.

Sebastian dreaded making the move out of the bed. He wanted to leap up and just get the hell out of there but was scared stiff he'd wake Taylor and there would be all sorts of ramifications. He needed to locate his clothes and his phone and then get back to Whistler and to Suzanne. He had no idea of the time as he lay motionless in the gloom, but the stillness of the night suggested to him that it was the early hours. He hoped it was, as there was far less chance of the young stranger he'd spent the night with waking up if it was the middle of the night.

Carefully, Sebastian eased the covers from him, swung his feet to the left and climbed out of bed. Cheap, scratchy carpet met his feet. He realised he was still wearing socks. Sebastian just sat for a few seconds, blinking hard. Little by little, he could see things a little clearer in the bedroom. His head thumped. It hurt to move it. The room started to spin. Suddenly, he felt queasy. Taking a massive gulp of air, Sebastian stood, and, on unsteady legs, he moved slowly across the murky room. He felt so dehydrated he could barely swallow. He found his phone quite quickly, on an upright chair, sitting on top of his neatly folded clothes; his boots on the bottom, his vest, trousers and sweater folded and piled on top. Beside them, his outside clothes were in a separate neat pile on a cluttered chest of drawers. Sebastian swore under his breath when he realised that the screen of the iPhone was totally obliterated. He tried to switch it on, but it was dead. He couldn't call Suzanne, and he couldn't call a taxi, but he knew he had to get out fast.

Bundling everything into his arms, he stumbled blindly out of the bedroom, down a short hallway, through an archway and into a dimly lit kitchen. There was a street lamp outside the window. Amber light peeped in. The room was no more than a large cupboard really, what you'd call a kitchenette. It had a microwave, a kettle, a two-ring hob, a chipped but serviceable enamel sink and an old yellowing fridge freezer. Sebastian opened the tatty old fridge and found a bottle of water. Necking it greedily, he downed the entire contents. Then, of course, he needed the loo but decided that using the toilet would make too much clatter; so cursing under his breath, he fingered his hair smooth, and then, as silently as possible, he began to get dressed.

Just a few minutes later, Sebastian took one last look at Taylor. She was still on her back, fast asleep. He was dying to know what had happened, but the urge to escape was a whole lot stronger; so with a heavy heart, he crept out into the still darkness of the early morning. It was 5.30 am.

THIRTY-EIGHT

SUNDAY 13 JANUARY

SEBASTIAN

A blast of chill wind attacked Sebastian as soon as he exited the street door. He was thankful he was dressed for the extreme cold, though was annoyed that he'd somehow managed to lose his gloves. He tightened his scarf around his throat. The road was covered in sheet ice and was dark and quiet. The occasional car drifted past him, snow tyres crunching on impacted slush. Sebastian walked, head bowed, his hands thrust deep in his jacket pockets, his shoulders hunched. He gulped in lungfuls of the crystal clean cold air as he trod carefully on the slippery frozen pavements, his inborn sense of direction taking him back towards the Beach House. The brisk walk cleared his head and within just a few minutes, he began to feel a little more human. His long legs striding out beneath his aching body, his foggy brain sharpening, Sebastian recognised his surroundings as he approached the car park, though he still had no recollection of actually leaving the restaurant.

With the deserted bar behind him, he gazed out at the smooth, navy waters. He felt numb and sad and cold. He was just contemplating his next move when, in the stillness of the early dawn, he heard a car pull up. Sebastian couldn't quite believe his luck when he realised it was a taxi. Passengerless, it slid into a parking bay in front of the restaurant, its engine still running, the diesel drone noisy in the quietness of daybreak. He hurried towards the yellow Toyota Corolla, a smile of hope gracing his weary face. An ordinary-looking, middle-aged man sat behind the wheel of the cab, a baseball cap pulled down low, a Styrofoam beaker of coffee in his hand.

By ten to six, and before sunrise, Sebastian was settled in the back seat of the taxi cab. He wasn't comfortable; he didn't feel good. He was utterly drained. He felt like he wanted to cry, but at least he was warm and on his way home. On his way back to explain to Suzanne. He was grateful for that. Sebastian sighed. He deliberated about asking the cab driver if he could use his phone, but as he didn't know Suzanne's number off by heart, he considered by the time he had located the hotel number and called and got through to the room, well, he just thought it would be better to make his apologies face-to-face. Anyway, he didn't want to have the conversation he knew he would have to have in front of the driver. Sebastian said a silent prayer that for the time being Suzanne would be sound asleep and not worrying about him.

He still had the mother of all headaches and felt sick. Sebastian sipped from a bottle of water the cab driver gave him, hoping it might settle his stomach. His tummy gurgled as the cold water trickled down. He suddenly realised he hadn't eaten since breakfast the previous day. Unless Taylor had fed him, of course, and he soon put that thought to bed as he'd surely have been in no fit state to be eating. His mind was a total blank from about twelve hours previously. He had no idea what had happened during those lost hours. No idea at all. More importantly right now, he had no clue what state Suzanne would be in when he finally got back to the hotel and no cunning plan to help him track down his birth father, either. Sebastian was just too exhausted to think about any of that right now. He laid his head back and closed his eyes. He exhaled noisily and tried to quieten his racing heart as the sunny yellow taxi devoured the miles of snow-laden tarmac on the highway.

★

It was almost eight when Sebastian located the pass card tucked deep in his trouser pocket. He was grateful he hadn't lost that as well. The sound of his breath rushing in his ears, he let himself into the hotel suite as silently as possible. The room was in relative darkness, lit only by the slender shafts of early morning light peeping through the curtain gap. Suzanne was on top of the covers, curled in a tight ball on her side on what was normally his side of the bed. She was facing the door. Sebastian stood rooted to the spot, looking at her. He felt his heart tug. He was so ashamed of himself for the worry he'd put her through. He gazed down, tears brimming in his eyes. He felt even worse, for some reason, because she was wearing his jumper.

As he watched her sleeping, Suzanne rolled over onto her back, and all of a sudden, her eyes burst open. Confusion and relief danced across her face. In a split second, she was awake. She sat bolt upright.

"Oh my God! Sebastian! Where have you been? I've been so worried." She began to sob.

Sebastian sank down on the bed and hugged Suzanne tight. He breathed her in as their tears mingled. He could feel her heart beating rapidly against his. Time stood still as they held each other, his exhaled breaths mirroring her inhaled breaths. Sebastian pulled away gently. He placed the palms and fingers of his hands on her jawline and cheeks. Remorseful blue eyes settled on hers. Suzanne looked haunted. Her eyes dazed and full of hurt, they were puffy and ringed with the remains of her make-up. The way she looked, and her obvious distress, made him feel like a total bastard.

"Suzanne, I'm so very, very sorry." Sebastian looked deep into her eyes and fought back more tears. "I found out some news about my father and it really fucked with my head. I went to meet him yesterday in Vancouver."

"Yes, I know. I spoke with Gloria," Suzanne managed between jerky sobs. "I know he's not your real father."

Sebastian hung his head. He was finding it hard not to dissolve into tears.

Suddenly, Suzanne seemed stronger. "That's awful, I know, Sebastian, but I was fucking frantic. I've barely slept. I've been throwing up all night." She looked embarrassed and pulled away from him. "God, my breath must smell horrible."

"No, it doesn't, baby," Sebastian said, pulling her back close to him and kissing her. "I'm so sorry to have done this to you."

"I thought something terrible had happened. Why didn't you just call me to let me know you were okay? I was ringing you all day and all night. I haven't slept. I think I just nodded off for a few moments. What time is it anyway?"

"It's around eight," Sebastian answered, not bothering to look at his watch. "I'm so sorry, baby. I know I should have called, but I was just on this emotional roller coaster. I should have told you I was going to Vancouver to meet him, but I just couldn't find the words. I thought you might try and talk me out of it, and it was just something I had to do. And then I got blind drunk and smashed my phone."

"I was going absolutely crazy. I found the address of the bar on a scrap of paper and I called them. They told me you were in a terrible state when you left. I was worried sick. I thought you could be dead in a gutter somewhere. My imagination was running wild." Suzanne sniffed loudly and linked one hand with his.

Sebastian said nothing. He was thankful they hadn't mentioned that one of their waitresses had taken him home. Probably because the person Suzanne had spoken to had no idea that she did. He hung his head in shame.

Their fingers intertwined, she continued: "It's okay, baby. I'm just glad you're back." Suzanne discharged a huge sigh and then buried her head against his big, strong body. As Sebastian held her tight, she mumbled into his chest: "When the guy that answered the phone told me that you were totally out of it when you left, I was so worried. Where did you go? Have you been wandering around all night? Where did you sleep?"

"I'm sorry, Suzanne. I can't remember much of what happened. I got so drunk I blacked out." Sebastian didn't say any more. *How could he tell her he was so out of it that he woke up half-naked in bed with a young woman he barely knew?*

214

A huge judder wracked Suzanne's body as she pulled away and rolled back the covers. "Get into bed, baby. I need a massive hug."

Sebastian offered up a chastened half-smile, kissed Suzanne gently on the forehead and then began to strip speedily out of his clothes.

Suzanne yanked the jumper up over her head and climbed beneath the sheets. She grabbed her phone from the bedside table. "I'd better text your mum and tell her you've turned up safe and well."

"Oh God, yes! Thanks, baby. Bloody hell, what have I done?" Sebastian mumbled desolately, as he stepped out of his trousers and let them drop to the floor.

THIRTY-NINE

SUNDAY 13 JANUARY

SUZANNE

Their embrace lasted a while. Two, three, four minutes passed in complete silence as two became one. The only sound to be heard was the soft whisper of their breathing above two quietening heartbeats. Suzanne had taken off her underwear, and, naked and warm, she buried her face in the curve of Sebastian's neck. She breathed him in, her nostrils flaring in surprise at the unfamiliar scent of his skin. She rested a cheek on his chest, her face tucked in, rising and falling in time with each beat of his heart. She lay across his torso with one leg curved over his. Looping her arms around his neck, she held on like her life depended on it. The two reunited lovers lay in each other's arms, not talking, just breathing, enjoying each other, their bodies entwined, their eyes closed. Skin to skin, heartbeat to heartbeat. Suzanne was delighted Sebastian was back safely with her, but the traumatic night had taken its toll. She was utterly exhausted. In just a matter of minutes, she succumbed to sleep.

★

Suzanne blinked her eyes open. As she came to, she smiled and admired the beautiful man in her arms. She extended her neck so she could stretch up and kiss him softly on the mouth. At the touch of her lips on his, there were fireworks, the intimate contact igniting a fire deep within her. Sebastian's eyes flicked open fast, blue and dazzling, drowsy, yet full of smouldering sensuality. Suzanne stared back into his gaze. She felt a delicious shiver pass through her. Sebastian's lips parted as she kissed him, his tongue hungry for her. Their mouths swiftly became a blur of lips and teeth and tongues.

Suzanne slithered up Sebastian's hard, tight body. She parted her legs instinctively, savouring the scorching heat of his growing erection pressing into her as she positioned herself on top and controlled the coming together of their lips. She adored kissing him in a dominant position. Raking her fingers though his liquorice hair, sweeping it back from his face, she feasted on his mouth. It was just so fucking sexy, his teeth gleaming white and like wolf's teeth; sharp and pointy. Suzanne was still sleepy, in that somnolent state where lovemaking is dreamy and hypnotic. She wanted to make love and couldn't bear to wait a minute longer. She needed that perfect fit right away. There was no doubt in her mind that he wanted and needed her too. They'd both had a terrible night, and making sweet love would make everything better.

Grinding the mound of her sex against Sebastian's throbbing cock, Suzanne moaned out loud. Their exchange of kisses became more frenzied, more desperate. Suzanne's mussed-up hair tumbled across

Sebastian's face. He pushed it away with a loving hand, then grabbed it in a fist and pulled it, taking her face up and away from his.

Looking deep into her eyes, Sebastian whispered: "I'm so sorry, Suzanne. I love you so much. Don't ever forget that," and then ran the tip of his tongue over the bow of her lips while a warm hand traced the contours of her nakedness. He skimmed her breasts, his long fingers brushing against her nipples, making them ache with desire. Suzanne began to tremble.

Suzanne arched up in ecstasy. She yearned to be possessed by Sebastian, filled full of him. He smelt different somehow, boozy and unfamiliar, and that excited her even more. Soft whimpers spilled from her lips as his fingers tormented her burning nipples. He stared up at her adoringly. His jaw was covered in stubble and he had dark shadows under his eyes, but Suzanne thought he'd never looked more desirable. His long hair looked teased to perfection by a top stylist, his eyes shone like priceless sapphires and his sensuous mouth curved into that smile that always set Suzanne's heart racing. She closed her eyes and let out a long, satisfied moan. She knew what was coming.

"I love you, baby," Sebastian mouthed as he slipped his cock inside her.

When he entered her, for some reason, it felt like the very first time. Suzanne's body blasted with pure adrenaline. Powerful pheromones ricocheted in her head, and a sense of serenity overwhelmed her. She raised herself up and opened her eyes so she could gaze at him while they made love. Her knees bent under her, on the edge of paradise, she clung on. Lacing Sebastian's hands in hers, she raised them above his head and rode him with an energy that startled her.

"I love you too, baby. I love you so much it hurts," Suzanne cried out, before quickly losing all control as a searing orgasm picked her up and shook her.

Mewing softly, Suzanne surrendered to a climax that made time stay still. Tears flowed freely down her cheeks as her undulating body was wracked with violent paroxysms. Collapsing on top of her lover, Suzanne felt as if she was floating. She was totally powerless over the tremors that took her. Still shaking, she hugged Sebastian like she never wanted to let go.

★

Hours later, when they were still cuddled up in bed and the sun outside the window was high in the cloudless azure sky, Suzanne needed to ask the question that relief and exhaustion had dispelled from her mind for a while. Now it was back with a vengeance. Tatiana.

"Have you been seeing Tatiana?" The woman's name stuck in her throat. Her mouth felt dry. Suzanne waited for an answer. She had to know, but she just couldn't bear it.

"Oh God, Suzanne! How did you find out about that? I'm going to call you Detective Perry-Jackson in future," he jested with a twinkle in his eyes.

"Suzanne was taken aback: "What?"

"I'm sorry. I know I probably should have mentioned it, but I didn't want to say anything because of our trip. Didn't want to worry you. I was going to tell you as soon as we got back."

"Tell me what?" Suzanne's heart was banging furiously against the walls of her chest now. *Surely, he wouldn't be so blasé if there was actually something going on?*

"I think it was a couple of days before we were coming away. She came to me for a consultation. That last-minute cancellation first thing in the morning, d'you remember? Some utter bollocks about an old skiing injury. I think she just wanted to check me out. Wanted to cause trouble."

"Well, she's certainly good at that. The fucking little bitch!"

Suzanne felt a huge weight lift. It made sense. Of course it did. She felt foolish to have thought otherwise, but after what happened with Edward, and Sebastian and his disappearing act, well, of course she'd have doubts. Blissfully happy now, she beamed at him, all the anxiety evaporating in an instant.

Sebastian pecked her on the lips. "I know it's shitty, baby, but it doesn't involve us. If Edward's stupid enough to get back with her, then it's his problem, not ours."

"Yeah, I know." Suzanne leaned in and gave him another kiss.

Sebastian kissed her back hard, then pulled away and said: "I'm absolutely starving. Let's go and grab a quick lunch and then hit the slopes. I bet your ass looks sexy in your new white salopettes."

"You think my ass is sexy, do you?" Suzanne giggled and pulled back the covers. She jumped out of bed and turning away from him arched her back and positioned her bare bottom right back at him. She gave it a little twerk.

As he grabbed handfuls of each buttock, Sebastian moaned: "Fuck it, let's have room service."

FORTY

SEBASTIAN

Suzanne lay on the bed, her face buried in a pillow, her hair splayed out around her like a child's crude drawing of a golden sun. Her breathing was uneven. Sebastian had just made her cum twice with his fingers and tongue. She always played coy, but he knew how much she adored his tongue buried deep in her ass. Still caressing her bare bottom, Sebastian got on the phone and ordered two cheeseburgers with French fries, a large bottle of fizzy water and two portions of apple pie with scoops of vanilla ice cream. While they waited for their food to arrive, they made love, slowly and leisurely in the shower stall with a cascade of steaming hot water raining down on their trembling nakedness. Their coupling was needy and intense, and the curtain of hot water splattering his fatigued body made Sebastian feel whole again.

By the time the waiter was knocking on their door with a shiny silver trolley bedecked with wonderful-smelling food, they were back in bed wrapped in hotel robes. The delicious aroma wafted into Sebastian's nostrils. He was starved. He hadn't eaten for more than twenty-four hours. As they sat cross-legged with their room service meal set out before them, Sebastian wished he'd ordered two burgers just for himself. He watched Suzanne devour every last bit of her meal as well. Crashing waves of guilt hit him all over again. He hazarded a guess that she hadn't eaten dinner either. And she'd been violently sick all night. *What the hell was he thinking, behaving like that? Getting so drunk he ended up sleeping with a total stranger. Unbelievable!* Sebastian concealed his unease with a disarming smile. He grinned at Suzanne, showing lots of teeth. She smiled back at him from beneath a fringe of still damp hair and took his hand and squeezed it. Somehow that made him feel even more of a shit.

★

It was gone two by the time they finally made it to the slopes. The sun was shining in a stunning winter sky. Their journey time to the Whistler Blackcomb range of mountains was swift. The hotel boasted exceptional ski-in, ski-out facilities that were pretty much bang on; the lifts being only a matter of steps from where the hotel's ski valet waited to assist guests with skis and poles. Which was fortunate as they didn't know quite how much time they'd have before the darkness of nightfall set in and the lifts started their downward journey back to base. Suzanne looked hot in her ski gear; figure-hugging salopettes and a dusky pink Prada ski jacket. Fluorescent ski goggles in hot pink completed her look and were a good match for her sexy mouth, glossed in strawberry pink. Sebastian couldn't resist sneaking a kiss from her sticky lips. She tasted of fruity mouthwash. Even though Sebastian felt drained, the crystal clean mountain air filling his fuzzy head and the taste of Suzanne made him feel horny all over again. She had that effect on him.

The slopes surrounding them once they'd exited the lift were bigger and badder and more beautiful than Sebastian could have ever imagined. Before starting their descent, they stood together and breathed in deeply, gazing in awe at the impossibly blue lakes overlaid with snowy blankets and the breathtaking vista awash with intense sunlight. Muffled up in his skiwear, Sebastian cooked under the sun's powerful rays. Time to ski.

The slopes were wide and vast, so although they were relatively busy as the conditions were perfect, there was still plenty of room to let loose. To get their ski legs, they started off on blues, but within twenty minutes or so, they took a chair lift to the top and skied down a long, expansive red run that tipped them out onto a diamond black. The exhilaration of speeding downwards at such an acute angle, slicing the blades into the shimmering snow, brought it all back. Sebastian hadn't skied for a while and he'd missed it. God, how he'd missed it! Suzanne was a proficient skier, though seemed a little more cautious in her approach, so he reeled in his mad streak and took it steady so they could enjoy skiing together.

With their cheeks ruddy and the sun beginning to sink slowly in the sky, they headed back to the hotel with plans to enjoy a glass of champagne in one of the hotel's open air hot tubs. Sebastian wasn't sure he could face any more alcohol, but he was determined to make it up to Suzanne and do whatever she wanted. Go along with any plans she suggested. He considered it was the very least he could do. He decided he could just have a very small one and leave Suzanne to do the serious drinking.

★

An hour later, the two lovers sat side by side amongst a handful of others in a hot tub designed for a dozen. There was little conversation amongst the group. Everyone sat in companionable silence. The views around them were spectacular. Sebastian exhaled. He freed his mind from the stress of the previous day and let the hot water take him body and soul. His aching muscles relaxing, he lay back and enjoyed the soothing sensation of the powerful jets pounding against the small of his back. Sebastian rested his head on Suzanne's shoulder. He closed his eyes and felt all the tension seep out of him.

All of a sudden, Sebastian felt Suzanne's touch beneath the foamy crests of frothing water, felt her fingers slip down the front of his swim shorts. Gripping his cock decisively, she held him in her grasp. A mischievous smile on her lips, she met his gaze. Sebastian tried to breathe easily as her fingers crawled up his shaft. Grinning, Suzanne looked straight ahead, like nothing untoward was going on down below. Sebastian breathed out, swallowing a moan. His cock growing by the second, Suzanne glided a well-practised hand up and down. He had no idea where this was going, so he closed his eyes and wallowed in the extraordinarily sexy moment.

FORTY-ONE

SUZANNE

Face to face with Sebastian, his strong arms wrapped around her, Suzanne stirred. She felt safe, she felt loved. So very different from Saturday night, when she spent half the night with her head down the toilet and the other half tossing and turning and getting no sleep. But that was all behind them now. They were together and that was all that mattered. And today was Sebastian's birthday! She sighed contentedly and nuzzled into his chest and breathed him in. The smell of his skin gave her goosebumps; a hint of Black Orchid shower gel mixed with his own special smell. She adored the romantic way he held her. She loved being cuddled all night long. Since she'd first spent the night with Sebastian, it had become the norm.

They'd both been totally shattered when they fell asleep, all snuggled up. Now it was barely 6 am and Suzanne was wide awake. After a few minutes of just enjoying the sensation of Sebastian's bare skin on hers, she reluctantly extricated herself. She had plans. Using the torch on her phone to light the way, she tiptoed to the wardrobe, and, making as little noise as possible, she

225

removed cards and a handful of gift bags and parcels of various sizes from their hiding place in her case. She assembled them, side by side, balancing the smaller ones on top of the one larger one. They made a small but colourful pile in front of the fireplace.

There was a Tom Ford tie in a smart presentation box. Wrapped up beautifully, the slim silk tie was a riot of royal blue roses over a black background. Suzanne hoped Sebastian would wear it for his birthday dinner. Two tiny gift boxes were tucked into a sparkly electric blue bag. One contained a sterling silver money clip engraved with his initials SJB. J being for James. And nestled alongside this in another cute box was a pair of sterling silver cufflinks, set with a shimmering Swiss blue topaz. There were also packages containing an indulgently soft, checked cashmere scarf and a chunky cable-knit sweater in the palest shade of baby blue. In addition to her presents, there was a shirt from the twins and the latest Lee Child novel in hardback from Pauline. Suzanne had two other gifts still hidden that she was saving for later. A vibrating cock ring and a handwritten list of sexual favours on offer from her to him. She planned to present them to him once they'd returned from dinner. Suzanne grinned. She was sure Sebastian would love his presents, especially the final couple. *Well, who didn't like being spoiled on their birthday?* Her grin broadened as she flattened down her hair and tucked it behind her ears. If she hurried, she could grab a quick shower and put some make-up on while Sebastian snoozed on.

But it wasn't to be. When she turned, Sebastian was bare-chested, sitting up in bed, watching her, rubbing his eyes and smiling that smile; a smile that never failed to make her melt.

"Happy Birthday, baby!" Suzanne exclaimed. She threw her phone on the bed and with one energetic leap was back beside him.

"Whoa, you're full of beans this morning!" He leaned a hand out and switched on a bedside light. Spotting his heap of presents, Sebastian added: "Are they all for me?"

"Of course!" Suzanne wriggled in next to him. "I've got some cool stuff planned, baby. We're going to have a perfect day." She licked her lips naughtily. "And now I think it's time for your first present of the day."

"Sounds thrilling," Sebastian laughed, his eyes all over her naked curves. He stayed exactly where he was.

Unhurriedly, Suzanne rolled the covers down to his thighs. She grinned at she exposed his sleepy cock. She didn't touch it. She was in full seductress mode now. For a second or two it crossed her mind that she wished she'd had time to do something with her hair, but she was confident that even though she didn't look her best, Sebastian still fancied the pants off her.

Sebastian linked his powerful arms behind his head and remained silent with a bemused expression on his darkly handsome face. He relaxed into the pillows, as Suzanne devoured his body with feral flashing eyes. Her mouth twisting with mischief, she ran her tongue exaggeratedly over her lips, moistening them, as she stared at the lower half of his body. It really was magnificent; muscular and defined. He didn't have an over-the-top six-pack of a gym slave, just a perfectly flush tummy with tight abs, pronounced, jutting pecs and that oh-so-sexy snake of soft, downy hair that trailed from his belly button to his groin. Nestling on his belly looking right back at her was his cock. Suzanne giggled as it twitched under her concentrated regard. Sebastian's eyes filled with amusement as he watched her. This morning, they were the colour of spring forget-me-nots.

Sebastian chuckled: "I reckon this is going to be some birthday!" He flicked a strand of tousled hair from her forehead and then palmed Suzanne's face and delved deep into her eyes. Their lips were so close his hot breath fell into her mouth. "You are so fucking sexy, Suzanne." His voice was a rich growl full of desire.

Sebastian's words made her tremble. She couldn't resist him. Suzanne kissed his mouth, her probing tongue swift like a serpent snaking between his soft full lips. He tasted sleepy and sexy. She combed long fingernails into his mass of hair and slammed her eyes shut, enjoying the darkness and just losing herself in the taste of him, feeling almost lightheaded with the sweetness of their first morning kiss. She felt light fingertips close in on her breast. Sebastian caressed it tenderly, bringing her nipple to life in an instant.

Considering it was high time to deliver the first gift of the day, Suzanne backed off. She clambered between Sebastian's legs, spreading his solid thighs as she did, marvelling at how tight and toned they felt. Kneeling up, she cupped his balls and gave them each a firm squeeze. Sebastian lay on his back moaning softly, looking like he was ready for anything.

Suzanne sucked his balls into her mouth, one by one. She toyed with them with playful nips of her teeth, before surrounding his shaft with both hands and lapping at every inch of him, dribbling saliva freely as she moved gradually

228

upwards. When she reached the head, Sebastian was fully hard, and, with a breathy whimper, she swallowed him whole. Suzanne welcomed his cock deep into her throat, his length and his thickness forcing her to gag. Coming up for air, she teased the point of her tongue into his minute sensitive hole and watched him squirm. Suzanne felt powerful. She had the upper hand and was loving every minute of it. It was Sebastian's special day and she wanted to give him the best blowjob ever.

She raised her eyes up to meet his and, between mouthfuls of cock, murmured: "I love sucking your big hard cock, baby."

"Aw, sweetheart, I love it too," Sebastian whispered back at her.

Suzanne sensed his fingers closing in on her pussy. Her belly contracted in anticipation as he made contact, his fingers heavy on her. She wanted them inside her. She craved his fabulous fingers working their magic. She was already dripping wet. Panting heavily, Sebastian slid her open. Suzanne was panting too. She let out a hoarse cry as two big fingers pushed inside her folds, homing in on her pulsing clitoris, widening her and finding her sweet spot with ease. Suzanne carried on sliding her hand up and down Sebastian's cock but had released him from her mouth. She was finding it difficult to focus. Sebastian always knew how to make her cum.

"Baby, you are so wet for me. I love you. I love you so much, Suzanne," Sebastian groaned.

"I love you too, Sebastian," Suzanne mouthed, her eyes half-closed. Every sinew in her body was taut with a delicious tension.

Suzanne was floating. Sebastian had taken over the

reins. He was in sole charge now as he held her on the edge, two fingers tight together, flicking back and forth. He watched her intently. His eyes never leaving hers for a second. Suzanne knew how much he loved to watch her cum. She was concentrating hard. Sebastian kept control until he knew she was really suffering and then moved in for the kill. It was a little game they played. As he teased her on the brink, Suzanne flashed him that pleading half-smile that said it all. He stared back at her with hungry eyes and upped the tempo, firm and fast, and that was enough.

A hot flush rocketed through Suzanne as an almighty climax seized her. Shuddering hard, she fell onto Sebastian who was now sitting up. She got her breath back and grabbed her lover around the neck. With her heart beating out of control, she watched in awe as Sebastian propelled his hard cock inside her. It took just one slick thrust. As he entered her, Suzanne wailed. Her soul surged with love and emotion. Adrenaline pumped through her veins. Their synchronicity was remarkable. She experienced the same intensity every single time they made love.

Facing each other, with Suzanne's calves crossed behind Sebastian's bottom, they started their dirty dance of love with a languorousness that bordered on drowsy. It was a position they rarely made love in, and taking it slowly made it feel dreamlike and ethereal. Without speed, there was more time for kissing and exploring. Sebastian's hands roamed her body. He caressed her cheeks softly, tugged at her hair and held her around the middle, supporting the valley of her waist in a firm grip as he moved into her agonisingly slowly. He rolled the flats of his hands over her searing nipples, then lifted her breasts and attacked them with his pearly white teeth. It was as if he was spoilt for choice. Suzanne massaged Sebastian's shoulder blades, grabbed fistfuls of his hair and kissed him like she was starved of oxygen. She was halfway to heaven again already. Sebastian's cock was so hard and so hot. She could feel every inch of the smooth fine skin that moved within her and filled her to the max. Every deliberate thrust lifted her.

As they fucked faster, they never took their eyes off each other. Not even for a second. It was as if they were both hypnotised, caught up in a moment of pure euphoria. Circling Sebastian's neck, Suzanne dug her nails in. Riding him effortlessly, she kissed his mouth with a burning passion. She couldn't get enough of him. She flicked her tongue all over his sharp teeth and gnawed at his lips. Sebastian bit back, snappy teeth nipping at Suzanne's lips and throat, his hands embedded in her wild hair.

As a second more lethal orgasm began to intensify, Suzanne whimpered and bit down hard on her bottom lip. Her body arched and spasmed, her nipples burned, and blood rushed to her head. She felt spaced-out and yet as if she was caught in a moment of perfect clarity. She wrapped her arms around Sebastian's back and pressed him tight to her as she let it go, let it take her, let it fly. Suzanne felt the heat of Sebastian's seed explode into her. She held on and let her orgasm engulf her. She felt incredible, the moment made ever sweeter by the knowledge that they were hitting the summit together, as one. Their bodies hot and wet and dripping with perspiration, they hugged each other tight and wallowed in the early morning coupling that left them both gasping for breath.

Still shaking with the aftershock, Suzanne didn't want to let go. She dropped her face and buried it in Sebastian's shoulder as she attempted to contain her convulsing body. Sebastian tilted her face to his. He kissed her forehead, each eyelid in turn and then found her mouth.

"I love you, baby," tripped from his lips.

Between a shower of baby kisses that she was busy planting on her lover's sensuous mouth, Suzanne murmured breathily: "I love you more."

With his cock still inside her, they sagged backwards in slow motion. They curled up together and tugged the duvet around them. Suzanne held him close and shut her eyes. *I'm going to make sure Sebastian has a birthday he'll never forget*, she vowed silently.

FORTY-TWO

MONDAY 14 JANUARY

EDWARD

Edward was worried. He wasn't sleeping well. Rick was turning into a liability. Sure, he'd laid out a lot of money on his recommendation, but as soon as the stock went public, they'd cash in, split the profits and they'd both be out of their financial holes. Rick just needed to keep his cool and stop calling him every five minutes. Everything would be fine. Puffing on a cigarette, Edward paced. Acrid smoke leaked from his lips and rushed from his nostrils. Unusually, he found himself alone in the smoking zone. He leaned back on the brick wall and took another drag as he gazed out over the City of London. There was a niggle in his gut. However much he tried to convince himself the information he'd passed on to Rick wouldn't be discovered and it would all work out, he was scared. He'd played it straight all his life and this just didn't sit right with him. But what choice did he have?

Tatiana deserved to be treated like a queen, his queen; but that took money. A lot of money. The mortgage on the penthouse was crippling him, and the twins' education didn't come cheap either. And, of course, his divorce was costing him a small fortune. Not that Suzanne was being especially unreasonable about their financial settlement, but even so, lawyer's fees were exorbitant. He knew he'd overspent massively. But he just needed to sit tight and wait it out. He was sure it wouldn't be long before he'd surprise Tatiana with that Tiffany engagement ring.

He was excited about going to the Maldives. Baros Island was their destination; an astonishing exclusive beach resort featured in the *Small Luxury Hotels of the World*. It looked amazing. A fortnight's holiday was just what they both needed. He'd been all for it when Tatiana had suggested it out of the blue over the weekend. It was somewhere he'd always wanted to go. A perfect romantic hideaway. They'd gone online and booked it right away. Thankfully, he still had a couple of credit cards that weren't hiked up to their limit and time off owed to him. He fantasised about going down on one knee on powdery, soft white sand and formally asking Tatiana to be his wife. She'd say yes, of course, and he'd slip the diamond rock on her finger before they made love on the beautiful beach with the crystalline waters lapping around them.

Edward sighed and took another drag on his cigarette. Couldn't happen though. As their trip was just a few days away, he couldn't risk blowing fifty grand on a ring. The water bungalow set on stilts above the Indian Ocean was costing more than twenty thousand pounds, when you factored in the first-class flights and just about every upgrade imaginable. He didn't mind. Tatiana was special. She was his world. They'd have a fantastic time. No shoes and no news. That should keep

Rick and his constant stream of calls at bay. Hopefully, he'd come back from their trip refreshed and a richer man.

Edward shivered. His smart city suit and thin cotton shirt weren't designed for standing around outside in the cool of the late afternoon. He took one last toke and then ground the dog-end in one of the sand-filled ashtrays on the wraparound balcony. He heard footsteps approaching, and a couple of guys joined him. They weren't from his department. He didn't really know them, but he nodded to them as they passed him.

He decided to text Tatiana. He missed her. On his way back through the large open-plan office, he started to type, one-handed. Just as he did, a message pinged in from her. That always happened. It was like total synergy between them. He was always thinking about her as she was thinking about him. A smile settled on his lips as he read it.

Hey, babe. Missing you!

She'd added lots of emoji hearts, devil faces and an entire line of kisses.

His smile was enormous now. He had just begun his reply when he was stopped in his tracks as an image followed. He clicked it open just as he rounded the corner towards his office. Edward swallowed and peered over his shoulder to check if there was anyone behind him. Thankfully not! Tatiana filled the screen. *Fuck, his woman was so hot!* She was reclining on the bed, their bed, totally naked, with her legs spread with two fingers inside her. Her pussy looked so wet and so pretty. Beneath the photo she had written:

I want you, Eddie!

Edward could feel himself hardening. He couldn't control it. He needed to head to the gents and have a wank, and while he was good and hard, he planned to text her and show her exactly what she'd be getting when he walked through the door.

FORTY-THREE

MONDAY 14 JANUARY

SEBASTIAN

Sebastian woke first. In the half-light he watched Suzanne sleeping. Tenderly, he brushed buttery blonde strands of hair from her cheeks. He loved Suzanne. Loved her like he'd never loved before. She looked truly beautiful as she lay on her side, her head tucked into his chest. Reluctantly, he gently nudged her awake. Suzanne woke up fast, gave him a sleepy smile, followed by a quick peck that converted into a deep kiss. She pulled away.

"Happy Birthday, baby!" she chirped and then hopped out of bed, grinning. "I can't believe we nodded off again."

"You're not planning on singing to me, are you?" Sebastian grinned back at her.

"Of course! Happy Birthday to you, Happy Birthday to you, Happy Birthday, dear Sebastian, Happy Birthday to you!" While she sang, Suzanne pulled the drapes halfway and a golden splash of sun painted dazzling shadows across the floor. Blinking in the sunlight, she got busy gathering up presents.

"Don't think I've ever had '*Happy Birthday*' sang to me by someone who was naked. And if I had, they wouldn't have looked half as gorgeous as you."

"You are such a charmer," Suzanne laughed. She began placing his presents on the end of the bed.

When she was satisfied with her display, she produced a bottle of Laurent Perrier rosé champagne she'd managed to squeeze into the dinky minibar. What else would they be drinking to celebrate his birthday? Suzanne told him, as she wrestled with the cork.

Sebastian piled the pillows up against the headboard, and Suzanne joined him back in bed with the champagne plus two chilled flutes she'd slid out sideways from the ice compartment of the minibar. Wholly at ease with their nudity, they sat up in bed and sipped pink bubbles as Sebastian opened his cards. There was one from his mother, his secretary, the twins and Suzanne, of course. He saved hers for last. It was big and boxed. The front cover was a collection of embossed red hearts. When he opened it, the centre was covered with hundreds of red Xs, and '*A thousand kisses from you are never enough!*' was written in Suzanne's hand, squeezed in amongst the numerous kisses.

"Ah thanks, baby," Sebastian beamed.

He kissed her hard, their tongues lingering for a moment. When they broke away, Suzanne gathered up the envelopes and threw them away and then arranged the birthday cards on the mantelpiece.

The presents were opened next. Sebastian loved them all. Especially the jewelled cufflinks. They were stunning and so him. She knew him so well. He felt overwhelmed by all the attention and Suzanne's generosity. For once he was in a relationship where everything just kind of worked. He even got on really well with Suzanne's teenage sons. The shirt they'd bought him was great. He planned to wear it tonight with his new cufflinks and tie. Yes, he truly was a lucky guy. He breathed Suzanne in greedily as he hugged her and thanked her. She smelt of sex and Chanel perfume; a winning combination in his book.

Even though the events of the last couple of days had been shocking and draining, Sebastian felt great. Today he was determined to put the uncertainty of his birth father and all the crap with the GMC behind him and just enjoy his birthday with Suzanne. Although his head was in a good place, Sebastian's body ached. His neck was stiff. He could barely turn it from side to side. Payback from the effects of his ridiculous drunken afternoon and evening. He hoped a long, hot bath would sort it out.

"Shall we take the champagne into the bathroom and have a lovely, long soak?"

"Oooh, yes!" Suzanne bounced out of bed. "You run the bath, while I order us a huge room service breakfast. The works!"

Sebastian made his way into the bathroom, naked, a glass of champagne in his hand. Suzanne was back on the bed, huddled up, perusing the room service menu. Grinning, he blew her a kiss. She blew him one right back.

Big and stylish, the bathroom was tiled floor-to-ceiling in Italian marble; two-tone bronze with flashes of molten silver. Sebastian parked himself on a corner edge of the bath. The floor tiles were half the size of the wall tiles, but in a similar amber shade and were toasty beneath his bare feet. Marvelling at the wonders of underfloor heating, he turned both taps on full and then added a generous blob of Suzanne's Far Eastern

Ritual foam bath. As it dissolved into the water, the wonderfully pungent aroma evoked fond memories. It took him back in time to a beachfront spa hotel he'd stayed at in Phuket, Thailand, years ago, when he was in his early teens. Just him and his mother. At the time he wondered why his father hadn't joined them on holiday. He now knew why, of course.

Sebastian grabbed a jumbo bath sheet in soft snowy white and wrapped it around his waist. The large slab of honey marble surrounding the twin sinks was awash with Suzanne's toiletries; smart bottles and tubs and pots lined up, facing forward, uniformly. Sebastian loved Suzanne's neatness. At the basin, he splashed cold water onto his face. Rubbing it dry, he stared at himself in the wide rectangle of mirror. Thirty-seven today. He looked just the same, though he had dark circles under his eyes and looked tired. He fingered his hair off his forehead, rubbed the stubble on his chin and decided he needed a shave. He quite liked the rugged look but knew it played havoc with Suzanne's sensitive skin.

After cleaning his teeth robustly, Sebastian had a quick shave. Just a minute with his electric razor and he decided he looked fresher and less weary already. He took a mouthful of bubbly. It tasted odd mixed with the remains of the toothpaste, so he rinsed his mouth thoroughly and then checked on the bath, leaning in and swishing a hand back and forth rapidly under the gushing water. The fragrant bubbles were rising and floating. Sebastian closed his eyes and inhaled deeply. The bathroom smelled just like that faraway five-star hotel, decades ago.

The water level had risen quite substantially, but there was still a way to go, so Sebastian decided to call his mother. When he walked back into the bedroom, he couldn't believe Suzanne was still talking to room service. It sounded like she was ordering for a family of six. That made him chuckle, but hell, he was hungry. He retrieved his mobile and mouthed that he was about to call his mother and headed back towards the bathroom. Suzanne was still in deep conversation on the phone but flashed her teeth and eyes at him.

Sebastian's phone screen was filled with notifications. There were WhatsApp messages and texts as well as Facebook birthday wishes. He browsed the messages hurriedly and decided to answer them later. There was also a missed call from his mum. He listened to her rambling heartfelt apology. Today he didn't want to dwell on her deceit. He decided not to mention it, though he knew it would be there hanging between them when they spoke.

Gloria picked up on the first ring. "Happy Birthday, darling," she said, the moment she answered.

Sebastian laughed. "Thank you. I'm having a great day and being thoroughly spoilt. Anyway, how are you?"

"I'm fine, thanks, Seb. Are you okay?"

"Yes, I'm fine, Mum. Really. Okay?"

"Okay. Well, that's good. I'm just about to head out to the hairdresser's, actually."

"Well, I'll let you go then. I can't talk for long anyway. We're waiting for a room service breakfast and I'm running a bath."

"Okay, darling. You enjoy your day. I'm just pleased you're having a good time."

Suzanne poked her head around the bathroom door. "Say 'Hi' to Gloria from me," she breezed and then disappeared again.

"Did you get that?"

"I did, thank you. Say 'Hello' back from me. Suzanne is such a lovely girl. I hope you two have a great day."

"I think she's got lots planned, so I'm sure it's going to be wonderful."

"Okay, darling. Enjoy yourselves and be careful on those black runs."

"Mum, I've been skiing on black runs since I was about eight years old!" Sebastian laughed.

"I know, but I'm still your mother and I still worry about you whatever your age."

"Yes, I know!"

"Anyway, enjoy your birthday, darling."

"Thanks, Mum, I'm sure I will. And thanks for the card."

"No problem. Pop round as soon as you're home so I can give you your present. We'll talk about the other matter then as well."

Sebastian's ears pricked up. "Is there any news?"

"No, there isn't, Seb. But we'll sort it, I promise. Just try to put it out of your head for today. Enjoy your day and pop in to see me when you're back. On Wednesday evening? I could make supper for you both?"

"Sounds great, Mum. We'll see you then. Take care."

Sebastian hung up just as Suzanne came into the bathroom, still naked, still drinking, the almost empty bottle of champagne in one hand.

"Breakfast is going to be about thirty minutes, so that gives us loads of time," she announced, a big fat smile on her face.

"Perfect." Dunking a hand in, Sebastian checked the temperature. "The bath's just about ready. Scalding hot, just the way you like it," he joked as he turned off the taps.

She stroked his cheek. "You are looking really smooth and sexy, baby."

Sebastian covered her hand with his. He moved her hand to his mouth and kissed her fingertips, before sucking them into his mouth one by one. He stopped sucking and stood back from her. He dropped his towel dramatically. His body looked magnificent.

Suzanne looked him up and down. "I want to eat you all up."

"If I remember rightly, you just did."

Steadying each other, the two of them climbed into the bath, hand in hand. Sebastian let out a whimper of mock pain. Suzanne always liked her bath water hotter than he would choose if he was bathing alone. He was getting used to it by now, though the heat still turned his skin pink. Wearing an exaggerated grimace, he lowered himself into the water next to her. The bath was double width, so they sat side by side. Once he actually got used to the heat, the hot water was bliss.

"What a great start to the day," he mumbled, closing his eyes and leaning his head back.

"Let's finish this, baby," Suzanne said as she upended the bottle and shared the last of the champagne between them. No wonder Sebastian felt so relaxed. He'd drunk almost half a bottle of bubbly on an empty stomach, before half nine in the morning, but he really didn't care. That's what birthdays were for. Today was going to be just perfect.

Beside him, Suzanne immersed herself in the water. When she came up to the surface a few seconds later, she smoothed wet hair behind her ears. It trailed down her back. She looked sleek. Carnal. She oozed sensuality. Suzanne caressed Sebastian's broad chest, her fingers combing tufts of damp hair. When she touched him like that, Sebastian felt the usual thunderbolt. He was getting hard. He wanted her again already. He wondered if it was too much. Maybe he should try and control it. He didn't hold that thought for long.

Drinking clumsily, Suzanne allowed a dribble of fizz to trickle from the corner of her mouth. The pink liquid travelled lazily over her skin and onto one of her breasts. Her beautiful breasts bobbed majestically, cresting the sudsy water. Sebastian couldn't take his eyes off them. He watched and waited. Suzanne chewed her lower lip in that magical way that she always did when she wanted sex. It always did it for him, always drove him absolutely crazy for her. With tentative fingertips, Suzanne began to massage the champagne into her left nipple. It elongated and hardened. Sebastian had an uncontrollable urge to bite it. Bite it hard. He parted his lips just enough and sucked her into his mouth. He tasted her skin sweetened with his favourite champagne. He closed sharp teeth on her puffed-up nipple, while twisting the other pink rosebud until it was just as hard. His heart was pounding. His cock was twitching. Suzanne was spreading her legs. Sebastian knew what she wanted.

As Sebastian found her, Suzanne sipped champagne. She peered at him over her tall glass but didn't speak. She said nothing as he slid a finger inside her. And then another. Finally, Suzanne let out a soft hum of approval.

"You want a third, baby?" he asked as he removed his fingers and began to drag three digits up and down her slick sex.

Suzanne swallowed noisily, her breath a series of short guttural pants, her heaving breasts causing tiny undulations in the water. With champagne still moist on her chin, Suzanne murmured huskily: "I love your fingers inside me, baby, but I want the champagne bottle."

They locked eyes. Sebastian remained silent. He was engrossed with his fingers.

"I want you to fuck me with the bottle, Sebastian." Suzanne's demand was a snarl through clenched teeth. Her words sounded harsh, almost angry.

Sebastian was taken aback only slightly. He loved it when they talked dirty. Loved it that Suzanne was confident enough to tell him exactly what she wanted sexually. Still working three fingers up and down her, he replied: "Oh you do, do you? You want a bottle in your pussy?" As he finished speaking, he pushed a finger inside her forcefully.

Suzanne whinnied as he penetrated her digitally. She bit down on her bottom lip. In a barely audible whisper, she said: "Yes, I do, baby. I want to be fucked with the bottle."

Sebastian loved the idea of seeing Suzanne's pretty pink pussy stuffed full with a bottle. Nasty but nice.

On unsteady legs, Suzanne got up. Holding Sebastian's hand for support, she got comfy on the edge of the bath. Soap suds graced her feminine curves. Drifts of airy foam flecked her nipples and smooth flat belly. Releasing a soft throaty roar, Suzanne leaned back against the tiled wall. She spread her legs and her eyes fluttered closed. Sebastian moved in fast, and with firm hands he took hold of each ankle and wrenched her legs apart. It was a dominant action. With a gentler and softer manoeuvre, he parted her lips. He splayed long fingers on the tops of each thigh as he gazed in awe at her wide open, pretty-as-a-picture sex. He scrutinized her clit. Swollen and dusky pink, it always looked darker when she was aroused. He loved to get up close and personal with her. Looking at her always made his cock rock hard. Sebastian swallowed. He just had to taste her. He needed to bury his face in her incredible pulchritude. Bending to her, he pushed his tongue all the way inside her sweet hole and groaned. He worked it in and out, savouring her amazing scent. Powerful pheromones exploded in his head. He trembled as he pulled out.

"I love the way you taste, baby. You taste like sweet nectar from the gods," he gasped, his voice thick with lust, his face glistening from her excitement.

Suzanne grabbed him by the hair and raised his face towards hers. "Stick the bottle in me and then use your tongue," she growled.

Sebastian opened her and then gingerly eased the bottle in. She was so wet, it slipped in with ease.

"Is that okay, baby?" he asked as he worked it slowly in.

"Harder," Suzanne breathed in reply, seemingly mesmerised, gazing down in astonishment at the bottle neck as it disappeared inside her.

Sebastian began to thrust the bottle in with a little more vigour. He scooted in close, so the action was his eyeline. The vision before him in glorious close-up was such a turn on. His cock bounced beneath the water. It was throbbing out of control. Mewing softly, Suzanne raised a leg and bent her knee. As she thrust her pelvis forward, her asshole opened just a tad. He couldn't resist. Sebastian loved the taste of her ass too.

Once Suzanne had the bottle in her pussy and a tongue teasing her ass, things moved quickly. Sebastian sensed the signs. A tremor moved through his lover and her entire body tensed in anticipation. Sebastian stopped rimming her and slid the bottle out. Her pussy stayed tantalisingly open. He recognised Suzanne was on the brink. She cried out as Sebastian stuck a finger in her ass and then homed in on her clitoris, slurping on it gluttonously between greedy pursed lips.

As Suzanne's climax closed in, Sebastian flicked his tongue from side to side vertically across her bulging clitoris. He was concentrating very hard on getting her there. She felt rigid beneath his tongue. She tasted of muskiness and passion. The sweetest taste of all. He pushed his finger a few more centimetres into her bottom, and that seemed to tip her over the edge. Suzanne was going crazy as she embraced her climax. Her moans amplified and her legs started to tremble. Cumming hard, she gripped Sebastian's head to steady herself as it washed over her. She threw her head back and keened.

Moaning softly, coming down from her peak, Suzanne was wilting. Sebastian slipped his finger from her ass, got rid of the bottle and guided her back into the bath with him. Still shuddering, she kissed him frantically, whipping him with damp strands of her hair. Sebastian took that as his cue to get inside her. He switched on the jets and all at once their bodies were assaulted with exploding bursts of soapy water from every direction. Seconds later, his cock entered her and they began their torrid tango of love. Face-to-face, they made love, sitting with their legs wrapped around each other, with Suzanne sitting on top, astride Sebastian's thighs. Their bodies pressed tight together, chest-to-chest, they kissed and hugged and fucked. Within a few minutes, they were cumming together.

Only moments after they'd climaxed euphorically as one and were hugging like koalas in each other's arms, there was a knock on their bedroom door. Breakfast was served.

FORTY-FOUR

MONDAY 14 JANUARY

TATIANA

Smoking a cigarette, Tatiana gazed out of the grand picture windows. It was already dark outside. The lights of London life twinkled like giant glittering stars. Tatiana thought the Thames looked black and exotic. Chilling in her chic kitchen, she was made-up for a night on the town, though she wasn't planning on going out. She looked stunning; her blue-black locks impressively sleek and hanging loosely down her back, her eyes heavy with liner, her lashes curled and densely coated in mascara, and her pouty lips a perfectly painted feast of cherry red. Wearing very little, Tatiana relaxed over the breakfast bar, a glass of Châteauneuf-du-Pape in her hand.

She stubbed her half-smoked Camel Blue out and picked up her phone. Nothing more from Angelo. *Thank fuck!* She checked her Facebook feed, scrolling through idly, before exiting the app and concentrating on the very graphic shots Edward had sent her. His fat cock filled her screen. It didn't look very attractive. No matter how much she loved cock, a snapshot of one just wasn't very pretty. Tatiana grinned, her lips twisting into a haughty smile. He really was a very bad man. That's why she loved him. Tatiana paused momentarily when that thought hit her and did a little somersault in her head. She did love him, didn't she? Actually, she really wasn't sure. Either way, she loved the life he could offer her. Only a few days now until they would be flying off to the Maldives. Lots of lazy days making love in paradise, lounging around and topping up her tan. God, she craved some sunshine away from the cold. Their holiday would be another dream come true. Sometimes she couldn't believe how far she'd come. From living in squalor in Tirana with her alcoholic mother to living the highlife in swanky Chelsea, holidaying in the Maldives and owning a flash car and more jewellery and designer clothes than she could ever have imagined possible. Everything was going brilliantly; well, it would be, if she could just get Angelo off her back. She'd heard nothing since she'd texted him on Saturday night. No news is good news, she decided optimistically. She'd outfoxed him. He'd be waiting for her at Dubai Airport on Wednesday, and she'd be getting ready for a holiday in the sun. *Go figure, asshole!*

She giggled when she thought of Eddie in a state, wanking over her at work. He'd be wanting her as soon as he got home. Which wouldn't be long. And she was ready for him. Dressed in high-heeled mules, a skimpy red slip and no knickers, she was glad she had the heating turned up high. Well, for now anyway, as she knew things were bound to hot up once he got home. She fancied being fucked bending over the kitchen counter. She'd be nice and upright and that way he could switch from one hole to the other. She was really into anal sex at the moment and Eddie certainly wasn't complaining.

Tatiana was feeling horny, planning her moves in her head as she heard his key in the door. She licked her sticky lips and turned to greet him with plenty of pearly white teeth on show.

"You, young lady, are seriously going to get it," Edward announced as he walked into the kitchen, grinning.

Tatiana stood and faced him. She said nothing as she lifted her skirt and flashed her pussy at him.

"Come here, you," he growled as he took his cock out of his pants and forced her to her knees.

FORTY-FIVE

SUZANNE

Suzanne felt stuffed and lethargic after their enormous breakfast. Together they cleared the plates away and then began to get ready. Suzanne had made plans for Sebastian's special day, so she shrugged off her lethargy and put her face and her ski gear on. Checking out her reflection, she thought she'd scrubbed up rather well. Wearing his new sweater and scarf, Sebastian cuddled her and thanked her for his wonderful presents. Suzanne held him close, cherishing his masculine scent. He kissed her softly, his lips as sultry as a tropical breeze. His mouth was peppermint. She nuzzled her face in the crook of his throat. His skin smelt fresh and clean, and utterly gorgeous, and the baby blue of his jumper made his eyes resonate with haunting, vivacious colour. Suzanne was so happy. She felt like she was floating on a cotton wool cloud.

It was almost midday when they left their suite. Sebastian had mentioned that he'd like to ski the alternative mountain range: Whistler Blackcomb. Doing her homework, Suzanne had pre-booked a return trip on the Peak 2 Peak Gondola, which connected Whistler with the Whistler Blackcomb Mountains. The four-kilometre ride, which features in the *Guinness World Record* books as the longest unsupported span in the world, promised an unparalleled perspective of British Columbia, and it certainly lived up to its promise. The aerial view was mind-melting. From the lofty comfort of their gondola, which was shiny brand new and the colour of a London bus, they gaped at the awesome delights beneath them; at the vastness of their world, at the colossal snow-dusted pines and towering alpine peaks. Through the bottom of their carriage, they even spotted a gigantic black bear scampering through the deep snow.

★

On the northern ridge at Blackcomb, the skiing was fantastic. The sun shone in an impressive blue sky, dappled with every shade of grey. Suzanne felt more comfortable now she had her ski legs back. They raced down a collection of wide red runs, keeping pace which each other, weaving across the mountain, picking up speed. Sebastian, ever-vigilant, followed Suzanne's progress at all times. They ventured onto a black. It was helpfully wide to accommodate the many skiers it catered for, but with an abrupt descent that was both daunting and exhilarating, after a valiant attempt, the steeper terrain and high speed became too much for Suzanne. She took a tumble and went down. She remained on her butt in the snow, her skis out in front of her. Raising her goggles up onto her head, she blinked upwards, grinning.

Sebastian hurried into a parallel turn at an acute angle. Powdery snow sprayed in an arc under the momentum of his blades. Confidently, he sidestepped back up the mountain to her. He offered Suzanne a wry smile and a helping hand.

On her feet again, Suzanne leaned in and elevated Sebastian's mirrored electric blue ski goggles. He looked so fucking sexy wearing them. Kind of mean-looking. Like a baddie. Laughter blazed in his spectacular blue eyes. Suzanne felt the pull of them. She needed to feel his lips upon hers. She moved in close and the lovers shared a memorable kiss. It was one of those moments. One of those spine-tingling instances that Suzanne knew she'd remember for a very long time. As their lips crushed together, it started to snow. A cascade of snowflakes twisting through the air, raining down on their upturned faces as they shared an interlude of kisses as soft and moist as the snowflakes that fell upon them. The snow started to accelerate; a million wet kisses descending from the heavens as the sky darkened. Since the sunshine had dwindled and the weather was definitely on the change, Suzanne and Sebastian decided to head down the mountain and seek shelter. They decided they'd stop for a hot chocolate in a mountain café.

It didn't take them long to find one. They stored their skis and poles and headed inside, Suzanne fluffing up her hair as she went. Without his ski beanie, Sebastian's hair was tousled. The look suited him, made him look even more fuckable. After she finished fiddling with her hair, Suzanne had a go at his. He let her for a while then caught her hand and kissed her fingertips.

The cafe was decked out in standard alpine style: heavy on the knotty pine, with massive unfettered windows and an old-fashioned linoleum floor, cracked and a little grubby with slush. The place was heaving; full of people struggling with their packed food trays while attempting to walk normally in clompy ski boots. The seating looked uncomfortable and the cuisine was obviously pretty simple fare, but being there with Sebastian, watching the snowstorm build outside, was everything Suzanne could ever wish for. She felt deliriously happy. She let out a contented sigh as she unzipped her jacket. Sebastian unwrapped his new scarf and then led her to a tight corner table that looked like it could do with a good wipe-down but had a great view. They sat down opposite each other.

"I'm loving every moment of my birthday," Sebastian said above the chatter. He brushed crumbs from their table and used a paper serviette to give it a half-hearted clean.

"Aw, I'm glad. And I'm loving it too." Suzanne glanced around her. "I suppose as it's your birthday I should be the one to go and queue. I'm pretty sure this place is self-service."

"I'm afraid it is. But I'll go. Can't have you queuing up. Not after your traumatic tumble," Sebastian grinned. "This is on me. What do you fancy?" he asked, handing over the plastic-covered menu and rewarding her with a smile that could melt her heart.

FORTY-SIX

SUZANNE

In their cosy hotel suite, Suzanne took ages applying her make-up. Tonight she wanted to look her very best for the birthday boy. En route, Sebastian had picked up a bottle of pink champagne from the bar. Laurent Perrier, of course. Suzanne couldn't help but smile as he'd ordered it. Their eyes had met and held. All knowing. Their dirty little secret. After having a boozy day so far, they were in agreement that they'd take it easy until dinner. Just have a glass each while they were getting ready. They'd save the rest for when they got back. Maybe make good use of the empty bottle again. The very idea made Suzanne tingle.

Smouldering green eyes all over her man, Suzanne sipped her favoured tipple and watched Sebastian dress. He really was something special. Contentment washed over her. A little over six months ago, she felt hollow, like she'd been hung out to dry, like her life was in free fall. And now, just half a year later, she was the happiest she could remember since the birth of the twins.

With the lights turned down low, the mellow strains of Ed Sheeran as their soundtrack chilling the mood, Suzanne sat on the edge of the bed. Her fine-knit dress pulled up around her thighs, she smoothed moisturiser onto her bare legs and feet. She smiled over at Sebastian as she creamed up. He looked striking in his new black shirt. It fitted him just right, hugged his wide shoulders and showed off his slim waist. The distinctive new tie and shiny cufflinks added that extra dash of class. Suzanne stared hard at his ass as he tucked his shirt into a pair of black dress trousers. Dressed all in black and moving around the bedroom on light feet, he reminded Suzanne of the Milk Tray Man; tall, dark and impossibly handsome.

Suzanne made her glass of champagne last. There was a long night ahead. She'd booked a table for two in the hotel's best restaurant: the Grill Room. Take two. They had his surprise presents to look forward to as well, and then lots of fucking, of course. Suzanne loved the feeling of being tipsy, but certainly didn't want to be too drunk to enjoy her lover to the full. She couldn't wait to witness that look of pure lust dripping from his glorious mouth when he realised what she had planned. Couldn't wait to have the pleasure of his cock complete with an all-singing, all-dancing cock ring adding that extra special something to their lovemaking. As she watched Sebastian smoothing on aftershave, she fantasised about him pushing her back on the bed, yanking up her dress and taking her without preamble or conversation.

"Great ass," Suzanne murmured, as she continued to rub body lotion onto the soles of her feet and between each French polished toe.

Sebastian flashed a dreamy smile and then came to her and sank to his knees. He gripped Suzanne's leg at the ankle. Moving upwards with a firm touch, his fingers rippled on her calf muscles as he massaged the moisturiser onto her skin. Just the feel of his hands on her sent shivers up her spine.

"You've got a wonderful ass yourself, you know. When people say to me 'nothing's perfect', I always want to say, 'except Suzanne's ass'."

Suzanne laughed out loud. She parted her legs just a little.

Right away, Sebastian noticed she wasn't wearing panties. "How d'you expect me to keep my hands off you at dinner knowing you're not wearing any underwear?" he asked. His tone was deadly serious.

"You'll just have to try your hardest, I guess," Suzanne replied huskily. The very idea that he might touch her at the table excited her. Suzanne's heart pounded in her chest as Sebastian lifted her dress and peered beneath. She could feel his eyes on her sex. She felt a warm flush between her legs. Moaning softly, she spread them wider for him.

"That is one pretty pussy, baby," Sebastian whispered.

When he talked to her like that, it gave her goosebumps, made her wet. Suzanne struggled to control the urge to grab him by the hair and force his head to her.

"Glad you like it," she breathed. "If you're very good, I'll let you taste it later, birthday boy."

Sebastian cleared his throat. He slid a hand to her. Suzanne gnawed her bottom lip and let out a soft cry. Their eyes met. For a moment it was touch and go. Sebastian stared deep into her eyes as he squeezed a handful of her wanting pussy. Holding her in his grasp, his eyes still glued to hers, he said softly: "It'll keep." Grinning like a naughty schoolboy, Sebastian let go and stood up.

Breathing deeply, Suzanne smoothed down her dress. "I reckon it'll be worth the wait."

"You bet, baby," Sebastian whispered. He turned off the music, grabbed his jacket and slid the key card into his trouser pocket. He stood still and gazed at Suzanne, his eyes snaking over her appreciatively. She felt as if he was making love to her already.

Suzanne checked herself in the bedroom mirror and made a few last-minute adjustments with her hair. Sebastian was still watching her as she squeezed bare feet into Manolo Blahnik clackety high heels and, tottering ever so slightly, strode across the room and grabbed her matching handbag. She unclasped it and dropped her lip gloss inside. She'd need additional applications throughout the evening as she and Sebastian were always snogging each other's face off. Suzanne knew she looked good. The coffee-coloured shoes matched her dress perfectly and were outrageously high. She loved the way they made her feet look tiny and her legs look long and toned. Suzanne was well aware that her knickerless state would drive Sebastian crazy. Make him want her all the more. If that were possible. She swallowed hard, held out her hand. Time to go.

As they walked out of the door, hand in hand, Suzanne said: "Don't forget, I've got two more presents for you when we get back. Sexy stuff. You are going to love them."

Sebastian couldn't wipe the smile off his face as he closed the door behind them.

★

The Grill Room seeped old-world money and was cleverly lit, not so dark you couldn't read the menus or see the delicious food on offer, but low and moody nevertheless. On arrival they were led to a perfectly positioned table by the maître d'. He had a sexy French accent and the look of Tom Hardy, but Suzanne only had eyes for Sebastian. Sebastian rested a hand on her bottom possessively as he guided her through the busy restaurant. His touch on her ass felt hot. He pulled out the seat for her and they sat. Their table was dressed exquisitely, with a pure white, crisp linen tablecloth, buffed shiny silverware and fine crystal glasses. Suzanne smiled as she noticed the pianist installed unobtrusively in the entrance vestibule. Easy on the ear, her voice was low and soothing and easy.

The restaurant was busy, with every table filled. The diligent staff moved at speed, working at full stretch. At their cosy table for two, within warming distance of the roaring log fire, the lovers sat facing each other. Beside them, a large window framed a snow-laden landscape backlit by a high moon. They shared a starter of rosemary grilled scallops and pork belly with a maple onion sauce and followed that with medium rare 12 oz New York steaks and salad. The beef was melt-in-your-mouth good, but so filling. Suzanne couldn't quite finish it all. They kept their alcohol intake to a minimum with just one small glass of white; a Chablis, followed by a small glass of deep red Merlot.

Once the plates were cleared away, Sebastian tucked a stray strand of hair behind his ear, grinned and said: "I'm curious about my other presents."

Suzanne reached over and interlocked her fingers

with his. She took a deep breath. "I've written you a list of sexual favours. You can redeem them with me at any time." She held his gaze and giggled nervously. "Maybe tonight would be a good time to start?" She felt her cheeks burn. She had no idea why.

Sebastian began to chuckle softly.

"And I've bought you a cock ring." Suzanne dipped her head timidly and then added: "I've never tried one before but thought it might be interesting!"

Sebastian raised both eyebrows in response. He squeezed her hands tightly. Before he had time to comment, a chorus of '*Happy Birthday*' rang out as two staff members marched in their direction, carrying a birthday cake, heavily frosted with swirly icing. Sebastian blew out all the candles. Suzanne didn't count, but she was sure there weren't thirty-seven. But who cared? Chocolate cake, followed by being made love to by the most beautiful man on earth. Could this evening be any more perfect?

FORTY-SEVEN

MONDAY 14 JANUARY

SEBASTIAN

Sebastian fingered Suzanne in the lift on the way back to their suite. Couldn't help himself. Just hiked up her dress and inserted two fingers into her sweet, sticky honeypot. Knowing she was wearing no underwear had kept him semi-hard throughout dinner. As soon as they were alone, he needed to touch her. Sebastian loved the smell of Suzanne's pussy. It drove him absolutely fucking wild. He'd have loved to have stuck his tongue inside her while they were alone in the lift. Instead, as they journeyed to their floor, wondering if the lift would grind to a halt and they'd get caught in the act, he fooled around with her clit, while she squirmed and moaned and parted her thighs to make fingering easy. He could tell she wasn't far off cumming, but there wasn't enough time. Sebastian took his fingers out and slapped her slit, once softly, and then again, a little harder. Suzanne trembled. She let out a tiny whimper and then flattened her dress back into place. Eyes on her, Sebastian pushed his sodden fingers into his mouth and sucked on them. And then, the taste of her excitement smeared on his lips, he kissed her hard.

By the time they got back to the room, Sebastian's cock was so cramped it was painful. Realising his dilemma, Suzanne unbelted and unzipped him, and then with a grin full of dazzling white teeth, she took his hand and invited him to sit beside her on the small sofa. Once he was sitting, her eyes twinkling, she presented him with a brightly coloured gift bag.

From the bag, Sebastian retrieved a handful of small square sheets of pale pink paper and perused them, one by one. Suzanne watched him as he read her handwritten notes, each one offering him a different sexual favour. There was a blowjob where Suzanne promised to swallow, an hour-long full body massage, an invitation to tie her up and gag her and even permission to fuck her in the ass.

"What the hell!" Sebastian exclaimed when he read the one offering him anal sex. "Is this for real?"

Suzanne smiled sweetly and nodded her head.

"Baby, you are too much!" Chuckling, Sebastian reached back into the bag and discovered the cock ring. "What are you like?" he laughed. He spent a few seconds examining it. He seemed lost for words for a moment and then murmured: "I've waited way too long for you tonight, baby. Come here."

They undressed swiftly and then Sebastian let her lead him to the window. His cock aching with desire, he watched Suzanne squat down and carefully place the cock ring over the engorged head and roll the tight circle of latex to the base. As always, he adored the feel of her hands on him. Absorbed in her task, strands of golden hair fell over her face and her breathing was heavy. Sebastian gazed down and regarded her. He shuddered as long pink nails glided effortlessly over the fine skin of his penis. Suzanne smiled up at him. A naughty smirk full of promise. She looked unbelievably hot, on her haunches, her knees bent in half, her legs spread wide. A light dusting of ginger freckles coated her legs. They looked so pretty. She was nude but for high heels and jewels. A heady waft of Coco Mademoiselle perfume stormed Sebastian's senses and filled his head. Suzanne was a veritable feast for all his senses. Iron-straight, yellow blonde tresses cascading down her bare back, her hair shone like spun silk. Groaning, Sebastian twisted his fingers in it and tugged. *Fuck, Suzanne was one in a million.*

The cock ring in situ, Suzanne glanced up at him, seeking his approval. Sebastian met her eyes with his. He truly loved this woman. Wanted to be with her forever, when he was old and grey and couldn't get it up. But right now, he wanted her so much. Couldn't wait to be inside her, making sweet, ethereal love. He yearned for a lovemaking session of such intensity that he could disappear, forget who he was and where he was, just exist in a moment of pure ecstasy. An ecstasy he never knew existed until he met Suzanne.

Sebastian inhaled and closed his eyes, his long lashes fluttering as he leaned against the window. The frigid glass cool on his bare back, it set goosebumps running all over him. All of a sudden, the cock ring began vibrating. Suzanne must have flicked some kind of switch, Sebastian realised. Whatever. It felt good. So fucking good. He clamped his teeth together and groaned as wave after wave of pleasure undulated through his cock. He felt his knees go weak as Suzanne swallowed him up in one ravenous mouthful. Her full lips possessing him, he was a prisoner incarcerated in her warm, wet mouth. In full cock-sucking mode now, Suzanne covered his helmet with lipsticky kisses. Saliva dribbled down his shaft. And, all the while, the rapid pulsing at the root of his cock felt amazing. Sebastian arched back against the cold pane of glass and released a long animal moan.

"Tell me what you want, baby. Tonight, I'm all yours to have any way you want," she breathed.

Sebastian stroked Suzanne's hair. She stared up at him, nibbling at his thighs while she waited for him to reply.

"Suzanne, you know what I want tonight more than anything else in the world?"

Big green eyes blazing, she purred: "Tell me."

"I want to make love to you. I don't want to tie you up or stick a bottle in your pussy or do you up the bum. I just want to hold you, want to breathe in your incredible smell, kiss you all over, lick your pussy until you've had so many orgasms you can't stop shaking, and then, when we're both ready, I want to make sweet leisurely love to you before we fall asleep in each other's arms."

"Perfect," Suzanne mouthed, her voice soft and low. Her eyes were wet with tears as she clambered up Sebastian's body. Raking her hands through his ruffled mop of ebony hair, her hungry mouth closed in on his.

FORTY-EIGHT

TUESDAY 15 JANUARY

SEBASTIAN

Sebastian always woke up fast. Eyes open, brain in gear. Usually with a sense of dread growling at the pit of his stomach. But this morning, it was different. He felt good; pretty amazing, in fact. Last night had been unbelievable. Their lovemaking had been astonishing. When he ejaculated into Suzanne for the final time deep in the early hours, he felt truly euphoric. Everything seemed surreal. As they came together in total unity, it was as if two had become one.

For a change, he'd slept really well. Slept the whole night through. No waking in the middle of the night feeling uneasy. He exhaled and rubbed his eyes. In the dim light they looked sharp ice blue. Their bed was chaotic. There were pillows heaped on the floor and the duvet was all bunched up and upside down. Suzanne was curled up in his arms, her head on his chest, her face partly obscured with a mass of flyaway hair. She looked so beautiful. He brushed soft wisps of blonde from her brow and kissed her temple. She didn't stir. He tidied the duvet around them and then stuck out one arm and retrieved his phone from the bedside table. It was a habit.

It was the first thing he did almost every single morning. Like most people. His shrink said it was because of his anxiety disorder. Sara had an explanation and a name for everything.

Sebastian scanned his phone for messages. There was a text that had come in overnight from his mother, confirming their supper arrangement for tomorrow. He hadn't mentioned it to Suzanne yet. He sighed quietly. It would be good to see his mother, though he couldn't help but wonder how the evening might pan out. *Did she have any news? His biological father couldn't be that difficult to locate, surely? Not with the way the internet had revolutionised absolutely everything.* Sebastian wanted to find out the truth, but dreaded what he might discover. What if his father was dead, or a total lowlife, or even worse, wanted nothing to do with him? Could he deal with the pain of rejection all over again? Sebastian sighed once more then turned his attention back to his phone.

There were a couple of WhatsApp messages from friends and several Facebook notifications, all of which he ignored. Instead, he checked his emails. It was mainly junk; *Groupon* offers and *Secret Escape* deals, cinema listings and special offers from his health club, plus a few that were work-related. Right away, he spotted one from Pauline that was marked as 'High Importance'. So he clicked it open right away. The message read:

Hi, Sebastian, hope you are having a wonderful time and that your birthday was fun. Wouldn't normally bother you with work stuff, but as this email is such good news, I thought I should forward it to you right away. See you Thursday. Enjoy the rest of your stay. Pauline.

"Hmm?" Sebastian grunted under his breath. He frowned as he scrolled down. His heart pumped hard as soon as he saw the email was from Alan Hamilton.

Dear Mr Black,

Just a quick note to inform you that my wife has withdrawn the allegations she made against you, some months ago. I'm sure the GMC will notify you directly, but I thought it only right to update you as soon as possible, as I'm sure this matter has been a cause of great concern for you. We apologise for the anxiety this must have caused you. My wife is not well at the moment and is currently undergoing medical treatment for her sex addiction.

Best Regards, Alan Hamilton

"What the hell?" Sebastian said out loud. He began to read the email in full one more time, just to make sure he'd got it right. As he read, under his breath, he muttered: "I told him the bloody woman was a nymphomaniac."

Suzanne stirred in his arms. "Baby, is everything okay?" she mumbled, big green eyes smudged with make-up, blinking rapidly as she came to.

"Yes, it is!" he beamed, kissing her on the tip of her nose. "Sorry to wake you. I've just had an email from Alan Hamilton, and the case with the General Medical Council is all done with, apparently. Finally, the man gets it that his wife is a bloody fantasist. He felt the need to tell me she's being treated for sex addiction!" He shook his head disbelievingly.

"What?"

"I mean, why would you tell anyone that, anyway? Madness, but woohoo, it's over! Thank fuck!" Sebastian's smile was immense. He returned his phone to the bedside table and hugged Suzanne.

"Oh my God, Sebastian!" Suzanne said, hugging him back. "That's such good news."

Suzanne wrapped her arms around him even tighter. He could feel her heart beating in time with his. It was as if they were synchronised.

"Is there really such a condition as a sex addict?"

"Therapists seem to have a name for every fuck-up these days," Sebastian said ironically, but he was still grinning.

Suzanne smiled back sweetly. Wordlessly, she pushed him down flat. Chewing her lip seductively, she slid on top of him. Her body flush on top of his, she crushed her breasts against his chest. Sebastian shivered. The closeness of her was almost too much.

Looking down at him eye-to-eye, her hands snaking into his oil black locks, she uttered under her breath: "Doctor, can you help me? I think I might be suffering from a sex addiction because when I'm with you, all I want to do is fuck you."

As her words fell into his mouth, Sebastian felt his cock twitch in arousal. A volt of electricity shimmied though his body as Suzanne ground her pubis against him. He breathed hard, taking in shallow, silent sips of her. Suzanne palmed his face and reeled him in for a long, deep kiss.

FORTY-NINE

TUESDAY 15 JANUARY

EDWARD

Edward was working from home today. At his desk in his orderly home office, he pored over his Mac screen as he methodically made his way through a ton of emails. Outside his window, the blackness of nightfall crept in stealthily like an uninvited intruder. The darkness sapped his energy. He'd made up his mind to give it another fifteen minutes and then call it a day. Tatiana should be home from her shopping trip in Knightsbridge by then. She'd just texted to say she was on her way back, and had promised him a fashion show.

He wondered idly how much her latest outing would cost him. She'd be spending outrageously, of course. Tatiana didn't even look at the price tag, just bought absolutely everything that took her fancy. This morning, she'd announced she needed a new wardrobe for their holiday. She'd been on his lap with her arms wrapped around his neck and her legs clamped around his hips, cosying up to him. *How could he say no?* Tatiana had purred like a contented cat when he'd handed over his credit card. She rewarded him with a lingering French kiss before clambering off and heading out, hours ago.

Edward checked his watch. Yes, it was bloody hours ago. But he wasn't complaining. She'd left him with a massive hard-on. He suppressed a self-satisfied smile.

He wasn't worried about his cash flow now. He hadn't heard from Rick for several days but was confident the deal they'd cooked up together would proceed with no hiccups. It had to. He simply couldn't allow himself to think otherwise. It would net him around a million, he reckoned. Certainly, enough ready cash to tide them over, finalise his divorce, and then pay for the extravagant wedding Tatiana deserved. Yes, his finances should all be in hand by the time they got back from the Maldives. Images of white sand and tantalisingly turquoise seas rolling onto deserted shores, danced like nirvana before his dark eyes. A fortnight's stay in one of the most beautiful beach resorts in the world with the most beautiful, fuckable woman on earth. What man could ask for more?

With his angular features, Edward liked to think he resembled a younger, slimmer version of the movie star Alex Baldwin. People often remarked on their similarity. Today he wasn't dressed like a film star. He was dressed for comfort in sludgy grey tracky bottoms and a Hollister roll neck sweater. He wore black velvet slippers on his bony feet. A mug of strong black coffee sat beside him on his massive mahogany desk which was neat as a pin. Papers and documents were housed in brightly coloured folders and formed one tidy stack within easy reach.

With dusk closing in, humming to himself quietly, Edward worked on. Capital played in the background; Taylor Swift serenading him with: '*I knew you were trouble when you walked in*'. Edward liked the catchy tune. He

271

joined in with the final chorus. Music always managed to lift his mood. Edward loved working from home. He'd managed to arrange it at least once a week now, which was fantastic as he knew how much Tatiana hated being left to her own devices, and for him, being apart from her for more than ten hours a day seemed like an eternity. It messed with his head wondering what she got up to. Not that she'd ever cheat on him, of course. No way. It was just he missed her like crazy. He'd never met a woman like her. She was always ready for it, night or day. When he was in the office, he missed being able to fuck her whenever the mood took him. And it took him ALL the time. The icing on the cake with working at home was that instead of taking a lunch hour, they always fucked. Doing the sexiest woman in the whole wide world was all the sustenance he needed. He never went hungry. Edward sniggered. No lunch break, no tea break, no cigarette break, just a fuck break. Tatiana was truly insatiable. Sometimes he really couldn't believe his luck.

Edward was chuckling away to himself as he clicked open an email from his immediate superior. He stopped laughing. The supercilious grin froze on his face. His stomach plummeted as he read it. The underlying message was that an irregularity had been reported at work and he was summoned to a meeting, first thing in the morning with the 'Big Cheese'. *Holy Fuck! What was that all about? Had someone spotted something?* He read the email again. It certainly wasn't giving anything away. There was no clear reference to insider dealing, but all of a sudden, Edward felt sick. A searing hot flush swept up his body. Blood rushed to his head and his stomach did a backflip. As he looked down, he noticed his right hand shaking on the mouse. He'd not go in. He'd call in sick first thing in the morning. Wait it out. See what went down.

At that moment, he heard a key turn in the door. Bad timing. Edward exited the email straight away. His heart was pumping so fast in his chest, he was scared that Tatiana would actually be able to see it beating. He exhaled hard, trying desperately to compose himself. Shoulder length, coal-black hair swishing, Tatiana slinked into the office looking as always like his very own erotic fantasy; her maquillage immaculate, green cat eyes made-up to perfection, her lips as red as tulips. He managed to force a smile.

"Hey, babe," Tatiana cooed. She was squeezed into tight leather trousers, worn with high-heeled, black, knee-high boots and a fitted red sweater beneath a grey gillet made from soft wispy fox fur. In each hand she clutched a selection of shiny carrier bags, designer names inscribed on each one.

"Hi, sweetheart. I've missed you," Edward said, getting to his feet. Tatiana dumped her bags where she stood and took him in her arms. As he held her tight, his head was spinning. *Surely his deal with Rick hadn't been discovered? How could they prove he'd done anything underhand? Fuck it! This has to be about something else, surely?* Edward tried to convince himself he was panicking unnecessarily. Everything was just fine. When Tatiana's fiery lips connected with his, distractedly, he returned her kiss.

Pulling out of the kiss, she whispered: "You okay, Eddie?" She scratched red talons through his shock of salt and pepper hair.

"All cool with me, babe," Edward fibbed. "How about my sweet girlie?"

"I am good, darling. I have bought so many beautiful things for our holiday. You want to see?"

Before he had time to answer, Tatiana's phone rang in her pocket. Easing away from their embrace ever so slightly, she took it out and stared at the screen. A look of sheer terror flashed across her face. It settled hard and fast in her eyes. She didn't accept or decline the call. She just let it ring. From the corner of his eye, Edward noticed the name *Angelo* light up the face of her phone.

"Aren't you going to answer it?" Edward asked, puzzled. Tatiana was always on her phone and usually hated it if she missed a call.

Tatiana shook her head mutely. She dropped her phone back into the pocket of her furry gillet. It went silent.

"What does Angelo want?" Edward pushed, unable to overcome his jealousy and curiosity.

"Oh nothing, nothing at all. I expect he is just keeping in touch. You know there is nothing in it, Eddie. We are just old friends."

Edward didn't buy it. He'd spotted the immediate look of horror as Tatiana had registered that the call was from Angelo, and all of a sudden it seemed like her heart was beating out of control as well. *Fuck! The pair of them were keeping secrets.* He had no idea how to deal with his problem, and even less idea how to discover what the love of his life was up to with that fucking violent nutjob, Angelo.

He decided to change the subject. Edward's voice was remarkably calm as he said: "So, come on then, show Daddy what sexy stuff you've bought."

FIFTY

SUZANNE

Fresh from the shower, her golden hair damp, Suzanne sat cross-legged on the bed, like a Buddha. While Sebastian was in the bathroom she spent time on her iPad updating information. She slid the super slim white tablet, a stack of leaflets and a binder filled with handwritten notes into a Louis Vuitton laptop bag. Wearing white panties and a matching bra, she got up off the bed. She could hear Sebastian singing in the shower. Sounding pretty pleased with himself, he blasted out Enrique Iglesias' '*Hero*'. He could be her hero anytime! Suzanne grinned. She longed to join him in the shower and make love one last time before they left the hotel, but she had to admit defeat; she'd run out of time. She needed to get herself together and then nip out to check out a few last-minute bits of information for her review.

★

Just over an hour later, Suzanne looked good to go. Her make-up was light and her gilded hair pulled back to the nape of her neck with a large pale blue velvet

275

bow. Topaz droplet earrings hung from her ears. She was dressed in a Wedgewood blue suit; the jacket was double-breasted with shiny gold buttons. The skirt was knee-length and pencil line, though not too tight. She wore a cream polo neck, Wolford nude pantyhose and baby blue Karl Lagerfield pumps with laces and a wedge. The wedges were high but comfy. Suzanne remembered her feet killing her at Heathrow and was determined not to repeat her mistake at Vancouver Airport.

There was a knock at the door.

"Shit! I'm not ready yet!" Suzanne announced, though looked perfectly ready. She blasted herself with perfume.

"It's okay, baby, I'll get it. You've got plenty of time," Sebastian told her soothingly, piercing blue eyes washing over her reflection in the mirror as she arranged a couple of loose strands of hair that fell decoratively over her cheeks.

Sebastian opened the door to an all-American cheerleader type. Cheerily, she introduced herself as Madison.

"Sorry, I'll just be two minutes," Suzanne shouted.

Sebastian confirmed that Suzanne would be right with her, and while the young woman waited at the door, he chivvied Suzanne along.

"Don't be gone too long. I'm going to miss you like crazy," he murmured.

"Not half as much as I'm going to miss you."

Suzanne gave him a squeeze. She wrinkled her freckly nose. Just the smell of him made her feel high. Lowering her voice, she said in a husky whisper: "I really wanted you to fuck me in the shower this morning."

Sebastian grinned like mad, flashing sharp white teeth at her. Suzanne couldn't take her eyes off him. She fingered his hair. Still wet, it glistened. It looked as if someone had sprayed it with tanning oil. Suzanne lost her fingers in it while they eyed each other, both very aware that Madison was waiting patiently behind the door, which was ajar. Sebastian kissed Suzanne then, hesitantly and briefly, his lips barely connecting with hers. His breath was minty fresh and moreish. Lust flickered in his eyes.

"I promise to make it up to you," he whispered.

"You make sure you do," Suzanne mouthed back at him.

Sebastian stared at her hard. A knowing smile spreading over his face, he nodded. Suzanne felt the dampness of his hair catch her, a few stray droplets of moisture hitting her face. She sucked in her breath. It felt incredibly sensual.

"Text me when you're done and we'll grab a bite."

"Great idea. I'm so hungry!" she said, still holding him in her arms. "Bye, baby."

Before Suzanne pulled away, she couldn't resist just one more kiss. She took it swiftly and then dazzled Sebastian with a sunny smile. She picked up her bag and dashed out the door, apologising profusely for her tardiness, even though she was no more than a few minutes late.

★

By midday, Suzanne had been shown around one of the hotel's most prestigious suites, which rather propitiously happened to be unoccupied, as were two family suites which she'd also had a nose around with the very chatty Madison. Suzanne snapped away, taking lots of reference photos. Once her last-minute tour of the accommodation was complete, and she was alone, she headed back towards the reception area. She texted Sebastian as she walked. While she waited for his reply, Suzanne found a seat in the lobby and texted Uncle Jack to let him know their trip had gone smoothly. Not that smoothly, of course, what with Sebastian doing his disappearing act, but she wouldn't be mentioning that, naturally. Finally, she typed a brief note to her boys to remind them she'd see them at the weekend. As she was just finishing typing, she got a response from Sebastian. He was waiting for her in the Portobello restaurant.

Suzanne was no more than a minute's walk away which pleased her no end. She was starving. As she hurried to meet Sebastian, her tummy let out an angry protest. It felt like several gallons of coffee were sploshing around noisily in her gut. This morning, she'd skipped breakfast. Images of mouth-watering food hovered in her mind's eye and had her salivating. As she walked through the restaurant's double doors, she drank in the heavenly aroma of freshly baked bread and pastries, and her stomach groaned again.

She spotted Sebastian right away. She only had eyes for him amongst a sea of faces. He was sitting at a window table for two, dressed all in blue; a blue suit, a blue shirt and a blue tie. His face was partially hidden behind the open menu, but his penetrating blue eyes connected with hers as he watched her weave her way through the tables to him.

They'd not dined in the Portobello previously, so Suzanne was pleased to have the opportunity not only to appease the grumbling in her tummy, but to appraise the place for her write-up. The place was pretty packed, evidently very popular, and it wasn't difficult to see why. It was homely and cosy and through vast panes of glass, it offered a wonderful view of the surrounding snowy terrain. From a snug position inside, they marvelled at the steady flutter of snowfall; tumbling and twirling, the ice crystals spiralled in the light breeze. The service was speedy, and they feasted on buttercup yellow, perfectly fluffy scrambled eggs, served up on giant platters with crispy strips of streaky bacon and buttermilk pancakes, all smothered in maple syrup. They washed their brunch down with a glass of Buck's Fizz. Suzanne thought it cute that they almost always ordered the same meals.

After they'd eaten, they finished their packing and once a porter had taken charge of their cases, they headed for the check-out desk and did the necessary. Sebastian insisted on settling the bill for all their extras, and, after just a little argy-bargy, Suzanne relented and let him pay. Sean and Stacey-Lou appeared out of nowhere and escorted them to their car; a sleek black Cadillac limousine with their luggage already loaded. Their transport was certainly showy and impressive. It seemed like the hotel was pulling out all the stops. There were handshakes and big smiles all round.

As she climbed into the car, her shapely legs restricted by her pencil skirt, Suzanne kept on smiling; but inside, her stomach knotted. The evocative smell of expensive hide twitched in her nostrils. She remembered only too vividly the last time she'd been in a limousine. The memories rushed at her fast. The psychotic Albanian was back in her head to haunt her all over again. Freeze-framed images collided in her cerebrum. Angelo Azzurro, his eyes as hard as marbles, as he dragged her from her house, threw her like a rag doll into a limo, straddled her and chained her up. Suzanne cringed as she remembered another time with Angelo. She was blindfolded, her clothes torn; a foolish, vulnerable woman in a speeding limousine, having rough sex. *What had she been thinking?* It seemed like a lifetime ago now. Brutal sex with Angelo was something she really didn't want to think about at all. Not ever. Suzanne tried to clear her head as she settled into her seat. She took Sebastian's hand and squeezed it so forcefully he shot her a quizzical look. She smiled back at him sweetly.

Suzanne kept her disturbing thoughts to herself. As the magnificent wintry landscape whizzed by, she snuggled up to Sebastian and sank back into the opulent leather seating. She tucked her knees up beneath her and rested her head on his shoulder. Sebastian wrapped an arm around her and dropped his head on top of hers. Suzanne could feel the softness of his freshly washed hair and the smell of his sweet, spicy aftershave. And yet, she had butterflies in her belly. Those alarming memories of Angelo troubled her. *Now Tatiana was back, could that mean that he was too?* And, now they were heading home, Suzanne was also fretting about how things would pan out with Sebastian and his search to find his birth father. She prayed his endeavours would have a happy ending.

As they sat in companionable silence, Suzanne inhaled and exhaled. *Everything would be just fine*, she told herself over and over again like a mantra. A night flight snuggled up in a business class double bed with Sebastian was really something to look forward to. Something to cherish. Something she would undoubtedly remember for a very long time. Just like she'd remember making love on his birthday. For all eternity.

Suzanne breathed out contentedly. Even though their trip hadn't been without its traumas, she'd had the most amazing time. She closed her eyes. A sense of serenity soothed her and all at once she felt the anguish release. Like she'd opened a secret valve and let it all go.

"I can't wait to get on the plane, get ourselves sorted and have a proper cuddle."

"Me neither, baby," Sebastian answered softly, threading his fingers through hers.

FIFTY-ONE

TUESDAY 15 JANUARY

SUZANNE

The jumbo jet soared majestically across the indigo sky. The window blinds were down, and the lights were dimmed. Suzanne gazed around the cabin. The low lights made her sleepy. The smooth motion of the enormous aircraft relaxed her. She felt safe. She'd kicked off her shoes and removed her jacket, and, after a light bite and a couple of glasses of champagne, she was looking forward to getting her head down. Suzanne was pleased when the smiley stewardess cleared their dining tables away.

Suzanne reclined her seat into a bed and Sebastian followed suit. Cuddled on their sides, their bodies moved together as if powered by an invisible magnet. Sebastian spooned her. His hands gripping either side of her waist, he dragged her in tight. A smile seeped over Suzanne's glossy mouth as she recalled the sweetness of the nights they'd spent together at the Fairmont. They'd lost out on so much sleep in favour of hot nights making love. Dreamy stuff; his face hovering over hers; inky black hair falling on her face, tickling her cheeks; the fullness of his lips; the heat of his breath and the flicker of her own reflection in his intense blue eyes. Suzanne had adored every thrust of his masculine hardness, shivered at every single touch, at every intimate caress, but she was paying for her pleasures now.

Her eyelids were heavy and she couldn't stifle a massive yawn. Suzanne fidgeted, getting comfortable. Behind her, Sebastian snuggled up close on their makeshift double bed. Suzanne sighed contently and together they tugged the blanket over them, so they were fully covered. She had no ulterior motive, but she quickly sensed that he had. She felt the shape of him pulsing against the curve of her bottom.

"D'you think your mum will have any news about your real dad?" Suzanne asked, pressing her body back against his.

"We'll find out soon enough. She's invited us round for supper tomorrow night. Is that okay?" he asked. His words blew hot against her neck. His cock was getting harder with every passing second.

"Of course. I'd love to see your mum." Suzanne giggled. "Are you horny, baby?"

"What do you think?" Sebastian breathed in her ear and then nibbled her earlobe.

Sebastian focused on her neck. His tongue tickled. The nip of his teeth made her squirm. Suzanne brought her knees up towards her chest and closed her eyes. He was moving fast, sending pheromones out into the atmosphere with his utter gorgeousness. Suzanne held her breath and trembled. Her woollen skirt bunched up as Sebastian's busy fingers slid beneath it. Once his fingers found their target, he trailed them up and down the split of her buttocks through her tights, tantalisingly slowly. His nails raked against the silky nylon, digging into her flesh. Ducking her head beneath the blanket, Suzanne moaned. Her pussy was already sodden.

The glossy tights were designed to be worn without knickers, so Suzanne was relieved there were few barriers as she longed to feel Sebastian's fingers slip inside her. She bit down hard on her lower lip as Sebastian traced the lips of her sex with his fingertips. He groaned in her ear. Suzanne heard a rip and then a second later, a finger tucked into her pussy. Sebastian's head was on her shoulder. His voice warm, he whispered: "Is it okay if I make you cum?"

Suzanne breathed out and managed a soft "Yes."

Sebastian grasped the seam and tugged. The tear enlarged as he forced a hand through the opening, and then another. A split second later he eased two fingers into Suzanne's pussy and then very gingerly inserted another in her ass. The latter was a tight fit.

"You like this, baby?" Sebastian's voice was a sleepy growl. His finger was gentle in her ass. In her pussy, his digits delved deeper.

Suzanne whinnied softly, nodding, giving him the green light, letting him take her anywhere he wanted to go. Her heart pounded in her chest. She could count every beat. The finger in her ass felt dirty and decadent sliding into her, only an inch, but it felt so fucking sexy. Suzanne wanted to scream out loud but made a supreme effort to stay silent. She was getting close, bubbling on the brink. The fingers on her pussy rhythmically skimming her clitoris were working wonders. Sebastian timed his tempo to perfection, bringing her to a rapid boil, the way he knew so well.

"Are you going to cum for me, baby?" Sebastian breathed in her ear.

"You bet I am," Suzanne replied hoarsely.

The heat from his lips burned her neck. Her body began to spasm. Suzanne longed to turn to Sebastian and kiss him as she was cumming, but she couldn't move. A toe-curling orgasm grabbed her and held her in a vice-like grip. It took her breath away as it rushed over her. Suzanne moaned and rolled over to face him, shaking uncontrollably as waves of exquisite pleasure overwhelmed her. She buried her face under the blanket and stifled her joy against his solid, heaving body.

When she came up for air a few moments later, Sebastian stared at her with an easy laugh that showed off his beautiful teeth to the max. Merriment danced in his eyes. In his hand he held a pink slip of paper. He handed it to her. Suzanne read it aloud.

"I promise you the best blowjob ever and I promise to swallow. Signed by me!" Suzanne giggled and fluttered long spidery lashes coquettishly. Eyes flashing with impertinence, she said: "So, when do you want it?"

"How about right now, in the loo?" Sebastian consulted his blue-faced watch. "At 19.32 precisely."

Suzanne raised herself on her elbows and mirrored him. She laughed and kissed him hard and then pulled back. Brow-to- brow, nose-to-nose, she licked her lips and whispered: "Come on then, big boy. Let's go and suck some cock."

FIFTY-TWO

SEBASTIAN

Gloria lived alone in an elegant ground floor apartment in a mansion block in Esher, Surrey. Her spacious flat was a ten-minute drive from Suzanne's former family home, though until Suzanne met Sebastian, their paths had never knowingly crossed. She'd lived there for almost a decade. It was stylish, with two large bedrooms and a southwest-facing private garden full of glorious natural light and prize blooms in the summer months. Gloria was a keen gardener. Inside, the décor was modern and eclectic with lots of gleaming silver and glossy black, ornamenting high-ceilinged pale grey walls. Several stunning chandeliers, an abundance of velvety cushions in an array of bright colours and an oversized comfy seating arrangement swamped with furry throws made the place look lavish yet homely. Gloria was a proud mum. Framed photographs of her handsome son at various stages of his life graced the walls and just about every shelf and available surface. Sebastian found it a bit embarrassing.

When Donald Black left their lives for good, a hasty divorce was arranged. Gloria never remarried. Sebastian did recall her having a few short relationships over the years, though no one had ever become a permanent fixture in her life. Sebastian didn't really know how he felt about the fact that his mother had had an awful time with Donald, and, even after he'd gone, she'd never managed to find love and companionship with another man. It was difficult not to be sad for the mother he adored, but he was placated by the fact she seemed content and had lots of interests and friends in her life. Being an only child, parented almost wholly by his mother, Sebastian cherished the strong bond they shared.

In the conservatory, which was set up as a fairly formal dining room, dinner was a heart-warming beef stew and dumplings served with a powerful kick of chilli, lemon infused couscous and a mound of steaming buttered broccoli. Homemade cherry pie and custard followed for dessert. The meal was delicious. Gloria was a good home cook and Sebastian was well and truly stuffed. He had to pop the top button on his Levi 501's. The food had made him full and so sleepy. Jet lag was steadily swallowing him up. He wasn't sure how long he'd last upright. He really needed to cut to the chase, but his mother had insisted they talk after supper. So, occupying just one half of the made-for-six rectangular table, they had chit-chatted about the trip; Sebastian's birthday, the beauty of Whistler, the hotel, the ski conditions and the long flight home. Sebastian's eyes glazed over as he remembered their return journey; Suzanne gazing up at him, on her knees in the cramped toilet cubicle with her mouth full, her lips and tongue mind-blowing on his cock. *Had he ever come that fast before?*

Sitting at the head of the black marble table, the sleeves on his midnight blue roll neck sweater rolled up to his elbows, Sebastian cupped a yawn. He really was so very tired. Suzanne was on his right side. He took her hand. He needed to touch her skin. Her palms were soft and warm as she squeezed her hand into his and let it sit on his lap. A waft of her perfume blew his way as she turned to him and awarded him a fleeting smile before turning her attention back to Gloria and a skiing anecdote from Sebastian's teenage years, when he almost came a cropper in the Alps. He'd heard it all before, several times, so he kept his gaze on Suzanne. She looked stunning, her hair the colour of set honey, hanging loose, framing her face. She was casually dressed in figure-hugging jeans and a cashmere sweater in army green. Sebastian longed to switch off. He wished they could just go back to his and fall into bed, Suzanne's smoking hot body in his arms as they drifted off, but he was well aware that right now, sleep would be unlikely to come. He needed to know. Needed to know if his real father was still around and interested in getting to know a son he never knew he had. Sebastian felt an overpowering need to track him down. He was convinced it could be a defining moment in his life.

After clearing the table and loading the dishwasher, they took their coffee to the sitting room and gathered on the sofa. Sebastian and Suzanne sat together on one arm of the L-shaped couch. Gloria faced them from the perpendicular. Dressed all in black, aside from a string of Tiffany freshwater pearls, she looked younger than her sixty-five years. Smiling, she handed Sebastian his belated birthday present: dusky blue suede loafers. He unwrapped them and tried them on for size. They fitted perfectly. He loved them. He thanked his mother, leaned in and kissed her cheek. He sat back down again and sipped his coffee. The suspense was killing him. He needed some answers and he wasn't prepared to wait a second longer.

"So, tell me, Mum," Sebastian said softly. For the first time that evening, he noticed Gloria looked truly pained.

"I don't know where to start, Sebastian," Gloria stumbled. She seemed older and hunched all of a sudden.

"At the beginning," he told her kindly.

Gloria sighed heavily and then began speaking. "His name was Micky Hewkin. He was a student working part-time at the hotel I managed. He'd only just turned eighteen. He was ten years younger than me." Gloria's words flowed out in a rush, as if she'd rehearsed it many times. "One night I discovered that Donald was seeing other women, using prostitutes, having one-night stands." Her voice thick with emotion, she buried her face in her hands.

"It's okay, Mum," Sebastian mouthed. He reached out and gently took one of her hands from her face. Her fingers were wet.

Gloria took a moment. She glanced up at her son teary-eyed and inhaled and exhaled deeply before continuing. "We'd only just got engaged, so I was devastated, but I had a hotel to run. It was an awful night and I'm not sure how it happened, but to make matters worse, Micky got drunk. He was usually such a reliable young man. I couldn't have the guests seeing him like that, so I took him to my room and put him in my bed to sleep it off." Gloria gulped audibly. Her voice hushed, she went on: "As soon as I got a chance, I called Donald and confronted him. He was so horrible to me that I slammed the phone down and I went to my bedroom sobbing my heart out. And Micky was kind to me, and... and..." Gloria's words dried up. "I'm so sorry, Seb," she mumbled as she hung her head in shame. Fat tears streamed down her cheeks.

"It's okay, Mum," Sebastian said again. He squeezed her hand comfortingly and shuffled around the sofa, so he was sitting close to her.

Gloria forced her lips tightly together. When she eventually met Sebastian's gaze, her bright blue eyes were faraway and watery. "The following day, Micky went home with a sore head and his tail between his legs. Donald arrived at the hotel only moments after he'd left, bringing flowers and false promises and I fell for it. I went back to him and we got married soon after."

"And Micky?" Sebastian pushed.

"We never talked about what happened that night. We just avoided each other as much as we could when Micky did his shifts. He'd gone off to Edinburgh University by the time I was showing with you. I don't know. I suppose I just blanked the possibility that the baby I was carrying could have been his. So stupid, I know; but I was ashamed, and Micky was just a boy."

"So, you didn't tell Micky and you haven't seen him or heard anything from him since?" Sebastian asked the question, although he was pretty sure he already knew the answer.

Gloria nodded solemnly. "As soon as I told Donald I was pregnant, he was over the moon, and the wedding went ahead quickly, for obvious reasons. We were happy, and everything was fine for a while. You were just coming up to five when Donald had the fertility tests because we were desperate for another child. Of course, once they told him he was infertile and always had been, everything changed. That same afternoon he broke my nose." She touched a hand to her nose as she said it. "Perhaps I got what I deserved," she added sadly.

Sebastian handed her a crisp white handkerchief, and as she dabbed her eyes, he circled her in his arms. "It's all right, Mum. Of course you didn't deserve to be smacked around and have your bones broken."

Gloria blew her nose. Sebastian waited a few moments for his mother to compose herself. He got all that. He understood how and why it had happened. Got that the man he had always called 'Daddy' when he was a toddler, changed totally when he realised he was bringing up another man's son. But what Sebastian needed right now was to find Micky Hewkin. Sebastian squeezed his mother's hand. He shot Suzanne an apologetic glance. She smiled back at him reassuringly, though he noticed her eyes were brimming with tears too. He loved the very bones of her. At that moment, he had never loved her more.

"Have you had any luck tracking him down? It's a pretty unusual name."

"No, I haven't done anything yet. I thought we needed to talk first."

"Okay," Sebastian said and swallowed hard. Nervously, he dragged a hand through his hair. *Where the hell do we start?* His tired brain felt frazzled.

Suzanne cleared her throat. "This might be a bit simplistic, but it is a very unusual name."

"Do you think we should just google him, then?" Sebastian said. He stood up as he spoke and then rubbed his eyes with his fingers. Man, he was so tired!

"Actually, I was thinking of Facebook." Suzanne made a mental calculation. "He'd be in his mid-fifties now. Hopefully, he'll have an account."

"Yes, good idea." Sebastian perched his bottom on the arm of the sofa next to Suzanne.

She opened the Facebook app on her iPhone, and when the screen loaded, she typed Micky Hewkin into the search space bar.

Huddled together, they stared at the screen as the results were displayed.

"Not one single match! I can't believe it's that unusual a name," Sebastian groaned, clearly disappointed.

"Micky is more of a young person's name," Gloria remarked. "Perhaps you should try Michael?"

"Good idea," Suzanne said as she carefully typed Michael Hewkin into the search bar.

Sebastian felt a deep churning in his gut as the results loaded. There were two. Even though it was a tiny thumbnail, the first photograph looked familiar. Suzanne clicked on it to enlarge it.

"Oh my God!" they blurted out as one.

Suzanne met Sebastian's stunned blue eyes as he grabbed the phone from her.

FIFTY-THREE

SUZANNE

"What is it?" Gloria asked anxiously.

"This is unbelievable!" Sebastian yelled and stood up. He looked radiant. His grin was huge. His lashes damp with tears, his eyes gleamed with elation. "I really can't believe this!" he said to no one in particular. Sebastian began to pace as he scrolled down Michael Hewkin's Facebook profile, taking a peep into his life. "It's definitely him. There are loads of photos of him and Abi."

"For goodness' sake, Sebastian. Tell me what's going on, please!" Gloria pleaded.

"We actually had dinner with my birth father a week ago," Sebastian said, looking totally bemused, like he was barely able to believe the words that had popped out of his mouth.

Gloria looked even more confused. Sebastian leaned over his mother and enlarged the profile picture for her and with a tremor in his voice, asked: "Do you think this could be him?"

Gloria's eyes grew wide. She hesitated for only a few seconds before saying: "Yes, yes, I'm sure it is. Look at his eyes. They're just like yours, Seb. But will someone please tell me; why were you having dinner with him last week?"

Suzanne decided to explain as Sebastian didn't seem ready to. He was still busy with her phone. She got up and sat down close to Gloria.

"Do you remember my girlfriend, Abigail?"

"Yes. Yes. She was the neighbour who helped out when that awful man abducted you. What's she got to do with Micky?"

"Micky Hewkin, now known as Michael Hewkin, just happens to be Abigail's new boyfriend. Oh my God! I just can't believe it."

"Me neither," Sebastian cut in, "but there's no question; it is him."

Gloria opened her mouth to speak and then closed it again without saying a word.

Suzanne took both of Gloria's hands in hers. "We met Michael for the first time at a dinner party at Abigail's last week."

"Heavens. That's incredible! What's he like? He was a lovely young man when he worked for me." Suddenly remembering what had happened between them, Gloria's cheeks flushed with colour.

Sebastian plonked himself down on the other side of his mum. "Actually, he's a really lovely bloke. We just clicked. He's a vet. We talked about playing a round of golf together sometime. We planned to exchange numbers, and then it slipped my mind."

"That's so wonderful, Sebastian," Gloria beamed. "What do you plan to do?"

Sebastian looked at Suzanne. "Can you text Abi and

get his number? Don't say why. Just say we planned to exchange numbers and then forgot."

"Okay. It's not late, so I'm sure I'll get a quick response."

Suzanne typed hurriedly.

Hey Abi, back now and had a wonderful time in Whistler. We must catch up soon! Any chance you could send me Michael's number to pass on to Sebastian? The guys got on so well they plan to hook up. X

She checked it and then pressed send.

A few seconds later, a message, followed swiftly by a shared contact, pinged through as two separate texts. Right away, Suzanne forwarded 'Hewy's' number to Sebastian's phone. As Sebastian took his own phone from his pocket, he looked bewildered. Suzanne and Gloria looked at him questioningly.

"I have no idea what to say," he said.

"Why not ask him for a drink after work tomorrow? Say you'd value his advice on something, maybe?"

He squeezed Suzanne's hand. "Thanks, baby. That sounds like a plan." Hesitantly, he started to type a message to Michael, aka 'Hewy', his real dad.

FIFTY-FOUR

THURSDAY 17 JANUARY

SEBASTIAN

The first day back after a break, Sebastian often found it stressful playing catch-up, but on this particular gloriously bright Thursday, he felt no such pressure of work. He felt high on life. As he sat at his desk, dazzling winter sun streaming in warming his cheeks and fooling him with its heat, Sebastian found it difficult to wipe the smirk off his face. He couldn't believe that finding his birth father had been that simple. Sebastian shook his head in disbelief, his muddle of jet black hair drifting lazily around his shirt collar. He was sporting a shadow of stubble. It suited him. He looked handsome and rugged.

Staring at the screen, Sebastian checked his diary for the rest of the week, scanning the scheduled operations and consultations. He raised his eyebrows when he noted that Tatiana Berisha had a follow-up appointment booked in for the end of the day, but he couldn't care less. Today he felt able to deal with the silly young woman playing her silly games. Sebastian steepled his fingers together and dipped his forehead to his hands. He let his eyelids gently drop. He was still so tired. Running on pure adrenaline. The time change made him feel like it was the dead of night. With his eyes still tightly sealed, he proceeded to bounce one knee on top of the other, the nervous rhythm he set accelerating swiftly through him. There was an army of butterflies swirling torridly in his gut, and yet, Sebastian was so excited, gearing up for the phone call he was due to make in less than fifteen minutes. At ten o'clock. To Michael. His father. Just contemplating their likely interchange made Sebastian's heart thump. Silently in his head, he rehearsed what he would say, over and over, even though this morning, he planned only to ask Michael to meet him after work. Sebastian knew the 'I'm the son you never knew you had' conversation had to be done face-to-face.

The previous evening, Michael had replied by text, suggesting that as it was quite late, Sebastian should call him the following day, around ten. Great timing. Sebastian's first appointment of the day wasn't scheduled until eleven. He'd arranged it that way so he could catch up. He wasn't doing much catching up, though, to be honest. He was far too preoccupied; clockwatching and contemplating how to drop the bombshell on Michael when they did meet up. Sebastian hoped that they would be having that conversation in only a matter of hours. He wasn't sure how much longer he could hold it all together otherwise.

Sebastian exhaled deeply. He tried a little yoga breathing. Some pranayama to control his racing heart. He inhaled and exhaled, making each breath long, easeful and smooth. It seemed to help. Sebastian's heartbeat slowed. He began to feel calmer. Everything was good. He'd found his biological father, and the Sylvia

Hamilton shit was over, thank God! The letter from the General Medical Council that had been waiting for him on his return had confirmed it. He'd read their letter several times and then duly filed it away, in his head and his filing cabinet as 'dealt with', both figuratively and literally. That done, he felt a tremendous weight lift from him.

Sebastian began to breathe normally again. The events of the last dozen or so hours had boosted his spirits immeasurably. This was a monumental day all round. Maybe he should ask Suzanne to marry him and make it a hat-trick of things to celebrate. Smiling to himself, a snort of laughter caught in his throat. He mustn't get ahead of himself. For one thing, Suzanne's divorce wasn't finalised yet, and two, he knew better than to take anything for granted. He really had no idea how Michael would react to his news.

There was a knock on his door.

"Come in!" he shouted gaily.

Pauline bustled into the consulting room, all smiles and smelling of Estee Lauder's Beautiful. Smartly dressed in the soothing colours of autumn, her caramel-coloured hair looked newly styled. She carried a mug of coffee. Sebastian took it gratefully from her hand.

"Thank you." He swivelled his chair and smiled up at her. "Just checking, my last appointment is at six, isn't it?"

"Yes, that's right, with Ms Berisha. For a follow-up, she said when she called." Pauline rolled her eyes.

Sebastian sipped his coffee as they exchanged knowing glances.

"Pauline…" Sebastian started.

"Yes?"

"I've got an important phone call to make in a few minutes. So, no calls or disturbances until, say…" he considered for a full couple of seconds before adding, "ten-fifteen?"

"Okay, no problem," Pauline answered jovially, before she headed out, closing the door behind her.

When his mobile phone's digital display changed in an instant to 9.59, Sebastian couldn't wait a moment longer. He typed in his passcode and then selected Michael's number. His heart was in his mouth as he waited for the connection. He took a sharp intake of breath when the call was answered.

"Sebastian, good to talk to you, man. How are things?"

"I'm good, thanks. Really good." Sebastian hoped he didn't sound as anxious as he felt. His hands were shaking, and he could feel perspiration building on his brow. "Just a thought," he ventured, "are you free tonight around six thirty or a little after?"

"Yes, sure; I could be."

"There's something I'd like to chat with you about. Sort of. Need to ask your advice about something," Sebastian supplemented, remembering Suzanne's words from the previous evening.

"Yes, sure. I can leave a little early and drive over to the hospital. Perhaps we should go and get a beer and a bite in Wimbledon village?" Michael suggested amiably.

Michael sounded nice. He sounded kind. He loved animals. He was the type of guy who would always help you out, the kind of guy who you'd want as your father. Sebastian couldn't help thinking all these things as he clutched his phone tightly in his hand. A sense of relief rushed through him. It was all coming together for tonight. The stark realisation that later that day everything would be out in the open and he could look his real dad in the eye, made him feel lightheaded. His stomach was in knots, but his smile was impossible to wipe away as he said: "Brilliant. I'll look forward to seeing you later, then."

"Me too, Sebastian," Michael replied, sounding genuinely like he meant it. As an afterthought, he added: "Can you text me the postcode of your clinic?"

Sebastian said easily, "Of course."

Sebastian didn't feel at ease at all. He didn't know how he felt. But when he said his goodbyes and hung up, he sat there for a full five minutes barely moving a muscle, just grinning. Then he called Suzanne to relay his news.

FIFTY-FIVE

THURSDAY 17 JANUARY

TATIANA

Tatiana loved to drive fast. She adored her white Range Rover Evoque with its black glass roof, big, wide wheels and just about every available extra. Another very generous present from Eddie. She giggled to herself. How she loved being spoilt. A late Christmas present he'd said when they'd bought it brand spanking new from the main dealer showroom. It was fast. It was classy. Men stared at her when she drove it around town. Tatiana hummed happily to herself. She couldn't believe she'd heard nothing from Angelo since she'd stood him up at the airport. But fuck him! She was on her way. By this time tomorrow she'd be in the sky on her way to the Maldives; a dream destination for a simple girl from Tirana. She'd top up her tan and they'd have loads of great sex. Well, they would if Eddie snapped out of his strange mood. She couldn't quite put her finger on it, but he was behaving very strangely all of a sudden. This morning he didn't even seem to want to fuck her. Though she'd persuaded him, of course.

Tatiana cleared her head of such niggles. She had more important things on her mind right now. Revenge for one. She flicked the indicator and made the sweeping turn into the entrance of the private hospital. She was a few minutes early. Time to check her make-up and make sure she looked good. This time she'd have that good-looking bastard and fuck up Suzanne's perfect romance. She'd flash her pussy on his couch, and this time the good doctor wouldn't be able to resist. She was sure. Tatiana visualised Sebastian on his knees going down on her and she smirked arrogantly.

Parked up, Tatiana switched off the ignition and switched on the interior light. Outside, there was a light mist. The car park was dark and cold and empty, aside from a few other cars. The Porsche she parked alongside was Sebastian's, she was sure. Tatiana was vaguely aware of another car arriving. Orange light swept across the tarmac as it parked up beside her car. Unperturbed by the new arrival, she took a silver lipstick tube from her bag and uncapped it. Angling the driver's mirror just so, she applied another layer. When she'd finished, her lips were as red as ripe strawberries and a true colour match for her dress; a knee-length, silky wrapover number that hugged in all the right places. She wore Kurt Geiger ankle boots in scarlet. Her slender legs were covered with patterned black hold-up stockings. She wore no panties, of course.

Tatiana checked the time on her phone: 17.55. Time to make her grand entrance. Smiling smugly at her reflection, she combed blood red talons through her curtain of velvety hair and then flicked off the light. She grabbed her bag and coat from the passenger seat. She was just about to open the driver's door, when all of a sudden the heavy door seemed to open all on its own. The interior light flicked back on again. She was dazzled. *What the fuck?* Tatiana could just make out a big, shadowy figure at the window. Stunned into immobility, she gazed open-mouthed as an oversized fist appeared in the car with her. A whimper of sheer terror escaped from her perfectly painted mouth. The sound froze on her lips as a man's rough hand gripped around her throat. Large spiteful fingers dug hard into her soft flesh, and in a flash the car door was wrenched away from her. A familiar face hovered in the darkness. When bright light settled on the sinister face, Tatiana's stomach dropped like a stone. Her heart clattered in her heaving chest as Angelo Azzurro closed in on her.

"Bitch!" exploded from thin lips that were set in a hard sneer.

"Angelo!" she started.

Angelo Azzurro didn't reply. He was silent as he grabbed her by the hair and began to drag her out of her seat by it. Tatiana was petrified, but she didn't plan to make it easy. Her screams pierced the night sky as she kicked and fought like a tigress protecting her young.

FIFTY-SIX

THURSDAY 17 JANUARY

SEBASTIAN

Sebastian was gearing up for his appointment with Tatiana, but his mind wasn't on it at all. As he washed his hands thoroughly, all he could think of was getting her in and out as quickly as possible and then meeting Michael. His thoughts were interrupted as Pauline came bursting through his door without knocking. She was close to tears.

"Sebastian, I've just called the police. It's all going on out there."

"What is?"

"A man has just dragged that Tatiana woman from her car kicking and screaming. I saw it from my window."

Drying his hands on a paper towel, Sebastian hurried to the window and flipped up a slat on the blind. He peered out.

"Ah, for God's sake! Angelo."

"You know him?"

"You could say that, Pauline, but it's a long story. I'd better get down there. How long did the police say they'd be?"

"I said it was urgent, that an assault was in progress, so they said a matter of minutes."

"I'll believe that if it happens," Sebastian said cynically, hurrying out of the door in his shirtsleeves.

"Be careful!" Pauline called after him.

"Don't worry about me. I owe that bastard big time." Sebastian's eyes burned with pure hatred. "Taking him on is going to be an absolute pleasure."

Leaving Pauline huddled at the exit looking both confused and horrified, Sebastian dashed down the stairway, taking the steps two at a time, concentrating hard so he didn't take a tumble. His mouth was dry, his veins pumped with adrenaline. As he opened the heavy street door, cold rushed in, but he barely noticed. From across the car park, he heard Tatiana yelling, her voice shrill, her harsh accent penetrating the stillness of the murky night. Less than fifty metres from him, she was putting up a hell of a fight, clawing and snarling as Angelo attempted to throw her into his car, a stretched limousine, just like the one he'd kidnapped Suzanne in. Sebastian had no feelings whatsoever for Tatiana, but at that moment, that memory buzzing in his head, he hated Angelo Azzurro with a stone cold heart. He knew he was a big man, so he had to be careful. But he also knew he was a coward. A fucking bully. He got off on hurting women. The man was a fucking beast and he needed to be taught a lesson. Sebastian's heart thudding in his chest, he took a deep breath of cold, sharp air into his lungs and then ran towards them.

Tatiana still had some fight in her. She looked impressive; bright red lips drawn back, her hair black and wild as she screamed obscenities at her attacker.

305

In a glamorous red frock, she really wasn't dressed for a car park brawl, though it was obvious to see that she wasn't going to go down easily. Angelo didn't seem to hear Sebastian's approach. He was too busy struggling with Tatiana's flailing legs as he tried to shove her into the limo. She was having none of it. She kicked out and caught him with a direct hit; a stiletto, square in the face. Angelo roared in pain and then went ballistic. With blood oozing from a gash in his cheek, he punched Tatiana full in the face. He hit her again and again. Sebastian felt sickened as he heard the heavy blows landing. He heard the cracking of bones. He was within a few metres of them now.

Tatiana was struggling to stay on her feet. She looked dazed and bloodied as she slumped against the limousine. She'd lost one high-heeled red boot in the scuffle. Wobbly and unbalanced, she held up both arms to fend off the next blow. Angelo batted them away. He stopped punching and started screaming at her. Sebastian spotted angry purple bruising on her face. There was a dark river of blood trickling from her nose. It looked broken. He knew he had to act and soon. In the melee and noise, Angelo turned suddenly. That's when Sebastian danced in on light feet, drew back his arm and elbowed him full in the face. One swift direct hit. Very *Jack Reacher*. As invariably happened in the *Jack Reacher* novels, the enemy was taken totally off guard and went down hard. As did Angelo. As he hit the ground, Sebastian kicked him in the balls. Kicked him with every bit of strength he had in his body. White noise rushed in his ears and time stood still. He heard police sirens closing in. He kicked and kicked. Angelo curled up in the foetal position squealing like a girl, but Sebastian carried on putting the boot in. He only stopped when he spotted the glare of approaching headlights.

Angelo lay on the floor in a ball, motionless and moaning. Sebastian was out of breath and breathing hard as he took Tatiana's hand and helped her up.

"You okay?" he asked, as he heard car doors open and the sound of hurrying footsteps.

Tatiana nodded and whispered so softly he could barely hear her. "I'm okay, thank you."

When she answered, Sebastian noticed she had lost most of her front teeth.

★

By a little after six thirty, the small crowd that had assembled in the car park had dispersed. The police steered a handcuffed Angelo into a squad car with very little due care and attention, bashing his head as he was unceremoniously slung in the back. A Middle Eastern man who had sat at the wheel of the limousine throughout the attack was directed into the same car, though he wasn't handcuffed and appeared to be treated with a little more deference. As Angelo peered out of the window his face was stretched tight with rage.

Wrapped in a blanket, her face battered and bruised, Tatiana looked very young and vulnerable. She kept her head down as she was helped into the back of the second police vehicle at the scene by a kindly looking policewoman. The cops had agreed that Sebastian could make his own way to the station to make his statement. He hoped Tatiana would get some treatment for her injuries before too long. Her once perfect nose needed resetting, and her dental bill certainly wasn't going to be cheap. Sebastian wasn't surprised to overhear that she was keen to press charges. You can only be friends with a man like that for so long. Sebastian felt drained, but good. He was elated that Angelo Azzurro was finally going to get his comeuppance. He couldn't wait to tell Suzanne. Sebastian suddenly realised how cold he was. He shivered and hugged his shoulders as he watched the two police cars drive away. He was still watching their tail lights as Michael Hewkin's silver Saab estate drove into the car park.

All was quiet and still now aside from the swaying movement of the tall bare trees and the persistent hum of late rush-hour traffic on the nearby A3. The two men shook hands, and in halting sentences, Sebastian explained what had happened.

"I'm sorry, Michael, but I have to go to the station now to make a statement. It looks like they're going to charge him with GBH." Sebastian's hot breath was clearly visible in the frosty night air.

"Ah, never mind, we can always reschedule. Look at you! You're freezing. You should go and grab a coat before you go."

"Yes, yes, I will," Sebastian answered distractedly. There was indecision in his eyes. He remained silent for a few seconds and then said quietly: "Michael, there's something I need to tell you." He was struggling to form words. His throat was dry. He had never felt so emotional in his life.

"Okay?" Michael responded quizzically.

Standing together in the cold, dark car park, Sebastian

stared into concerned blue eyes that matched his own. He scanned Michael's face. *My God, we even look alike!* Tears started to run freely down Sebastian's cheeks.

"Look, mate, it's all over. You're in shock." Michael squeezed Sebastian's shoulder sympathetically.

Sebastian swallowed hard. There was no going back. He had to speak out. He had to tell Michael the truth. His voice shaking, he said: "It's not that. This is about something that happened thirty-seven years ago." He paused. Michael was staring at him, vapour trails rising from his mouth. Sebastian exhaled and said: "You knew my mother, Gloria Scott."

"Gloria Scott," Michael repeated slowly, as if he was taking a trip back in time. "God, yes. She was lovely. She was my boss for a while before I went off to uni. That's your mum, you say?" Michael looked puzzled.

"You're my father," Sebastian blurted out as a hard, jolting sob overwhelmed him.

Michael stared at him. He opened his mouth to speak, but no words formed. Instead, he wrapped his arms around his son. Somehow it didn't feel awkward at all. Sebastian rested his head on his father's shoulder and began to weep.

EPILOGUE

SEBASTIAN

Eyes brimming with tears, Sebastian gazed at the two identical babies, tiny and wrinkled and safe in the crook of his arms. The most precious cargo. Sebastian felt his heart swell with a love he'd never thought possible. Two incredible baby girls swaddled in white; all big blue eyes and new pink skin with a dusting of downy blonde hair covering their diminutive heads. They looked just like their mother. Exquisitely beautiful. Baby One came into the world weighing 5 lbs 9 ounces and her even tinier baby sister weighed 5lbs 5 ounces. Born at thirty-seven weeks, although pocket-sized, they were both perfectly healthy, Sebastian had been reassured.

He smiled over at Suzanne sitting up in bed; she looked tired. Her face was pale, and her golden hair was wild, but the intense happiness in her glowing green eyes was unmistakable. She'd managed to birth their twin girls naturally, as once again both her babies were head down just waiting to get out into the world. Sebastian had been there throughout, holding her hand, feeling her pain, sharing the most remarkable celebration of love. There had been white-coated professionals and

310

nurses all around them during the five-hour delivery, but to him it seemed there was just the two of them, and then all of a sudden, in one magical moment, there were three, and eight minutes later, there were four. Sebastian was a happy man. His world was complete.

After the main event was over and the babies checked and cleaned up and returned to their mother, Suzanne's private room at the Portland Hospital filled up with family. Rayan and Christian crowded around the bed, excited to welcome their new baby sisters into the world. Gloria was there, of course. She hadn't stopped crying. Meeting up with Michael for the first time in almost four decades had been something of a moment for her too. It was a real family affair. Sebastian felt a hand rest on his shoulder.

"What a pair of beauties," Michael whispered softly.

"And their mum is pretty gorgeous too." Sebastian grinned at his father. He still couldn't believe it. One minute, this man was a widow with no real family and the next thing you know, he's gained a long-lost son, swiftly followed by two granddaughters. Sebastian was delighted he seemed to be taking it all in his stride and the two men were finally getting to know each other. Making up for lost time. In a little more than eight months, they'd formed a wonderful bond. He looked up to Michael, admired him as a man. "Do you want to hold them, Dad?"

"Yes, I'd love to, but give the girls to Gloria first."

Gloria came around the bed and one by one she took her new grandchildren in her arms. She balanced them both with ease. The look in her eyes made Sebastian well up all over again.

It had been a hell of a year. A little more than twelve months ago, Suzanne walked into his consulting suite and he felt that thunderbolt. Since that monumental moment, when he found his true love and soulmate, and soon-to-be wife, he'd become the proud father of two perfect baby daughters and discovered a brilliant father he never knew existed. Not forgetting inheriting two fine stepsons as well. They'd need him too, now their father was serving time in Ford Prison for his part in some City dodgy dealing. Tatiana had dropped Edward like a hot stone once he was charged. Bizarrely, after being the star witness in Angelo's trial, she seemed to be making a name for herself as a Z-list celebrity. With her nose reset and some expansive dental work, she looked as stunning as ever. According to Rayan, it was rumoured that Tatiana might be one of the housemates going into the *Celebrity Big Brother* house. Unfortunately, the police had only managed to secure a conviction for ABH for the car park assault, but at least the psychotic Albanian asshole had been handed down the biggest sentence possible: five years. Sebastian grinned. Yes, all in all, it had been a hell of a year.

"I think Mummy might want a cuddle now," Gloria said. Big fat tears slid down her face as she and Michael stood side by side and clucked and cooed over their bewitching twin granddaughters.

Sebastian watched his mother return the girls to their mother, tenderly laying a baby in each of Suzanne's arms. Serenity flooded her fatigued face as she gazed down at her daughters. She looked exhausted and yet radiant, truly beautiful with their baby girls clutched to her breast. Sebastian's heart soared with joy as he stared at the three most beautiful girls in the world. Tears began to form on his lashes as he sat down on the bed beside his wonderful threesome. Suzanne smiled at him, her eyes soft and full of love. He leaned in and planted a gentle kiss on her forehead. She smelt of motherhood and milk. The sweetest smell of all.

"Come on, let's have a selfie," Rayan suggested, waving his smartphone about.

Everyone crowded around the bed. Six adults huddled around the sleepy new arrivals and smiled at the phone camera. Rayan held his phone at arm's length and took a perfect family portrait.